STRINGS DETACHED

Chris Riffle

For Ferguson, my cat

CHAPTER ONE
2019

Jake's duffel bag rattled beside him on the gently rocking train. He put a hand on it to stop its babble. Outside, to his left, he could see the Hudson River. How beautiful it looked that morning. A soft rain had just begun to fall. He watched as the drops met the water of the river and thought deeply about the contents of the duffel at his side.

Many people, even non-New Yorkers, know of the robustness of the New York City subway system: of its numerous never-ending lines that stretch from Brooklyn to Manhattan to Queens to the Bronx; of its patrons ranging from Hollywood celebrities to homeless folks looking for a warm place to sleep; of its screeches and rumbles, and its mantra: "Stand clear of the closing doors please."

Those not in the New York Metropolitan Area or in the surrounding areas on the frigid banks of the East Coast may not know of another of its sprawling train systems: the Metro North Railroad. The Metro North is run by the Manhattan Transit Authority, the same company that owns the NYC subway system. These lines are more expensive, tidier, faster. Lines can go as far north as Poughkeepsie, or Wassaic, as far east as New Haven, Connecticut. These are the commuter lines. You can drop your kid off at preschool in Stamford and still make it into your job in Midtown by 9am for $23, avoiding the second-rent that is Manhattan garage parking. City dwellers take various lines to escape. They go hiking at Breakneck Ridge or to get some shopping done in Cold Spring. Only once they're out of the city for even a small amount of time do they grow anxious and itchy. Call it too much oxygen.

Jake was on his way back home on one of these very lines. Grand Central Station to Tarrytown, NY: $12.15 off-peak one-way rate. Lately, he traveled into the city almost every other Saturday. He took to walking to the train, a 12-minute walk from the door of his apartment to the station, unless it was rainy, in which case he'd drive and pay for parking in the lot. Used to be he'd stay in the city for much of the day, but as of late, he'd stay only for enough time to fill his bag and get on the next train back home. Tarrytown wasn't necessarily a small place, but it seemed there were eyes everywhere. He couldn't risk being seen in town, even in a neighboring town, doing what he was doing. An alcoholic pastor is not something the members of his congregation would accept.

Springtime trains started becoming more crowded than the winter trains, and Jake was dreading the quickly approaching summer season where the train would be packed to the brim with city people eager for some space. Some summer afternoons, he would have to stand for the entire 40-minute ride home, his heavy duffel weighing down on his shoulder, sweat dripping down his brow. The thought of this saddened him, not because of the thought of the upcoming summer but because of how he'd been doing this long enough to know what would happen when the seasons changed.

It started to rain harder as Jake stepped off the train. He wished he'd looked at the weather forecast that morning when he left his apartment. Maybe he would have driven or at least packed an umbrella. His apartment was north of the train station, almost as far north as Sleepy Hollow. The name of his neighboring town always gave him chills. Even at 32, he was vaguely afraid of the headless thing that may come out of it. He didn't believe evil could stay in one single town in upstate New York—evil, in his experience, was everywhere—still, he tried to avoid Sleepy Hollow if it could be helped. By the time he made it home, he was dripping wet, and his mind battled two scenarios:

1. He could strip down and jump in the shower immediately. He could put on some fresh clothes, make some lunch, catch up on some TV.
2. He could open the duffel and break into a new bottle. He could shower later. He could eat later. Being drunk made watching TV better.

Of course, scenario two would win out. He knew this before he even made it into the front door of his apartment. He'd already been figuring which bottle he was in the mood for today. He preferred whiskey, but sometimes he'd break into some tequila or gin. Maybe he'd just reach into his duffel and pull out the first bottle he put his hand on. He could play a fun little game he liked to call Duck, Duck, Booze.

His apartment was one of four units in a large, converted home. He had the south unit on the bottom floor. It had everything he needed: one bedroom, one bathroom, one scarcely used kitchen, a living space. Even with these bare minimums, he could hardly afford the place on his pastor's salary. Unlike megachurch pastors who lived in mansions and took helicopters to their Sunday services, Jake didn't like to exploit the members of his church. He didn't get down on his knees and beg the wealthy members to get them to donate more. He didn't pick on the poorer members and pretend that their donations, no matter how small, would make a huge difference. Only sometimes, at the bottom of a bottle, he'd find a little bit of regret. Why not exploit this legal loophole in the fucked-up system? Why not steal and cheat his way into wealth under the guise of beautiful and everlasting salvation? If people were stupid enough to do it, what difference did it make to him? From what he'd understood when he went through the process of interviewing at this church, its members had never given much back, and previous pastors hadn't pushed them to. The church survived off of faith-based grants and forgiven taxes. Lately, the administration had been pushing him to ask for more, and he'd nod his head and say, "Sure, sure," and then change nothing.

Jake unzipped his duffel, rainwater still sliding down his fingers, legs, nose.

Duck.

He wondered, as he often did before the crack of a fresh bottle, how he'd gotten here. He knew he needed help. The thing was that he didn't really *want* help. He liked to drink, as his father no doubt had before him, and unless he was hurting anyone, he didn't see how it really mattered. As long as he could function at work, make it to Sunday morning sermons on time, who was he hurting? He didn't have a social life. He had no friends.

Duck.

He didn't go on dates. He was celibate and wasn't sure what the point of going on dates was when there wasn't the possibility of a good hard fuck afterward. On one of his Saturday trips into the city, he met up with a group of Asexuals, thinking he'd be able to find common ground with their views on sex. Instead, he left early and stopped at a nearby bar for a Guinness; or was it two, or was it three? The church hadn't asked him to remain celibate—it wasn't that kind of church—but rather it was a choice he'd made long ago as a result of a childhood of which memories mostly eluded him.

That is, of course, until he was good and drunk and weeping on the floor of his living room.

Booze.

"Ah, excellent choice sir," Jake said to himself when he pulled out a bottle of whiskey, his hand wrapped around its neck like the limp neck of a dead turkey. It was time for his Thanksgiving feast (Thanksgiving in April?) and he would stuff himself to the brim, right up until he felt like exploding; and then it would be time for dessert. He took his first drink right out of the bottle. This was a habit he'd picked up at no time, no place in particular, just something he did that felt right. Having tested the murky and spicy waters, he went to the kitchen to grab a glass and some ice and poured himself his first plate of wonderfully carved turkey, perfectly-mashed potatoes, that jelly cranberry stuff that maintains the shape of its tin prison, a cob of corn. A second drink from the bottle was the gravy on top of it all. Glass full, he went to sit on the couch, either unaware or uncaring that he was still dripping wet.

Time slid by, then. He'd put something on the TV, but by his third drink, he wasn't really watching. At some point, he did force himself to strip down, take a shower, and put on some fresh clothing. When he did this, he didn't know. Either before or possibly after the showering, he went to his fridge and found something to eat. It wasn't as wonderful as the feast in his glass, but the rational part of him—this was only really a sliver of him at this point, a single atom amongst octillions of them—knew that he needed real food to survive. Before a blackout might attack him out of nowhere, Jake made sure to set his alarms for the church service in the morning. He knew out of experience that he needed to set multiple: 7:05, 7:08, 7:10, 7:11, 7:15, 7:20. He even set a 7:30 just in case, though he knew that one would make him late. He needed to be there early to greet people and be awake enough to come up with valid responses like 'Mhmmm' or 'I'm glad to hear that' or 'I'm so sorry' or, the golden boy, 'I'll be praying for you (or them, or whomever)'.

And at some point later in the night, the memories came. They played on the glowing TV in front of him. The screen showed rain and a yard with a pool. Blurry movement in the corner of the screen caught Jake's eye. The TV said 'Fuck' and the figures came into view. Two naked lovers dripping wet and laughing or screaming or crying, or a crash or something like it. *"Jacob. Sweetheart. Call 911."* Benny leaving for college. The death of their mother. Lily Scarlett, the pornstar, tits falling out of her satin gown. These memories came flooding in, and Jake screamed, "Stop!" He threw a napkin at the TV. The TV said 'Asshole.' Jake fell to his knees and screamed it again, "Stop! Stop!" And then the TV went dark. Jake could feel the consciousness leaving him. Was it sleep? He wasn't sure. He wouldn't be sure until the ring of his 7:05 and 7:08 and 7:10 alarms sounded. Even then, he wouldn't truly be sure.

CHAPTER TWO
1996

In the early-internet days of the '90s, Huber Heights, Ohio, a suburb of Dayton, had a place of worship on nearly every other street corner. Each church or synagogue showed off its unique denomination—Christ's Episcopal Church, St. Mary's, Church of the Scientist, Hope Catholic, Shul of God, Hope Eternal and so on—and Jacob found himself on any given Sunday morning in Christ's Nondenominational wearing a tie and horribly itchy black pants. Each time his mother and father drove Jacob and his older brother, Benny, to church, Jacob would wonder as they passed all of the other churches: *how can all of these religions think they are the right one?* This thought would evolve into something deeper and more complex as he got older, but for now, it remained quite simple and matter-of-fact. As a 9-year-old, Jacob knew very little of other religions. His only Jewish friend wasn't religious. He had never even heard of Buddhism or Hinduism or anything not dominated by the white American culture.

"Job endured," their wrinkly old pastor spat into the mic one Sunday morning. Jacob was munching on the final bite of a stale jelly-filled donut and could smell his father's coffee beside him. Just before the service started, he saw his father take something out of the pocket of his suit jacket and pour it into the coffee. Jacob assumed it was to make the coffee sweeter. "You see, God gave Satan free rein to do whatever he wanted to Job. Satan, too blinded by hatred, could not see the trick that God was playing on him. You see, God knew Job, as he knows all of us here in this room. He knew that Job would never condemn Him no matter how much Satan tormented him. And as we know, God was right."

Benny tapped on Jacob's shoulder. Jacob didn't notice as he was fascinated, or perhaps disgusted, by the story of Job. He wondered why they were worshiping a man who could be so cruel. Certainly, this test of Job's will could have been done differently. He scratched his butt through his black pants. Certainly—"Psst," Benny interrupted. Jacob looked over at Benny, mildly annoyed. Benny looked around with a cunning smile and then opened his hand for Jacob to see what was inside. It took Jacob's sight a moment to adjust and see the image on a small piece of paper, and when they did adjust, his eyes widened in horror and uncomfortable curiosity. Benny had used a church pen and the back of a membership card to draw a crude image of a woman with huge breasts and an immensely hairy private part. He moved the pen back and forth across the private part and grunted quietly. It took Jacob seconds, too many seconds, to tear his eyes away from the piece of paper. And even after he looked away, he felt something like a bubbling in the bottom of his belly and a strong urge to look again at the picture Benny had drawn. Instead, he looked forward at the pastor, who was spewing something into his microphone that Jacob couldn't quite comprehend.

Jacob's father took a long sip of his coffee and Jacob wondered how it didn't burn his mouth. He looked up to his father as any proud son might. He wore a thick brown mustache and glasses that were always falling down his nose. Jacob used to put them on just so he could slide them up his nose with his pointer finger like his father was always doing. He hoped that one day he could drink coffee too. He liked the smell of it on his father's breath. He liked to watch the steam rising out of his father's cup. It felt, to Jacob, like the absolute peak of adulthood.

His mother sat on the other side of his father and had neither donut nor coffee but held on tightly, with both hands, to her Bible. It was white, and worn down from frequent use. When she read to Jacob from it, he would notice notes throughout all its open spaces, highlighted passages, circled words. It seemed to Jacob that it was the most important thing on earth to her, perhaps besides himself and Benny. In church she always wore a dress, bright and floral in the spring and summer and dark or bland in the fall and winter. She straightened her curly amber hair and wore earrings, a different pair every week. Jacob had never seen where his mother kept her earrings, but he imagined boxes and boxes full of them, all different shapes and colors and styles.

"Dear heavenly Father..." Jacob noticed too late that everyone had closed their eyes and bowed their heads in prayer. He clapped his hands together and closed his own eyes as the pastor continued, eager to join him in this prayer, though unsure why it really mattered. "Bless these folks who have decided to join us here today. Let them hear your voice through me and come away from today's service with a newfound respect for you, almighty God, and the knowledge that you are always watching, you are always there even in the darkest of times. Dear Lord please continue to keep these fine people safe as they make their way to lunch, soccer games, relative's homes—" Jacob noticed movement beside him and opened his eyes very slightly to see his father taking another long drink of his coffee, finishing the cup, and frowning slightly. Jacob scratched the other side of his butt. He peeked toward Benny who was looking intently at the picture of the woman he had drawn. Jacob wanted to look again at the picture but shut his eyes quickly. "Our Lord, amen." The congregation repeated this last word and Jacob shuttered. He found collective voices rather unsettling.

When the service concluded, people were in high spirits, all feeling accomplished having tithed away their hard-earned cash. Jacob's mother had given Jacob and Benny each a dollar they were allowed to put in the tithe bucket. Benny tossed it in and moved along as if he'd just tossed away a piece of trash. Jacob tried to find meaning in the moment. He thought of all the things his dollar could help. Only, he made the mistake of looking inside the bin and finding hundreds of bills and checks the total sum of which he couldn't even figure. His last thought as the dollar bill left his hand was, *Will God even notice this dollar? Will he care?*

Standing around in the church after services was Jacob's least favorite Sunday activity. His parents seemed to know every single person at the church and would stop and talk to every single one of them. At least, their mother did. Jacob, Benny and their father had no choice but to follow along. While he wasn't really interested in their conversations, Jacob didn't have much else to do but catch snippets of them here and there. Mrs. Kindler's cat went to the vet on Tuesday, and they still hadn't figured out what was wrong with him. Brent and Jessie are getting a divorce, said Mrs. Whiting, and then she whispered something of which Jacob only caught the word "Gay" and a very concerned look. His father looked disinterested, but his mother's mouth was agape. Aaron Tillson, who was very close with Jacob and Benny's father and always insisted they call him Uncle Air, stopped to give them each fist bumps and asked his parents if they'd be going to Chet's after. Jacob thought it was a pretty stupid question because they always went to Chet's after service.

Chet's Grill was Jacob's most favorite Sunday tradition. Every week, after church wrapped up and the conversations were finally over, Jacob's parents would drive him and Benny down the street to what would look to anyone not in-the-know like the blandest-looking restaurant in the entire Dayton area. It was a small brown brick building, perfectly square, with a peeling yellow roof and a nearly unreadable sign out front that said ' het's Gr ll'. The parking lot would be nearly full when they got there, the rest of the church crowd having rushed there just after the service ended to get a good spot. Only, Jacob's mom was very good friends with Chet. She said they'd known each other since grade school, so he always saved them a seat inside and had drinks waiting: a Pepsi for Jacob, a lemon-lime Slice for Benny, a bottle of beer for their father, and ice water for their mother.

They sat down at their table. Jacob's father took a long, ritualistic pull from his beer. His mother had her Bible with her, as she always did, and sat it down next to her water, careful not to touch it to the spot where the condensation had pooled by her cup.

"That was a lovely service," Jacob's mother said. "Did you enjoy the service, Jacob? Benny?"

Jacob said, "Yeah," and shrugged.

Benny said, "Sure," and shrugged.

Their father took another drink from his beer.

"I always love the story of that Job. I'd like to think I'd be as strong as him, but then sometimes I get a headache and I'm already asking God why he would do this to me."

She'd said this as a joke. It didn't land well amongst the family, but Jacob laughed so that she didn't have her feelings hurt. It struck Jacob as odd that his mother would joke about that, because what she was really saying was what Jacob had been thinking during the service: God is cruel.

"How are we today?" Chet said beside them with a big smile. Jacob had never seen Chet in normal clothes, always in a black shirt, an apron, and thick black shoes. He had a net on his graying hair that always struck Jacob as hilarious, but he never said so to Chet. Jacob's mother stood up to give Chet a hug and a kiss on the cheek. "Let me guess," Chet started when she sat back down, "cheesesteak for the Mister, turkey club for the Missus, cheeseburger for Benny, and two hot dogs with ketchup for my man Jacob?"

They all nodded except Jacob's father, who tipped his beer lazily toward Chet.

"So, school starts next week," Jacob's mother said to him and Benny, "are you excited?"

"No," Benny said.

Jacob had been about to say 'Yes,' but having heard Benny's no and his apparent annoyance at the question, Jacob instead said, "No."

"You're going into high school, that's a big deal. You're not excited about that?" Benny shrugged. "And you," she said to Jacob, "you're going into fourth—isn't that exciting?"

Jacob lit up at the thought of fourth grade. He could hardly wait for it. He was excited to see his third-grade friends again and maybe meet some new friends. He was excited to meet Mrs. Hyman to see why it was the fourth-graders were always laughing when someone said her name. He thought she must be really funny for people to be laughing when they weren't even around her. Despite this excitement, Jacob only shrugged and took a sip of his Pepsi.

"Don't shrug so much," their father said.

"Anyway, I'm excited for you both," their mother continued. "I can't believe how old you boys are getting. I thank God every day for both of you."

Jacob tried to exchange a glance with his brother but Benny wasn't paying any attention. He had his face pointed down at his hands where Jacob could see the piece of paper with the drawing on it Benny had made earlier.

"Shrugging will wreck your posture," their father said.

Their mother said, "Benny, what is that you're looking at?"

Benny's eyes got wide, and he closed his hand so that the piece of paper was no longer visible. He smiled at his mother and said, "What are you going to do all day when we're at school? It can't be very fun at home all alone without us."

"Posture is important. Posture is what gets you ahead in life. Posture—"

Jacob scratched his butt.

"You know I work at the café on weekdays during the school year. I might have to pick up an extra shift this year." She paused and briefly glanced at their father, who took a sip of his beer. "But you're right, it won't be as fun as having you around."

"Who will be there to beat you at Boggle?" Jacob said with a grin.

"My brother had scoliosis when we were growing up. He had to get surgery to have it corrected and even now his posture is—"

"How do you always beat me at Boggle?" their mother asked.

"Excuse me, miss, could I please get another beer?"

"Miss? You know my name is Cheryl. I've been serving you beers for eight years."

"Thank God we don't live in one of those towns where you can't buy beer on Sundays."

"Yeah. God forbid," Cheryl said with a smirk. She went to get him another beer.

By the time their food came, the family was in good spirits. Even Benny seemed happy to be there, which was a very rare occurrence. Jacob ate his hot dogs with little regard for how much ketchup was smeared on his face. His mother often laughed when he would eat this way and tell him he eats more like a five-year-old than an almost-fourth-grader. His father would just roll his eyes and tell him to clean himself off. Benny ate his burger without a word. He was notoriously silent whenever he ate food, hyper-focused on the task at hand. He ate without regard to food order. He'd take a bite of his burger, and while he was still chewing, he'd throw a fry or two into the mix. He seemed to be constantly chewing, only stopping to take an occasional sip of his Slice, food still in his mouth, of course.

Their mother drove them all home, a Christian radio station playing softly from the dashboard. It seemed like more and more lately their mother was driving them home from Chet's. It was strange at first, to Jacob, because their father would usually drive them everywhere, but Benny had told him one afternoon that it was because of the beers their father was always drinking. He said he heard their mother and father fighting one night and that she told him she didn't want him driving after having alcohol anymore because he'd almost gotten them into a crash. Jacob wondered if the same thing could happen if he drank too much Pepsi, so that night, he decided to test it. He had five cans of Pepsi within a few hours and the only thing he felt was sick to his stomach. He thought he might throw up, but then the feeling passed and the only thing he was left with was a very full bladder.

It started to rain just as they pulled into their driveway. The sky had been clear and blue only moments before, and the rain seemed to come out of nowhere. Their home, a three-bedroom Cape Cod style house, always felt out of place amongst the two-story craftsman and colonial-style houses. Their yard had always been impeccable. Until recently, Jacob's father owned a landscaping company, so he'd have his team come at least once a week to ensure his yard was the best in the neighborhood. More recently, though, he'd been trying to get Benny to do the yardwork for him. In trying to teach Benny hard-work and discipline, their yard had started becoming less and less perfect. The lines from Benny's mowing zigged and zagged; grass was spilling over the edges onto their driveway and into the gutter on the street. Their dad didn't trust Benny with the hedge trimmer, so at least the hedges still looked pristine.

Their father handed Benny the key to the house and asked if he wouldn't mind running and opening the front door for them so they could run in from the rain. Benny groaned but took the key and did as he was asked. Probably it was easier than putting up a fight with their father. When the door was opened, Jacob hopped out of the car and made his way to the house. He sprinted as fast as he could, the rain coming down heavily now. In trying to get up the two steps that led to the front door, the tip of his foot hit concrete and he went flying forward. When he realized what had happened, blood had already started pooling under his left kneecap. Before he could react, he felt the strong arms of his father scooping him up and bringing him inside.

The gash in Jacob's knee was deep, but it didn't hurt too much. His mother cleaned the wound, put some Neosporin on it, and bandaged it up. He was still dripping wet and decided to go upstairs to his room to change.

Jacob's father had let him have free rein on what he wanted to do to his room when he was seven years old. At that time, he had been fascinated by dinosaurs. He liked that even after all this time, people were still studying them and learning new things about them. His mother had taken him to see *The Land Before Time* and it had quickly become his favorite movie. His bedroom reflected this love for dinosaurs almost excessively. The walls were covered in stenciled paintings of dinosaurs, his bedspread was of the characters in *The Land Before Time*, and he even had a bookshelf full of dinosaur books and dinosaur toys. This was perfect when he was seven, but now, at nine, he was embarrassed by it. The sight of his room always made him cringe as he crossed the threshold of the door from the hallway he shared with his brother.

Benny had run up the stairs as soon as they made it home. His door was shut, but Jacob could hear the arcade-like sounds of *Sonic the Hedgehog* coming from behind it. Jacob wanted to go in and play with him, but Benny had a rule that if his door was shut Jacob could only come in for emergencies. He rarely had his door shut, so Jacob did his best to keep his promise, scared of what Benny might do to him if he did.

Jacob put on a fresh set of clothes, this time a pair of basketball shorts and a long white t-shirt. He didn't mind wearing nice church clothes, but he also enjoyed getting out of them very much. The patter of rain on the window made him feel comfortable and he sat on his bed and wondered what it might be like to be a bug in the grass outside. He pictured a lone ant being carried away from its family on a quickly rushing bead of water. He pictured grasshoppers perching atop blades of grass and holding on for dear life. How big he, Jacob, must look to them, even though he was one of the smallest kids in his class. He stared at the T. rex painted on his wall and thought how large a T. rex must look to a bug.

From Benny's room he could hear the sound of the Sega Genesis being turned off and a TV show or movie being turned on. The very first word he could hear was the word 'Shit', and he knew he could absolutely not venture over to Benny's room now. Jacob wasn't allowed to watch anything with bad language in it, but he'd heard Benny watch enough of it that he could make out bad words here and there. He thought some words, like piss, might be bad but was too afraid to ask his parents. They might scold him for saying the word even though he was really just asking about it. Benny would tell him if he asked, but he didn't want to ask him either. Benny would play little tricks on Jacob whenever he had a chance and Jacob just knew that if he asked Benny about any of that stuff, he would find a way to trick Jacob into saying something he shouldn't say. This would then lead to him getting banished to this room, which made him so embarrassed. No, some questions were better left unasked.

Jacob walked downstairs with the intention of asking his mother or father to play Boggle with him. He knew his mother always let him win, but it felt good to him anyway. He found his mother and father lying together on their sofa with the TV on, both of them softly snoring. He went to the sink and poured himself a glass of water and brought it back up to his room with him. On his way, he heard Benny's TV say 'Ass.'

Back in his room, Jacob sat on his bed and tried to figure out what to do. He thought again about the bugs, but really, his mind got wondering about the true scale of things. He started to consider raindrops themselves. He thought about how he'd learned in class that our world was mostly made of water, in fact even our bodies are mostly made of water, so wouldn't it make sense that there would be something living inside of those droplets of rain? Maybe, if he looked close enough, he'd see another world within each one.

He remembered a Christmas a few years back when he'd received a pair of *Teenage Mutant Ninja Turtles* binoculars. He went around the house for weeks looking at things in the binoculars. He liked the sensation of being far away from something but being able to see it as if it was right in front of you. He liked the way you could adjust the dial in the middle to be blurry and then clear again. Of course, as with any new toy, he got sick of them and eventually forgot that he even had them. He went over to a bin with a bunch of old toys and rooted through it until he found them.

Jacob went to his window, which faced the front of the house, and pulled his blinds all the way up. He had to squint his eyes from the brightness; for a rainy day it was immensely bright. From the TV, he heard the word 'Penis.' He pointed the binoculars out the window and peered into them. Everything was blurry at first and so he adjusted the center dial until things started coming into view. He squinted, willing his eyes to see inside the rain drops, to see the worlds that might be within, but all he could see was falling rain and an empty front yard. He looked down at the grass to try to find some bugs but had no such luck.

It occurred to him that he might have a better view from back of the house. There was a bathroom in-between his room and Benny's room that had a small window facing the backyard. He went to it and again looked through the binoculars. He looked to the left first where he could see their neighbor's yard. Their grass had gone un-cut for a long time and even Benny's lines were straighter than theirs. Jacob had heard his father remark that the people that lived there were criminals and that he was just looking for his chance to call the cops on them. Jacob had never met them, but if his dad didn't like them, then neither did he.

He shifted his view to the right and into focus came their other neighbor's yard. Only weeks before Jacob's mother had said that a new couple had just moved into the house, and she had baked them cookies to welcome them. Jacob remembered asking if he could use their pool now, since the old neighbors didn't like kids, and his mom said they'd have to see. He saw the pool first, rippling in the pouring rain. He saw their tall fence blowing very slightly in the wind. He heard the TV say, 'Fuck.' As he scanned their backyard, he noticed two blobs of movement beside the pool. He adjusted the dial again and two figures came into view. Jacob's mouth dropped open as he saw what they were.

The TV again said: 'Fuck.'

On a long chair next to the pool, a man and a woman were naked. The woman was on top of the man, and to Jacob she looked like she might be writhing in pain. Her head was thrown back, her mouth wide open, and her lower half was grinding into the man. The man grabbed the woman's hair and started to pull. The woman's mouth got wider, and her eyes were shut in what could only be agony; or was it pleasure? Jacob felt bubbling in his gut, the same thing he had felt earlier when Benny showed him the picture he had drawn. He watched the woman closely, scanned every bit of her body, dripping wet in the rain.

"What are you doing?"

Jacob shot around, his eyes wide with fear and embarrassment. Benny stood in the doorway of the bathroom with a look of amusement on his face.

"Nothing," Jacob said. He hid the binoculars behind his back praying to God that Benny hadn't noticed them.

"What are you hiding back there?" Benny asked. Jacob gulped.

"Nothing." Even he could sense the feebleness of his lie. Fear enveloped him.

"What were you looking at?"

"Nothing."

Benny smirked and moved toward Jacob. Jacob knew he could fight this, but he also knew he would lose, so instead he just handed the binoculars to Benny and moved out of the way. Benny smirked again as he looked through them and out the window. Jacob was relieved at first when Benny looked to the left. He'd see nothing but a neglected yard and falling rain. Only then he shifted to the right and froze. His mouth dropped open. The TV said, 'Bitch.'

"Get out," Benny said in almost a whisper. Jacob didn't move, his legs simultaneously felt like cinder blocks and like jelly. "Get out!" Benny yelled, looking back at Jacob. "And shut the door."

Jacob managed to rush out of the bathroom. As he was shutting the door, he noticed Benny unzipping his pants. Everything was quiet at first except for the chatter of the TV in Benny's room. Jacob was calming down. A moment ago, it felt as if his heart was working so hard it might stop working completely. The TV said, 'I love you.' And then he heard a sound from down the stairs. It was his mother's voice, but he wasn't entirely sure she had really said anything. He positioned himself on the top step and turned his head so he could hear better.

"Oh my God!" his mother screamed. This startled Jacob and his heart started beating hard again. "Oh my God, Oh my God, Oh my

God," she whined. The TV said, 'Death.'

When the shock left him, Jacob ran down the steps toward the sound of his mother weeping. When he turned the corner, he saw her holding his father in her arms. His father appeared to be sleeping.

"Please, God," his mother said, not noticing Jacob standing by the sofa. "Please, God, no. Please, God, let him wake up."

She was shaking Jacob's father back and forth and he was not waking up. Finally, she looked up, tears streaming down her face, and saw Jacob. She stopped sobbing then. Went silent and looked very calm. She petted his father's head. "Jacob," she said, calmly still. "Please, Jacob. Call 911."

Jacob stood, frozen, not sure whether or not he should be crying. He felt pain in his knee where earlier there had been none. He wondered if the wound had re-opened and there was blood running down his leg but he was too afraid to look.

"Jacob. Sweetheart. Call 911. You remember, like we taught you?"

She cradled his father's head like it was a newborn baby.

"Jacob. Please, honey. Please call 911."

Jacob walked slowly to the phone and looked at the numbers. Everything was blurry. He realized that he was crying. He wiped his eyes and found the number 9, then 1, then 1 again. The line rang and he felt a chill run down his spine. It sounded ominous, that ring. His mother just went on rocking his father's head back and forth, back and forth, back and forth, back and forth, back and forth, and Jacob wondered why he wasn't waking up. The phone rang again, and he heard the sound of someone picking up on the other end. "Hello, this is 911—" Jacob couldn't hear what the person on the other end was saying. He couldn't hear anything. The only thing in his head was that ringing. He thought it might go on forever.

CHAPTER THREE

"I'm so sorry," Jake said to Tara Sorenson. He'd made it to the church early enough to get in some facetime with the members. That morning, he brushed his teeth twice and washed his face in case there was any dribble from the night before. He put on a dark gray blazer with jeans and a white t-shirt. He took his role as a 'young pastor' very seriously, which, these days, meant that he had to pretend to not take things too seriously. "It's good to see you," he said to Marcus Torrey. How he retained these people's names, he really wasn't sure. Looking at them before the service, he truly hated them. He hated how content they were with the free donuts and bagels that were donated to them in lieu of going in the trash at the bakery. He hated how they sipped on bad coffee and maintained a healthy chatter with the other members. Hate was bad, he knew, but he didn't really care; nor did he truly believe it.

"Jake, hey," Kendall Brandon said. She was the youth pastor at the church. That pretty much meant intern in church speak. "You look terrible, is everything okay?"

"Hey. Yeah. Just tired is all. I'll wake up before the sermon."

Kendall took the young pastor thing even more seriously than Jake did. She had on a pair of tennis shoes, jeans, and a tucked-in black halter top. She had a pretty face, very slim and moisturized. She seemed to have a different hair style every time Jacob saw her. Spending no time at all to do his own hair, he always admired the effort she put into it.

During her interview, she confided in Jake that she was a lesbian, but that having been in churches and Bible school for so long, she had learned to keep it a secret. He thought of his mother in church that morning that his father died. That word, *gay*, and that face she made when she heard it. Jake didn't care either way, though he was in agreement that it was probably for the best that she keep it under wraps. He wasn't sure if he trusted his congregation, and he certainly didn't trust the people that paid their salaries. After all, she was already the first black woman the church had had on staff; a point, Jake imagined, of contention amongst the administration.

Her sermons often hinted to the church youth that all people should be loved regardless of their lifestyles and backgrounds. That said, she never said the words she meant to say outright—call it a self-preservation thing—but she was under impression that her little hints were paying off. Jake himself didn't like to touch that topic. Tarrytown was a rather liberal place where most people were accepting of other ways of life, but the God-fearing churchgoers of the world, historically, don't have such a good track record of acceptance.

"Anyway, I wanted to let you know I'm taking some time off. Alex and I are heading on vacation."

Alex was the name they used for Kendall's girlfriend when the members were around. Her real name was Talia. Jake knew Kendall wanted him to ask her where they were going, but he didn't feel like chatting if he could avoid it, the hangover being what it was this morning. He wasn't anti-social, not really. In fact, he'd gotten to where he was today by being someone people felt they could talk to. Confide in. He supposed he was good at pretending.

"That sounds really nice," Jake said, "you deserve some time off. You've been working hard."

"Yeah. Thanks. Barry is going to take my spot." Jake didn't like Barry. He didn't think Kendall liked him either, but Barry was the guy that volunteered to take over if either of them needed some time off, so they didn't have much of a choice but to endure him. He had a habit of spitting when he talked. Not just little spritzes here and there: he was a full-on Super Soaker. The kids created a sort of splash zone when Barry was subbing in; it was the late kids, or the ones that weren't liked so much, that had to sit in the front. "We're going to L.A."

Jake said, "I have a brother that lives there," and then remembered he didn't really want to chat.

"You have a brother?"

Did he? It felt like it had been a lifetime since they'd seen each other. Are brothers still brothers if they've lost touch?

"Benny," he said. "If he still goes by that."

"What is he doing in L.A.?"

"I don't really know. We don't talk much."

Jake did know but he certainly wasn't about to tell his church's youth pastor that his older brother made porn. He looked at his watch and saw that (praise the Lord) it was time for him to go to his office, pop some Advil, and get up to the stage.

"I have to get ready. Hope the kids don't give you hell today."

"They always do. I'll see you around."

And to his office he went. It looked like the kind of office you see at dead-end jobs in movies. There were cubicle walls set up, desks with computers on them, stained rolling chairs that someone had oh-so-kindly donated. It always disoriented him to walk into his office from the relative beauty of the rest of the church. It was like a portal into mundanity. The bottle of Advil was in a cabinet in his desk. He pulled two pills out, thought about it, and then pulled out one more. He stared at them sitting on his desk in a little triangle. He knew he should dry swallow or else wash them down with water from the fountain down the hall. But. He fingered the cross necklace he wore around his neck. It was thick and heavy for its size. He looked toward the drawer above the cabinet where he had gotten the Advil. This drawer was locked, he knew, and he was fingering the key to it. He also knew that, once unlocked, he would find a half-full bottle of whiskey, and next to it his mother's old Bible. How nice it would be to wash the pills down with the whiskey.

He poked his head out of his office to make sure no one was around. When he was sure the coast was clear he bent down, slid the fake back off of the cross and put the key into the lock. In a swift motion he opened the drawer, pulled out the bottle of whiskey, put the pills in his mouth, and swallowed them with a gulp and a slight sting. Instantly his sprits improved. He felt like jumping and clicking his feet together. He imagined himself running into the hallway and sliding like a cartoon that can't catch its footing.

He put the bottle back in the drawer and locked it away. Until next time, old friend.

He grabbed the Bible that was on his desk and flipped the page to where he had his sermon written down on a piece of paper. He had tabbed the passages he needed to turn to so that it could appear as though he was reading his Bible, though the passages were typed out for him on the piece of paper. His sermon, like Christianity, was an illusion. He was a magician. Is this your card? Sit in this box and let's cut you in half. If you have faith, maybe God will spare you. If not, well, then it must have been your destiny; we should celebrate, we should rejoice, we should lap up the blood like dogs and soak it into our daily bread.

He smiled and nodded at the members of his church as he passed them in the aisle. His smile looked genuine. At least, he thought it did. It said, 'I love you, God loves you, praise Him!' He maintained this all the way to the stage, behind the podium, and while he launched into his sermon.

"Good morning," he started. "It's so nice to see you all here. To those of you who I haven't met, if it's anyone's first time, welcome to the Tarrytown Church of Christ. Before we begin, I wanted to give you notice that our friend Barry will be taking over the Youth Group next week while Kendall is out on vacation." Jake could have sworn there were a handful of groans in his audience. Apparently, it wasn't just he and Kendall who didn't like Barry.

"Now. Two weeks ago, we started a series I like to call the trifecta. There was Trust, such a powerful weapon. Then Hope, in which Paul told us to rejoice in our sufferings because we are a people of hope. And in this final week, what are we learning?" he beckoned the congregation.

"Faith," most of them said in unison. A shiver went up Jake's spine.

"Faith. That's right. For this week I'd like you all to open your Bibles to the book of Job." There was the sound of shuffling, of books being quickly thrown open for fear the message might be missed.

He'd been dreading talking about Job again Though he rarely thought of his past, at least sober, preaching the book of Job always seemed to open old wounds. His mouth was moving, and he hoped it was saying what he'd written down on his slip of paper, but his mind was thinking about another slip of paper. He remembered in exact detail the drawing Benny had made next to him the day their father died. He could have drawn it from memory. He remembered the way it had made him feel that day in his childhood church, the bubbling in his belly, the longing to see it again, again, again. The TV said, 'Tits.'

Jake blinked and the sermon was over. Someone in the crowd was sniffling.

"Before we go, I'd like you to join me in prayer." Heads lowered, hands slapped together. "Dear Heavenly Father. Let us be like Job. Even when things get hard, when things around us are falling apart, let us have the courage to believe you're still watching over us. Heavenly Father, send us home with faith in our hearts, love in our souls. Our Lord, Amen."

"Amen," the crowd said.

As people sidled out, some stopped by the exit doors to put small bills in an offering box. Some tossed their sticky napkins and semi-empty coffee cups into the trash bins. They smiled and held onto their Bibles as if they were rescue tubes and they were drowning in an open sea. Perhaps they did feel that way. Jake himself often felt like he was drowning in the sea, but his lifesavers were his good friends Jack and Jim and Evan. Nothing like more liquid to save you from drowning.

Most of the room had cleared out, and Jake started making his way toward the door. On his way there he was stopped by a voice. It was a strong, high-pitched voice. All it said was, "Hey." He turned around to where the voice had come from and saw a girl standing there. She was wearing a cream-colored dress that ended just below her knees. There was a floppy straw hat atop of amber hair. There were two bright blue eyes.

"I didn't get your name," she said.

"What?"

"You never said your name during your sermon."

"Oh," he laughed nervously, "it's Jake." He stuck out his hand. She sort of snorted, but then took it.

"I'm Lily."

Jakes heart leapt. Lily. Of course her name would be Lily. A flash of his old family computer went through his head. A loose satin robe. His pants at his ankles.

"Nice to meet you, Lily. Is this your first time here?"

"Not my first time, but it's been a long time. I was a kid the last time I was in here."

"What brings you back?"

Lily shrugged. She suddenly looked like she wanted to run out of the room. Then she smiled and said, "Story of Job. That's a classic."

"It's one that means a lot to—"

"Do you believe it?"

"Believe what?"

She said, with all seriousness, "Do you really believe that someone could go through all that and still have faith?"

Jake shrugged now. "The Bible is a book of metaphor and allegory."

"Children's stories," Lily said.

"We're all children in the eyes of God."

Lily's eyes narrowed. Jake had gone so long pretending to believe in all this that he feared he might let something slip if he talked to this girl any longer. But O' God, did he also want to stay near her. He needed to get himself out of this situation. He needed his booze.

"Cool hat," he said.

"I looked up 'what do people wear to church,' and this came up." She waved her hands from her head to her waist, and Jake couldn't help but scan her strong legs and black-heeled feet. "I probably should have been more specific about the time period and type of church I was going to."

They stood and stared at each other for a moment. Did she love him? Did he love her? A love at first sight kind of thing? He knew it was impossible, yet his brain told him it was true. "Anyway," he said, "I should go and talk to the other members. Put in facetime and all that."

"Sure," Lily said. "See you around I guess."

Jake didn't go and mingle. He went back to his office and employed the use of his cross necklace once more. Just a sip, he told himself, just to get him through the next service. One sip turned to two. And then another just for good measure before he locked his cabinet once more. He wondered what would happen if he was caught drinking back here. What would happen if someone smelled the liquor on his breath? He thought of Kendall. It saddened him that if both of them were found out, they would probably send him to a meeting and fire her. The fucking church ad(men)istration. The never-had menstruation. Even if they did fire him, they'd do it quietly. The most shame he would have would be the knowledge that he was the most cliché man on earth. "Oh, an alcoholic," they'd say with a smile, "we have to fire you, but don't sweat it. It's all part of the profession, my boy. At least it's not as bad as what those Catholic priests do, am I right?" If they found Kendall out, they'd tell everyone exactly why. They'd encourage the slanderous mommy groups. Every religious institution in the state of New York (and parts of New Jersey) would know about it and she'd have to find some more progressive church in, say, Portland.

Worse, given his career trajectory, wasn't he liable to become one of these old white men himself? Wasn't it just like a young white man to think he was different from the rest of them, only to turn around and become what he'd always hated most?

These hypotheticals had gotten Jake so worked up that he unlocked the cabinet for one more calming sip of his whiskey. He locked it away again and slid the false back of the necklace into its proper place. In another cabinet he had an open roll of breath mints; he peeled back the paper just enough to pop the one on top out and toss it in his mouth. He enjoyed the way it cooled his mouth. He was already feeling much less angry, and he felt more than ready to tackle the second service. He put on a toothy smile before he hit the threshold of his office door. The thought of going home and drinking where he couldn't get caught is what really propelled him forward and toward the noisy chatter of his congregation.

***

Out of life-long habit, Jake maintained a ritual of going to the same place, Ava's Diner, every week after church services were over. If he had any friends at all in Tarrytown, it was Ava and Thomas, who ran the diner together. He never saw them outside of the diner, and if he did, he'd probably have that sort of brain confusion you'd get as a kid seeing one of your teachers out in public. They belonged here. They had everything they needed, why leave? What he liked most about Ava's was that almost no one else from his church went there. He tried to assure himself it wasn't because Ava and Thomas were black, but he never quite could. The thought always sat there, a deadweight in the back of his mind.

"Ah the good pastor himself," Ava said coming out from the kitchen soon after Jake sat down in his usual spot. "How are you?"

"I'm good," Jake said, "and yourself?"

"Can't complain," Ava said, smiling. Jake had never asked Ava her age, but if he had to guess, he'd place her in her early sixties. That's not to say she looked that age. In fact, she was slender, and her kind face held very few wrinkles. Jake wasn't even sure what basis he had for thinking she was in her sixties. Maybe she just had that motherly, or grandmotherly, way about her. He missed his own mother dearly. "You're looking too thin. Do you eat when you're not here?"

"How could I eat any other food? Nothing can live up to yours."

"Well, then you better come by more often and we'll fatten you up."

"You'd get sick of me," Jake said.

"That's probably true." Ava smiled at him and put a hand on her hip. "You want a beer?"

"Yes. Please," Jake said. He tried to hide the eagerness in his voice.

The bell at the door rang, but Jake had his back to the door and didn't look to see who it was. Ava said, "I'll be right with you," and then looked back at Jake. "You know what you're eating today?"

When Jake started coming to Ava's, he thought it might be nice to have a usual, like he had when he was a kid. Only after a year of eating cheeseburgers every single Sunday did he decide to branch out. He'd tried much of the menu, but recently he decided to start at the beginning and make his way to the end each week. Last week was a french dip. He looked below it and gulped.

"I guess it's hot dogs today," Jake said.

"Anything on 'em?"

He gulped again. "Ketchup, please."

She walked off, presumably to put his order in to Thomas or someone else in the back.

"Hot dogs, huh?" A high, strong voice behind him said. As he was turning around the voice said, "Interesting choice."

Lily was sitting at the table behind him with a grin on her face. She no longer had the hat on her head.

"Most people go out to eat when their service is over. Did you have errands to run or something?"

"Most adults don't order hot dogs for lunch."

"We're still talking about the hot—"

"Unless you're at a baseball game or—"

"I'm doing this thing where I make my way down—"

"A cookout! Or Coney Is—"

"Anyway, I come here to get away from church peo—"

"But not at a diner."

"Would you like to join me?"

Jake's eyes widened. He didn't know where that came from. Had he really said those words? What would they talk about? He was out of practice on the real-conversation front. He couldn't use his stock phrases in a face-to-face conversation that lasted more than a minute or two. In the old days—days not even really so much old as forgotten—he could carry on long conversations, but given his current lifestyle, it had gotten difficult. He felt relieved that he had enough alcohol in his system that his hangover was gone and his brain felt less fuzzy.

"You look like you regret asking that," Lily said. The smile on her face was incredibly pretty. Her teeth were an imperfect off-white that, to Jake, felt like perfection. Too white is creepy; too yellow is gross.

"No," Jake lied. Or was it a lie? "It would be nice to have some company here for once."

Lily stood up and made her way over to his table. Her eyes were radiant even under the horrible lighting in the diner. He thought momentarily of standing but then thought better of it. That felt like something men did in old movies. Did people do that anymore? Suddenly he couldn't feel his legs, so it really didn't matter one way or the other; he would not be able to stand.

"It smells like hot dog over here," Lily said as she took a seat across from him. As she was sitting, her knee brushed Jake's.

"I haven't even gotten them yet."

Ava was walking over to their table with a beer, and when she saw Jake had company, she smiled and tilted her head. "And who is this?" she asked, setting the beer down in front of Jake.

"Lily," Jake said. "Lily, this is Ava."

"Jake's my father."

"She means pastor."

Lily smiled and said, "Nice to meet you."

"Would you like anything to drink?"

"I'll have one of those," she said, pointing to the beer, "and the hot dogs please. Ketchup."

Ava narrowed her eyes wondering if this was a joke. When it appeared as though it wasn't she said, "Sure. I'll have that right out for you."

When she was gone, Jake said, "Did you order those hot dogs as a bit?"

"Maybe," she said. "Or maybe talking about hot dogs just got me hungry for some."

"Doubt it."

"Anyway, this feels weird, having lunch with my pastor." Ava walked over and set a beer in front of Lily. As she walked off, she gave Jake an eyebrow-raise and a smile. Jake felt blood rushing to his cheeks. "Even weirder having a drink with my pastor," Lily said. She lifted her beer and tipped it toward Jake. He lifted his own and they tapped them together. "To Jesus?" she said.

"And hot dogs," Jake said. Lily laughed, and they both drank their beers. He'd been good at banter, once, but hadn't employed it in a long time.

"Are you even allowed to drink?" Lily asked when they put the beers down. "I'm very new to this whole religion thing."

"Sure, we can drink. We're just not supposed to get drunk."

"And do you?"

"How old are you anyway?"

"And do you?" she repeated.

"Do I what?"

"Get drunk?" Lily asked. She was studying Jake closely, perhaps anticipating catching him in a lie. Instead, he just shrugged and took an awkward sip from his beer. "I heard a rumor," she said, "that you're celibate. Is that true?"

She'd been at his church only one day and already she knew of his celibacy. Was there nothing else exciting going on in town?

Was the only thing to talk about in the moment before or after a church service that the guy spitting Bible verses and lessons at them wasn't having sex? Did they feel sorry for him? Did they envy him? He'd preached about saving yourself for marriage many times, but never did he breach the actual subject of celibacy. Maybe it was time. Maybe he should make up a reason for his own celibacy and preach it as if he'd wanted them to know all along. Would that stop them talking about it behind his back?

"You're very direct," Jake said.

"I don't like rumors. I'd rather ask about them directly than take it from someone who probably doesn't know you at all. So. Are you celibate?" She was staring directly into Jake's eyes. He felt more uncomfortable with that stare than he did telling her the truth.

"Yeah, it's true."

"You've never had sex before?"

"Nope."

"Do you masturbate?"

O', if only Benny were here. Benny would know what to do. He would know what to say. Jake wasn't even sure where Benny was these days. Last he'd heard he was working in the porn industry in Los Angeles, but there was no way of knowing if he was still there. He'd never seen any of his brother's works, of course. He never really asked him about his job. When was the last time they even talked?

"No, I don't. Can we talk about something else?"

"If you want to," Lily said. He could tell by her face she really meant it too.

"What are you doing here?"

"In the diner?"

"No," Jake made a little movement above himself with his hands, "here. Tarrytown."

Ava came out of the kitchen with two plates of hot dogs with ketchup, and a basket of french fries. She sat the hot dogs down in front of each of them and the fries in-between them. The bell at the door rang again at the entrance.

"Fries are on me," Ava said, grinning at the both of them, "you two enjoy your meal and let me know if you need anything at all."

"Thank you," Jake and Lily said in unison, and Ava walked off toward the new customer.

Lily reached for the fries and ate a few of them. As she munched, she said, "Just home for a bit while I find a new job." Usually someone talking with their mouth full would disgust Jake, but when Lily did it, it seemed perfectly normal. Cute, even.

"You're from here?"

"God this is boring," she said, but she answered anyway. She breathed in deeply and all in one breath she said, "IwasborninDetroitbutwhenIwastwomydadleftandmymomdidnthaveenoughmoneytostayinDetroitandshehadacousinwholivedhereinTarrytownsowemovedhereandthenIwenttocollegeatNYUandthenworkedinthecityforawhileandnowimbackhereinTarrytowneatinghotdogswithapastor." And as her air ran out, she breathed in heavily again and then sighed. "Anyway, I probably won't be here long." She took another bite of the fries.

"Sorry, I missed that. Can you say it again?" This made Lily laugh.

"You could've asked me anything, like do I masturbate, and instead you asked why I was in Tarrytown."

"People don't typically want their pastor asking them if they masturbate." He took a big bite of his hot dog and failed to catch the subtle innuendo in it.

"Well, I do," Lily said. "I mean, I do masturbate. And it would have been nice if you had asked." Lily took a bite of her own hot dog and did not miss the innuendo in it. Just what Jake needed, an attractive woman teasing him for being celibate. Her mouth very full she said, "God I hate hot dogs."

"Then why did you get them?"

She swallowed. "For the bit, of course. You can never waste an opportunity for a good bit."

"Was this one worth it?" Jake asked.

"Absolutely," Lily said with a grin. There were still tiny pieces of breading in her teeth and a dab of ketchup on the side of her mouth.

Jake looked back toward the door to the kitchen where he saw Thomas' head peeking out at them, Ava just behind him whispering something in his ear. He had on a white t-shirt and a greasy apron, his standard work garb. When he saw Jake was staring, he shifted his eyes and shut the door. Jake shook his head, amused.

CHAPTER FOUR

During the week, Jake tried his best to be of service to people in need. This was the only part of his job that made him feel useful. He might not make much of a difference taking people's money and telling them for the hundredth time in gruesome detail how Jesus was nailed to a cross, but when he visited people in the hospital or at their homes when they were in need, at least then he could feel like he was making a difference. Prayer is strong. Not in that your prayers actually reach anybody, but because they give people hope. Liver failure? Pray about it! Mother of a family of four died? Pray for her kids! Cancer? Prayer, prayer, prayer. Who knows, maybe some of them do make it through somewhere. Jake could get behind the idea of manifesting things. I want a girlfriend, I want a girlfriend, I want a girlfriend and poof, girl drops some strawberries in front of you at Trader Joes and your hands touch as you're helping her pick them up. Your eyes meet. You get a dog together and name it Spot and suddenly there are baseball games and weddings and then you retire and move to a home together and still on some occasions you'll steal some fresh strawberries from the abusive kitchen staff and let your hands touch them together until they find you both that way, both of your fingers red with goopy bits of strawberry.

The Tuesday after his meal with Lily, Jake was headed to Sleepy Hollow Hospital (during the day, of course) to visit a ten-year old boy who had recently come down with pneumonia. It was one of those out-of-season sicknesses that somehow seemed stronger than the in-season ones. He was the nephew of one of his weekly members. She emailed him, pleading for him to come and pray over the 'poor child.' Jake always had toys ready for occasions such as these. One of his favorite days he could remember was walking to a dollar store with an empty grocery bag and filling the thing to the brim with cheap toys. There were knock-off superhero dolls, cheap water guns, those glasses with the springy eyes, helicopter caps. He came across a dinosaur grabber thing and thought about the room he had until he was thirteen. He took joy in reaching into the bag and pulling out whatever his hand touched whenever he had a check-in with a kid. Even the slightly older ones would get a kick out of what he brought them. Today's gift was an army guy with a parachute that no-doubt wouldn't work. Jake probably had the same one when he was a kid.

His cell phone rang as he pulled into the parking lot of the hospital. His Aunt Beth was calling. When was the last time they talked? Jake wasn't sure.

"Hello?" he answered. He put the car in park and turned off the engine. A rain drop plopped down on his windshield.

"Jacob, it's Beth, how are you?"

"I'm doing great, and you?"

"I'm just so glad to hear your voice, it's been so long."

"I know, I was just thinking about you," Jake lied. Truth was, for a woman who raised him for his entire high school career, he often forgot that she existed. At least these days he did.

The rain fell heavier now, and Jake wished he had brought an umbrella.

"Benny and I were just having a conversation about you, and I thought maybe I'd try to see if you weren't busy." Jake's heart leapt at the mention of his brother.

"I have to run into a hospital to meet this boy with pneumonia, but I can talk for a second. Or maybe I can call you after."

"Oh that sounds serious, I don't want to interrupt."

"Well, he'll still have pneumonia either way," Jake said. After a moment, he winced and said, "Sorry, bad joke."

"Smartass," Beth said. He could sense her smile through the phone. It was a smile he suddenly missed greatly.

"Everything going okay at the school?" Beth was an administrator at the high school Jake went to in Akron.

"You know I retired there," Beth said. Beth *had been* an administrator at the high school Jake went to.

"Right, right, I knew that," Jake lied again, "habit, I guess."

"Well things are just fine with me regardless. I," she paused uneasily, "I miss your mother. I always miss her. But I'm doing just fine. I'm glad to know you and Benny are doing so well."

"I miss her too," Jake found himself saying. He was a little surprised he said it. It's not something he would usually say out loud except maybe to himself in the late hours of the night with a mouth full of low-to-mid-shelf liquor.

"You go and meet with that boy. I'll pray for him, for whatever that's worth."

"I've never seen you pray."

"Everything's worth trying once," she said.

"Thank you. Love you, Beth. I'll call you soon, okay?"

"Please do. I miss you. I love you too."

Jake hung up the phone with a sigh. He'd missed her too, but he knew he wouldn't call her again anytime soon. He'd probably never talk to her if she didn't call him from time to time. He knew that probably hurt her. After all, she'd done so much for him and Benny when she wasn't forced to. He didn't like to think of the burden they'd probably been. More so himself than Benny, who was off at college most of the time. It was as simple as turning on his phone, finding her name, and pressing a button. He could even ask his phone to do it and he wouldn't have to touch a thing.

But he knew he wouldn't.

He looked around his car to see if he may have left an umbrella somewhere inside of it, but with no luck, he took a deep breath, exited his car, put his Bible above his head, and ran for it. By now it was pouring down rain and he was saying curse words that were drowned out by the rain and the Bible above him. The entrance had seemed so close when he parked his car, but now it felt miles away. When he finally made it inside, he found himself panting and wheezing and felt some regret for not having been to the gym in years. He didn't let himself think that, in reality, it was probably the alcohol slowly killing him from the inside out.

Naturally, Jake hated hospitals. From the moment you walk in the smell lets you know that you're not welcome. It's not only medicinal. It's bare feet and bedpans and puddles of tears. It's mop water and latex gloves and laundry. One of Jake's biggest fears was getting sick enough to have a long stay in the hospital, to have to make one of the rooms his very own hotel room. Scratchy sheets and bad TV all day. Hey doc, what's going on, we just have to run some tests, well you already ran a bunch of tests didn't they tell you anything, just a few more tests, a few more tests and we'll get you right on out of here okay bud?

Jake made his way to room 408 where the boy's aunt had directed him. Jake didn't know a lot about the boy other than that his name was Philip, he was ten, and he had pneumonia. People forget that you're supposed to have an actual conversation with these kids to put them at ease, and to have a conversation with someone, it really helps to know a thing or two about them. Jake had done enough of these to get him through, but he always struggled with the first part: the introduction. Once he got to the prayer part, it was all essentially autopilot.

He knocked on the door, which was slightly ajar. He heard nothing. He might have knocked too quietly, or the boy could be asleep. Jake thought he might knock again, but as he lifted his hand, a nurse came to the door and gave him a look as if he was a crazy person. She had short, platinum blonde hair, and Jake could see the beginning of a tattoo on the spot between her left shoulder and her neck. Her scrubs were plain burgundy, and she had her hands in her shirt pockets. She pushed the door open with her elbow and went inside. Jake followed.

"How are you today?" the nurse asked the boy with a smile.

"I'm okay," Philip groaned. He was very thin and pale in the face. There were dark circles around his eyes. His brown hair stood up on the left side and in the back.

"I'm just going to take your temperature, and then I'll get out of your hair. There's someone here to see you."

Jake had been cowering behind the nurse and Philip hadn't even noticed him until now. The boy looked confused, even slightly fearful.

"I'm Jake," Jake said as the nurse put the thermometer near the boy's armpit. "I'm the pastor at the church your aunt Kate goes to." The boy was silent. "Have you been to church before?"

Philip nodded but remained silent.

Jake looked around the room awkwardly while the nurse finished up. A bag of Philip's things was in a chair beside the bed. Sticking out was a Nintendo Switch. He could work with this.

"All set," the nurse said. She looked like she was surprised by the result of the measurement. "Looking good. I bet you'll be out of here in no time." She walked off.

"You like Nintendo?" Jake said, moving closer to Philip. Philip lit up.

"Yes," he said.

"I haven't touched a video game in a long time, but my brother and I used to have a Sega Genesis. Do you know what that is?"

"Is that what *Sonic* was on?"

"That's right," Jake said, "have you played one?" Philip shook his head. "Anyway, I had some friends that got a Nintendo 64. We used to play *Mario Kart* and *Super Smash Bros.* all the time. Do you play those games?"

"*Mario Kart* is my favorite," the boy said, sitting up in his bed. "I'm not very good at *Smash*, but I play that sometimes with my friends.

Jake moved to the chair beside the boy, sat down, and said, "I always play as Bowser in *Mario Kart*."

"He's so slow!" Philip said.

"But he handles like a dream. Who's your go-to anyway?"

"Luigi."

"Luigi! You know how I think of Luigi?" Philip was listening intently. "I think of him as the big green butt I pass right after the start."

This got Philip laughing. It was a weak laugh, but a laugh nonetheless. He said, "Bowser has a way bigger butt."

"Your mom has a big butt!" Jake said.

"You have a big butt!" Philip retorted through bouts of laughter.

And then he started coughing. It was one of those coughs synonymous with hot medicinal drinks. With soothing honey and cooling ice cream. It was loud and crackled with a ferocity that suggested throat blisters popping and phlegm loosening. It was enough to cut both of their laughter short and for Jake to remember why he was really here. Enough butt talk.

When the coughing died down, Philip went silent, clearly trying to pretend it hadn't been painful. He seemed to be holding back tears.

"Your aunt sent me to pray over you. Would that be okay with you?"

The boy nodded for a moment, but then the tears that had been welling escaped and he began to sob. Through sobs, he asked Jake if he was dying.

"No," Jake said, alarmed, "no, you're going to be fine." He put a hand on Philip's arm. "Sometimes prayer just helps hurry a sickness along. It's like how if you blow on hot soup, it helps make it cooler faster, cool enough to eat."

"Ok," Philip said, sniffling. He seemed less frightened. Jake heard a squeak by the door, and he looked back to see the nurse from earlier peeking out from behind it. When she saw him looking, she jumped backward and out of sight. He realized he was still holding Philip's arm and he snatched his hand away. People were suspicious of men touching boy's arms these days. For good reason, too, Jake supposed.

"I'm going to bow my head. You can too if you want, or you can just listen." Philip bowed his head and put his hands together just like Jake did when he was a kid. "Dear Heavenly Father," Jake started, "I ask that you watch over this boy, Philip. I ask that you please remove the sickness that is ravaging his body. I ask that you get him back safely to his family so that he can talk and laugh and play with them again. And above all, father, I ask that you give Philip the courage to play as Big Butt Bowser at least once so he can see how amazing he is." Jake peeked out at Philip, who couldn't help but smile. "Our Father, amen."

When they both opened their eyes, Jake could swear the boy actually appeared to have gotten better. He knew it wasn't possible—he knew that his prayer did nothing but perhaps lift the spirits of the boy, but cure him? No. He still had a long way to go. Jake stood to leave and told Philip to take care. He made his way to the door and then stopped and turned back around.

"I almost forgot," Jake said, reaching into his pocket. "I have this bag of silly toys I like to give to," here he paused, "friends."

He pulled the army guy out of his pocket. The parachute was wrapped tightly around him so that you could only see his head and his feet. He went to hand it to Philip who looked puzzled. "Have you seen one of these before?" Jake asked. Philip shook his head. "You unwrap this plastic, and it'll become a parachute. Then you can throw the guy in the air or off of something tall and, in theory, his parachute should catch, and he should float down." As he described, he moved his hands in demonstration. "Anyway, it probably won't work, but part of the fun is seeing if it's a good one or not." Jake tossed the toy to Philip across the room. Philip caught it and tried to hide a smile.

"Thanks," Philip said.

Jake said, "You bet," and then walked out of the room.

He started to walk down the hallway when he heard, "Hey," from behind him. He turned to see the nurse from Philip's room. His eyes moved first to the tattoo poking out under her scrubs and then to the name on her nametag, Eve, and then to her eyes. "I haven't heard that boy laugh since he came in."

"Boys twelve and under, just move the conversation to butts or farts." He paused. "Who am I kidding—boys of any age, really." The nurse smiled.

"I use the same trick when I'm on a date. I bring up my ass." Had she said this to be funny? Was she flirting? Jake wasn't a good judge of these things having been solitary for so long. If it was flirting, he knew he should end it right now lest he—

"You go on a lot of dates?" Jake said.

"I go on a lot of bad dates."

Jake's heart started pounding wildly in his chest. He could feel his cheeks getting hot and hoped Eve didn't notice. His eyes moved between the tattoo and her eyes. This she noticed. She pulled the arm of her scrubs down over her shoulder so that more of the tattoo was showing. Jake felt as if he couldn't breathe.

"It's a snake tangled up in ivy. I'm thinking about getting it touched up. I've had it since college."

Jake suddenly wanted to touch it. He wanted to rub his hand up and down the tattoo. He wanted to kiss the spot where it ended just at the base of her neck. What would it be like to take this woman to dinner like a normal person? He'd wear a nice button-down, maybe even a sport jacket, she'd wear something just a little revealing, something that could show off that tattoo, that ass that she so willingly brought up. They could get a dozen oysters to start. She'd get the lobster ravioli; he'd order the veal. He would make dumb jokes and she would laugh, and then he'd pay at the end of the date. Maybe they'd even kiss in the parking lot before driving to their homes. Maybe Eve would text him before she even got back to her house to tell him what a great time she had. Jake would say he had a great time too; maybe they could do it again next week? And then the next week maybe he'd get to touch her ass or her breasts. And then the next—

"Anyway, I think it's really nice that you come do this for the kids," Eve said pulling her sleeve back over her shoulder.

Snap out of it snap out of it snap out of it.

"It's just part of the job."

"You don't really strike me as the pastor type."

Jake noticed his dick was hard in his jeans. This made him feel like fainting. What if she could see it? What then?

He shifted his feet and said, "Well, you should come to the church sometime. Tarrytown Church of Christ."

"Church isn't really my thing. But I'll see you around, yeah?" She smiled at him and then turned around and walked away.

Jake stood still for a long time. He felt his hard-on relaxing in his pants. He did everything he could to keep his mind off of the shoulder tattoo, his dating fantasy, her beautiful eyes. He hadn't even registered their color, he only knew they were entrancing. Finally, after he wasn't sure how long, Jake started moving. He made it out the door of the hospital with no incident. He made it to his car much the same. He looked at the clock: 2:36. His heart was still pounding. He made a long sigh and then said out loud, to nobody, "I need a fucking drink."

CHAPTER FIVE
2000

Jacob, a quiet and timid 13-year-old, sat next to his mother and Benny in another Sunday church service. He had pimples on his face now. Two fresh ones had just sprouted on the right side of his mouth. It hurt him to talk. His newly cut hair was parted in the middle, and he could see it bounce in his peripherals when he turned or bobbed his head. He'd grown taller and skinnier so that he looked nearly skeletal. He was very interested in girls. In fact, he couldn't keep his eyes off of the girl directly in front of him. He could only see the back of her head, a long, curly wave of blonde, but he imagined all sorts of things about what she looked like from the front: possibly she looked like Kelly Kapowski from *Saved by the Bell*—yes, she definitely looked like that, and not only that, but she also had on the nurse outfit from that one episode, only her top was falling off and slowly, slowly you could see her breasts appearing, but they were in church and Jacob knew you weren't supposed to see those things in church, but then again, it wasn't a sin to just not tell someone their top was falling off, and still the top slowly fell and Jacob just couldn't stand it, he wanted, needed, to see them so badly, maybe he could even reach out and touch them, and he felt as if in a trance, he felt his body go almost numb except for his arms and hands that were reaching out for a feel, just a small feel, and he was almost there, he almost had them, he—

"What are you doing?"

Jacob snapped out of his fantasy and noticed that his arms were raised almost like a zombie's. His eyes widened, and he desperately tried to cover up what he had been thinking about (in church nonetheless!!!) and grabbed a pen from the seat back in front of him (her seat back). He let his hands linger maybe a little bit too long on the chair before pulling the pen back to his own body. He lifted it up to show Benny, who was looking at him like he was an insane person.

***

Benny had grown muscular where Jacob had grown skinny. He had just finished his Senior year of high school where he'd been a second baseman on the school's baseball team. He was all set to go to Ohio University in the fall. Not his first choice, but he wanted to stay close to be there for Jacob and their mother. His hair was thick and dark, and he had the beginnings of a beard growing on his face, albeit a patchy one. He was frustratingly handsome and even more frustratingly very popular. Especially with girls. When their mother wasn't paying attention, which was a lot in those days, Benny would sneak girls up into his room. It seemed to Jacob like it was never the same one, but they'd always do the same humiliating thing to him. Up the stairs they would come, Benny leading the girl up with his hand, and Jacob would peek out of his room. The girls would stop and smile at Jacob and whisper to Benny, "Aww, your brother is adorable," and give Jacob the sort of look you might give to a cute puppy dog; and then they'd go into Benny's room and quietly shut the door.

Jacob could only remember Benny getting caught one time. It was a result of bad timing; or was it bad luck? It was late, later than Jacob should have been awake and later than their mother was typically awake. Jacob heard movement from outside of his door and got up to peek through. Benny was leading a girl quickly and quietly out of his room. This wasn't a girl Jacob recognized and he wondered how Benny had snuck her in. He kissed her in the doorway. She smiled at him. Jacob jumped when he saw that Benny was looking directly at him. He held his finger to his mouth in a shushing motion. Jacob nodded. Benny led the girl down the stairs and to the door. Jacob left his room and peeked down the stairs. Once again Benny stopped to kiss her, a quick but intense kiss, and then she was gone. He shut the door.

"You ought to be ashamed of yourself!"

Jacob noticed the yell was coming from the kitchen. He found out later from Benny that, at the exact moment he'd gone down the stairs with the girl, their mother had gone to the kitchen to fill a glass of water. Had he led her down the stairs thirty seconds earlier or thirty seconds later, their mother never would have found out.

Benny was silent. Frozen. Jacob was sure Benny would handle this coolly. He was always so cool, he'd surely find a way out of this. But there he stood, motionless.

"Who was that girl?" their mother yelled. It was a weak yell. She was out of practice. Since their father had died, she'd been aloof, near-catatonic, her only real activity outside of church was reading and writing in that damn Bible of hers.

"No one," Benny squeaked. Jacob was alarmed by Benny's unease.

"Did you sleep with her?" An unexpected firmness now. Such anger—or was it disgust?

Benny said nothing, his silence all the answer she needed.

A scream came. A glass shattered in the kitchen. Stomping, then.

And suddenly their mother appeared in Jacob's view. He quickly turned to hide himself from her, but his curiosity made him turn back around. His mother stood fuming in front of Benny, Benny still motionless except for a light trembling. There was a hesitation, a pause in the confrontation, and then suddenly, as if in a flash, there was a slapping sound. Benny held his cheek in astonishment. Their mother shook her hand as if to whisk the pain, and the action she had committed, away. Jacob must have made a noise, because their mother's head shot up toward him, and for a moment, he was afraid she would stomp up the stairs and slap him too. Instead, she just stared at him as if she was looking at the killer of their father. Jacob felt tears on his cheeks.

"Benny will burn in hell for what he's done," she said, still staring at Jacob. She did something neither of them expected, then; how could they have? She thrust her hand, the non-slapping hand, to Benny's crotch and squeezed. She looked him dead in the face as he sobbed. "I ever catch you again, I'll cut it off."

She let go, gave Jacob one last burning look, and then stomped to her room and shut the door. Benny fell to the floor, sobbing. Jacob ran down the stairs and held him. They cried together like that a long time.

***

Jacob gave the pen a twirl and it fell into his lap. A boy at school had tried to teach him to spin a pen on the back of his thumb, but Jacob had yet to master it. He picked the pen up and tried again, unsuccessfully. And then his attention went back to the girl in front of him. He imagined running his fingers through that long hair. Now she looked like Rachel Greene from *Friends* with her shoulders and belly showing. And again, her top was starting to come off, except this time it was her pulling it off for him, staring at him as she did so. He could almost see them, and his mouth again dropped open.

"Amen," he heard the entire crowd around him say. He'd missed the entire prayer for his impure thoughts. He was embarrassed but very glad that no one else could live in his head. Though that wasn't true, was it? God could hear all of his thoughts. He knew everything. As they were getting up to leave, he sent God an apology in his head and said it wouldn't happen again; he promised.

The girl that had been in front of him turned around. She really was very pretty, but she looked nothing like she did in his fantasies. She looked older than him, maybe Benny's age or a year younger. She smiled at Jacob, and he blushed. And then he realized she'd actually been smiling at Benny, who was smiling back at her coolly. She looked him up and down in a flirty way and then turned to leave. Jacob watched as Benny checked her out from behind.

Where Benny had often been cold to Jacob before their father died, he was now kind and included Jacob in lots of things. He never closed his door unless he had a girl in there with him, an open invitation for Jacob to come watch movies or play games with him. Except for that night their mother had caught Benny with the girl, she paid little attention to the two of them. This gave Jacob a free pass to watch Rated R movies (though, he made Jacob close his eyes at nude scenes) and play games full of violence. Benny spoke often of internet porn. He said that he'd heard about a site through a friend of a friend of a friend of a friend where you could find some porn clips for no charge at all. He said they didn't even ask you for a credit card. Jacob begged Benny to tell him what the website was, but Benny would just shake his head and say, "Maybe in a couple of years. You don't need to be watching that stuff now." He'd nonetheless continue to bring it up, perhaps to taunt Jacob or perhaps because it was the only thing that was going through his head all the time. Either way, Jacob wanted in.

After the church service ended, their mother went to talk to one or two people, but the conversations were kept very short, and within ten minutes or so, they were already out in the car and on their way to Chet's. At this rate, they'd be one of the early arrivers, something that had happened increasingly often after the death of their father.

The three of them were mostly quiet at Chet's. They ordered their usuals and sat in an uncomfortable silence. Instead of their mother trying to start a conversation, it was Benny who tried.

"So," Benny started while chewing some ice from his cup, "I'm supposed to get the information on my roommate soon."

"Oh. Good," their mother said.

"It will probably be someone from the baseball team. They try to keep teammates close so we can build friendships off the field."

"Can I come watch you play baseball in college?" Jacob asked.

"If you can get a ride, sure. Or when you learn to drive."

"How far is it?" Jacob asked.

"How far is what?"

"Ohio University."

Benny looked down at his hands and said, "Only a few hours. Pretty close huh?"

Jacob's eyes widened. That sounded far to him. Their mother stood up and walked into the ladies' room.

"Well, I'm excited for you," Jacob said, "even if it means I don't get to see you as much."

"I'll call you all the time," Benny assured, "you and mom."

Their food came then, and they started eating without their mother. They didn't talk anymore. Jacob found his mind wandering to the girl who had sat in front of them at church. Now he pictured having a magic remote where he could have paused everyone in the church and gone around to the girl and stripped her clothes off. He pictured the scene in detail. She was wearing a baby blue bra and matching underwear. He fantasized he got the bra off in one go, something he'd heard Benny talk about being able to do. He imagined her perfect breasts falling out of them. He chewed his hot dog and felt that familiar bubbling in the bottom of his gut. And then the memory of their mother grabbing Benny's crotch flashed in his mind and he tried to ignore it.

Eventually, their mother came back and had decided not to eat her food. Chet put it in a box and said something quietly to her. He appeared concerned. When she walked off, he turned to the boys.

"Is everything okay at home?" he asked.

Benny said, "Yeah, everything's fine."

"Your mom is okay?"

"Her husband died a few years ago, you think she's okay?"

Chet lowered his eyes but then looked at the both of them sternly. "If you ever need anything, please call over here and I'll come right away. You both still know the number?"

"Yeah, we got it." Benny seemed annoyed with Chet and Jacob wasn't sure why. Jacob always liked Chet.

"Ok. I'll see you boys next week. You take care."

"Bye," Jacob said. He followed Benny, who had already walked away, out of the door.

Back home, Jacob and Benny went to Benny's room and played *Street Fighter II* while their mother went into her room and shut the door. The TV said, "Huyyah!" Benny always won at these games, but Jacob was just glad to get to play with him. They wanted to get a PlayStation or a Nintendo 64 like all their friends had, or even to hold out for a PlayStation 2 that was supposed to come out later that year, but every time they asked their mother, she just sighed and shrugged. They could never make out if the shrug was a 'sure' or a 'you've already got a video game system.' And so, they continued playing their old games.

Hours passed, and they decided to put in a movie instead. They watched *Batman Returns,* and Jacob thought he would just about pass out from the look of Catwoman. His mind played fantasies again, only this time he didn't undress her, he just ran his hands up and down her shiny leather suit. He thought it must feel like heaven to touch her body over that suit. He snapped out of it when Benny got up to go to the bathroom. He touched his penis and felt how hard it was. He looked around the room. Benny must keep the porn website written down somewhere. Quickly, he moved to the one place he could think that Benny would keep it: his backpack. He shuffled through old math homework and crude drawings, and just as he heard the toilet flush, he found the name of a website written on the corner of one of the pages and he had to hope it was the right one. Jacob ripped the paper off and went back to where he'd been sitting, adrenaline rushing through him. Benny came back and they watched the movie some more, though Jacob couldn't get the thought of the website off of his mind. It consumed him. It tortured him.

It was evening when it finished. It was dinnertime, though he wasn't sure dinner would even be made for them that night. Their mother had forgotten about dinner on multiple occasions. Jacob would wait until he was too hungry to wait any longer and then just find himself something to eat in the fridge or in the pantry. On one such occasion, he found that they were very low on supplies, and so he made himself a makeshift sandwich: bologna, mustard, bologna. He didn't like bologna, nor did Benny, and apparently it had been left in the fridge too long, because shortly after his consumption of it, he threw it up directly on his dinosaur bedspread. He was so nervous to say anything that he washed it off himself as best he could and then slept in it night after night until eventually his mother stripped all of their beds for washing. Even when she'd put it back on his bed, Jacob swore he could still smell the sour spot.

On this night, he wasn't particularly hungry, at least not for food. When Jacob left Benny's room, Benny shut the door behind him. Heart pounding, Jacob snuck down the stairs. At the bottom, he looked to his right where the computer room was. It was dark and empty. He looked to his left where his mother's bedroom was still closed shut. He walked toward it and put his ear to the door. He could hear the rushing of water from the bathtub filling up and grinned because this bought him some time; their mother always took terribly long baths.

He turned back around to the computer room. There were towering shelves of books on either side of the wall. Besides novels, much of the space was filled in with old photo albums, art projects that Jacob and Benny had done, textbooks from his parent's college days, decorative vases, random junk. The carpet on the floor was scratchy below Jacob's feet as he walked to the computer: a large hunk of plastic and glass that took up the entirety of the desk that it sat on. He sat down at the chair in front of it and pressed the power button. His heart jumped as he realized how much noise it would make as it powered up, and he threw himself to the right of the computer where there was a speaker with a dial on the bottom. He turned the dial all the way to silent just in time. The screen flashed a bright white, and then the Windows symbol filled the middle. He clicked into the World Wide Web, where he had to wait eagerly for a few minutes for it to load. He grabbed himself in his pants and squeezed lightly. He knew of masturbation through his friends and through Benny, but he still hadn't done it himself. It sounded easy enough. Just put your penis in your hand and bob it up and down. The tricky part, he thought, was how you're supposed to know you're done. No one had told him that part, and he had been too embarrassed to ask.

The internet booted up while Jacob took the slip of paper out of his pocket. He typed the web address in and hovered his finger over the enter button. He gulped and looked behind him. His mother's door was still locked, the faint sound of rushing bathwater still there. He looked back to the computer and pressed enter. The screen, once loaded, filled with a page of nude thumbnail photos with text underneath. Both sides of the screen were red and had big words of text: Anal, White, Ebony, Teen Girls, Big Breasts.

Jacob pictured the two neighbors in the rain. Water dripping off of them as they rode each other. He'd been too young to fully understand what a gift that had been to see. And now he could feel his heart beating wildly at the thought that he might get to see it again. But there was fear there too. *Jacob, honey, call 911.*

He scrolled down and found a video titled: Lily Scarlett Makes Breakfast in a Satin Robe. The image was grainy, but her breasts appeared to be falling out of a blue satin robe. Jacob clicked the image, which brought him to a page where he could download the video. Again, he looked behind him to make sure his mother hadn't come out of her room. He could hardly breathe he was so nervous and excited. He clicked it. The video downloaded, and then all at once came up on the screen. Jacob pulled down his pants, just enough so that he could pull them back up if his mother or Benny came in.

The video opened with Lily Scarlett walking into a kitchen with her blue satin robe on. Already Jacob was wondering what it must feel like to touch her over that robe. He fantasized about taking it off but then realized he didn't have to fantasize anymore. In time it would happen for real. He put his hand on his penis and started to move it up and down. The sensation was incredible. He felt his eyes close and roll slightly back. But he didn't want to miss what was happening on screen, so he pulled himself together.

Lily Scarlett was making breakfast. He would wonder, later, why she only had out corn flake cereal, flour and orange juice; can't have been a great breakfast, but then again, he'd think, she was about to get a better one. She poured the cereal into a bowl. As she bent over to pour, her satin robe looked like it might fall open. He could see the top half of her breasts. They were very large and shapely. He moved his hand up and down faster, hoping it might somehow move her along faster. He wanted so badly for her to take off that robe. As she opened the orange juice a shirtless man came up behind her and grabbed her around the waist from behind. This seemed to please her. He rubbed his hand all over her satin robe, on her waist her shoulders her breasts her ass her stomach. Jacob saw all of this as if it were happening right there in their computer room. And then there, finally! He was pulling off her robe! Slowly, he pulled the robe open, exposing the full front of Lily Scarlett's body. O' God, how wonderful it was. O God', how glorious those large breasts were.

As if in a flash, the man's penis was in Lily Scarlett's mouth. He was leaning up against the counter, his elbow dangerously close to knocking the bowl of dry cereal onto the floor, and she was on her knees bobbing her head back and forth on his penis. Jacob thought of how it must feel for a mouth to be around his own penis, considering how good it felt in just his dry hand. And then suddenly he felt the sensation that he had heard about. He stopped moving his hand a moment, scared of what might happen. But it had felt too good, and he didn't want to stop; no matter what, he didn't want to stop. So, again, he started, and the feeling came back almost immediately, maybe even more strongly. His breathing became shallow, and he felt his as if his whole body, save for his penis, was completely numb. Suddenly, it reached a peak and he felt something let go. He let out a sound between a grunt and a squeal. A liquid came out of his penis, something white and sticky and smelly. It flew onto the keyboard in front of him, onto the wood of the desk, onto the floor, into his hand.

And then he noticed his feet were wet.

That couldn't have been from himself, right? Jacob didn't know much about masturbation, but he thought that if it made the floor fill with water, he would have heard about it. Nonetheless, there was water at his feet. A lot of it. He had already been stunned when the stuff came out of his penis, and now he was all the more stunned at the water soaking his feet. The computer said, 'Slurp.'

He sprang into action. He closed out of the web page and shut the computer off. He looked behind him to see that the water had been rushing through from under his mother's bedroom door. She must have fallen asleep as she was waiting for the tub to fill. Surely that must be the explanation. Before he could go and check, he ran to the kitchen to get some paper towels to clean up his mess. His pants fell to his ankles as he did so, and he could feel them soaking up the water, making it difficult for him to move. The water would wake her any moment and she might come out. He would be so ashamed if she saw what was all over the desk. Would she scream like she had at Benny? Would she grab the scissors and cut it off? He didn't often commit sins, but it was dawning on him now that that's exactly what he had just done. He had sinned, and now he felt awful about it. He apologized to God over and over in his head as he wiped the desk and keyboard and hands off with the paper towels. *Never again*, he pleaded, *I promise I won't ever do that again.*

By the time his mess had been cleaned, his mother still hadn't come out of her bedroom. Jacob did one last inspection of the computer room, his feet and hands and pants dripping wet, and when he was sure it was all cleaned, he pulled up his pants and walked over to his mother's bedroom door. He knocked quietly. "Mom," he whispered. Nothing. He knocked louder and then said, "Mom," again. He tried the doorknob. She had locked it. "Mom," he said again, louder still, a tremble coming from his voice. Nothing but the sound of rushing water.

Things went dark for him then, and later Jacob could only recall a few details. He remembered screaming and pounding on his mother's door only to continue hearing no response. He remembered

Benny coming down the stairs at some point and pounding on the door with him. Eventually, Benny broke the door in, the flimsy door no match for a big brother's strength, and even more water rushed out from their mother's room. He didn't remember finding her motionless in the tub, her face bloated and purple. He didn't remember holding onto her body, crying while Benny tried to tell him to call 911. "Call 911, Jacob," Benny had said. How many times Jacob had to hear those words. "Jacob, please." He didn't remember Benny giving up and calling 911 himself, knowing full well there was nothing they could do. He does remember that the water kept running. Neither he nor Benny had thought of turning off the faucet in the bathtub.

When the police and the ambulance arrived the whole first floor of their home was covered in water. When Benny would describe it later to his friends in college, he would say it was three feet deep. When Jacob described it to his school guidance counselor the following year, he said he had to swim to keep afloat. In reality, it was less than an inch deep, but who can argue that to those two boys it felt deep enough to swim in?

CHAPTER SIX

"Great sermon today, daddy," Lily said, sitting down across from Jake. It had been three weeks since their original hot dog lunch at Ava's, and since then she'd come in every Sunday and sat with him. She'd recently taken to calling him 'daddy', seeing how uncomfortable it made him, only she didn't know—or he hoped she didn't know—it also turned him on. He'd be lying if he said he didn't like her company. But even after all this time, they seemed to know very little about each other, instead choosing to engage in useless, but fun, banter. Lily seemed to be very committed to bits. For example, still, three weeks after the original hot dog bit, she continued to order hot dogs and ketchup while Jake was still working his way down the menu.

Ava had walked in as Lily was sitting, and at the word 'daddy', she shook her head but couldn't help smiling. She liked to see Jake like this: with company, with an uncomfortable but nonetheless happy look on his face. Ava herself knew of Jake's celibacy pact, only she didn't believe for a second that it was a real pact. If she knew Jake like she thought she did, that poor boy was afraid of something. *What a shame it would be to go a whole lifetime without sex*, Ava thought, and was very glad that she and Thomas still did it semi-regularly after all these years. It probably helped that they never had any children of their own. A niece and two nephews and a pet cat were quite enough for Thomas and Ava. *Maybe that's what the boy needs*, Ava thought, setting beers down in front of Jake and Lily, *a cat*.

"Hot dogs today?" Ava asked Lily, who smiled and nodded. Jake shook his head. "And for you?"

Jake gulped. "Clams, I guess. You have such a," he paused, "colorful menu."

"You gulp like that at a menu item again and I'll consider your word 'colorful' a hate crime and get you kicked out of town." Ava could play her little games with them too. Why should she miss out on the fun?

"Jake's been kicked out of hundreds of towns for being a racist," Lily said.

"Is that so?" Ava asked, eying Jake suspiciously.

"And for the murders."

"Well that I don't care so much about. Just don't be a racist, you hear?" Ava walked off with a grin. There were other customers to serve but none were quite as fun as Jake and Lily. She really did look forward to these Sunday afternoons.

"Well, I'm very comfortable now, thanks."

"You're welcome," Lily said, clinking her beer into Jake's. "Anyway, we have to talk."

"Isn't that what we're—"

"I was thinking about you the other day when I was masturbating." Jake almost spit out the beer that was in his mouth. He looked around to see if anyone had heard. "Jesus, not like that," Lily said. Though Jake was pretty sure she had chosen her words perfectly well. "I mean I was masturbating, to *porn*, and I couldn't help but wonder, do you really not masturbate? I mean if it's just something you want to keep secret, I won't tell anybody. I don't talk to anyone in this town anyway."

"I wasn't lying."

"You've *never* masturbated? Not even one time?"

The register said, 'Cha-ching!' Lily Scarlett's tits fell out of that blue satin robe. The neighbors bobbed up and down in the pouring rain in pain or in perfect ecstasy.

"I did once," Jake said. The only person he'd ever told about it was that first guidance counselor, who'd told him he'd done a bad, horrible, terrible, awful, stupid thing—how dare he even think about touching *down there*, didn't he even believe in God? He had to take a long drink of his beer to hide his discomfort.

Lily's eyes lit up. "You did?" She leaned in and touched his shoulder. O', how nice it felt to have her touch his shoulder. O', how it radiated through his whole body, his arm then his torso then down to his stirring crotch. "And how did it feel?"

Dirty, nasty, icky, repulsive.

"It doesn't matter. I don't do it anymore, so it makes no difference how it felt. Besides, I was a kid, so I barely remember."

Lily took her hand off of his shoulder, leaving a warm spot where it had been. "You're going to ruin masturbating for me. Now I'm going to think of you every time I do it." Again, she'd chosen those words perfectly.

"Don't you have a boyfriend or anything?" Jake asked.

"Nope," Lily said.

"You've still never told me how old you are."

"I'm 28," Lily said. Jake couldn't tell if she was being serious or not. He'd asked her this question about five times now and she always dodged the answer. How strange that she'd just come out and say it now.

"Really?"

"29 on Wednesday," she said. Jake understood why she was telling him now.

"Happy Birthday," Jake said and lifted his beer to her. She didn't return the lift.

"Tell me on my actual birthday."

"On Wednesday?"

"Jesus, this is a long conversation."

"All I mean is I only ever see you on Sundays."

"Right. So, see me on Wednesday."

"This Wednesday?"

"Jesus Christ. Yes, Pastor Jake, this Wednesday. As in three days from today. As in not tomorrow and not the next day but the one after that. As in—"

"Okay I get it," Jake said. "Sure. I can see you then."

"I'm meeting some friends in the city for drinks. I'll text you the name of the bar."

"You don't have my—"

She was holding her hand out to him. Instead of saying one more embarrassing word, he just reached in his pocket, grabbed his phone, put the password in, and put it in her hand. She put her number in the phone and then texted 'It's Daddy Jake' to herself. What a great thing to have texted a member of his congregation.

"There," she said, handing his phone back. He slid it back into his pocket thinking he should remember to delete that text later.

Just then, Ava came by with a steaming plate of clams and some hot dogs with ketchup. Jake tried his best not to pinch his nose at the smell.

***

On Tuesday, Jake went to the church and pored over scripture he thought might bring him comfort, might ease his mind, which had gone completely rogue at the thought of drinking with Lily the next day. Often, scripture was more of a discomfort to him than any real comfort. The more of the Bible he read, the more he memorized and preached out loud, the more repulsed he was by it. He read 2 Timothy 2:22—a near-perfect verse in numerical symmetry, 2T222—in which it asks him to rid himself of the yearnings of youth, a verse which had brought much comfort to him in the Bible college days when he'd come across a particularly attractive classmate and found himself fantasizing about the lips between her legs opening wide enough for him to fit his entire body into. He read Galatians 5:19 in which it highlights how normal it is to have impure thoughts; if only he could rid himself of them! O', how wonderful would it be if he didn't have to think of what it might be like to wrap himself into a ball and put himself in his mouth! 1 Corinthians 6:18 says to flee! Run from those thoughts, O' aberrant one! But how can he run from them when they were consuming him? How do you run when your thoughts find every hole a new possibility for mental exploration? Tailpipes, donuts, bottles of Gatorade, potted plants (that oh so moist, penetrable soil), jacuzzi jets, that space between airplane seats, enlarged pores, binder rings. This Bible didn't give answers; it only led to more questions, more frustration in which it tells you to look deeper, deeper, please please please deeper.

Jake took off his cross necklace and opened his special drawer. A long pull from the bottle of Jack eased his mind; never mind that the clock still hadn't hit noon. After a pause, he took another drink and set the bottle back in the drawer. Before he could close it, his mother's old Bible caught his eye. He looked at the cover from time to time but couldn't bring himself to open it for fear of what she'd written in it. He remembered her avid note-taking with fondness but was afraid of what had been added in the days after their father died. Would he find what was to come in these skinny margins? Had her cry for help been clearly written there? And if so, where was her God to save her? He fingered the cover of the Bible. He'd always liked its worn feel, like a detective novel that had been sold time and time again to various used bookstores.

For good measure, he took one more drink of the Jack and noticed that it was getting low. He'd need to bring a backpack with a replacement and swiftly make the switch. He wasn't sure he could make it through a moment like this without it. Oddly, that thought brought him more comfort than any Bible verse ever had. He liked that, no matter how bad it was for him, there was something immediate that could ease his racing mind. You pray your whole life only to die in the end never having known if your prayers were answered. At least with alcohol, you knew that it was working. Your head starts swimming and your thoughts become muddy. Dear Jack, I pray that you make it all bett—and Jack answers you before you even finish.

He set the bottle back in the drawer, locked it shut, and put the cross back around his neck. Where before his mind was conjuring possibility after possibility of what could happen the following day, his newfound courage had him thinking it might be fun. He could have a few drinks, meet a few new friends—friends, how strange— and make it back home in time for a game he liked to call Drinks and Jeopardy or Wheel of Forgin or The Price is Rye. Dare he say a perfect Wednesday?

He knew he should work on his sermon for that Sunday. They hadn't started another series, so he didn't even know which direction to take it. He had a log of all the sermons he'd done since he'd been made the head pastor. He flipped back to the same day the previous year. Infidelity. He'd laughed a lot while writing that one. He wondered what it would like to be an infidel and then wondered if that was even a word. Upon Googling it, he found that he in fact was an infidel, or at least these days he was pretty sure. How do you believe in a God that gives you all bad and little good? Was he supposed to wait this all out like Job? Had he not proven himself at least enough for God or Satan or whoever to pull their hand out of his ass and let him move himself, dress himself, bathe himself? He felt his asshole pucker at this thought and had to shoo away another thought, which was about how pleasant someone's hand might actually feel up there.

Jake looked back near the beginning of the log and landed on another that made him chuckle. Excessive drinking. In those days, he drank, but in not the same way he did now. They were the days before his cross necklace, when his trips into the city were meant for fun and exploration, not just for restocking. The sermon hinged on a single passage: Noah, having saved the entire universe, starts to drink and doesn't stop. The Bible says this is bad but to Jake this seems like the correct course of action. God just killed off everyone but Noah, his wife, and his children. He's going to have to watch his children fuck his children and his grandchildren fuck his grandchildren. What about his wife? Maybe he'd have to watch his children fuck her too. Wouldn't anyone take up drinking? He decided to do this sermon anyway. It had been long enough, and even if anyone still remembered that one, they could get something different out of it than they had years before. He'd still hinge it on that section but could find new passages and supporting detail to make it feel new and crisp. He himself would have fun with the complete hypocrisy of his message.

After writing out his sermon for that Sunday, he felt he had worked sufficiently enough to sneak back home and start drinking. Duck, Duck, Booze yielded him a bottle of vodka. While dark liquors he tended to drink straight up, he had to be sufficiently drunk before he could do the same with clear liquors. He kept soda water and limes around for his first four or five drinks of gin or vodka or some tequilas. As he was cutting a lime for his vodka soda, his knife slipped, and he sliced into the side of his thumb. It didn't hurt so much as it gave him a shock. Blood spilled quickly, covering the slice of lime he had intended to use for his drink. He rushed to the sink to run water over the cut. The water below his hand ran red for a few seconds and then was clear. He didn't have any bandages, so he pulled off a paper towel and wrapped it around his thumb a few times. Then he grabbed the slice of lime and ran it under the faucet. Again, the water ran red and then cleared. The lime looked good as new. He squeezed it in his drink, tossed it in, and mixed it all up.

The night slid by. By the time it was dark, Jake had consumed enough vodka sodas to move on to iced vodka. He'd bled through a few paper towels, but the cut had since stopped bleeding, and all he could feel of it was a dull, distant throb. He was watching *Batman Returns* on TV, and he was drunk enough that the thought of him and Benny watching the same movie the day their mother died didn't even cross his mind. He felt that he connected with Batman in a way. He had a secret that he couldn't tell and that he hid well. Only, his Bat Cave was his duffel of liquor and instead of a billionaire he was a preacher. Instead of a Batsuit, he had on his own skin. He was his own alter-ego. Jacob, Jake. He wondered what he would find if he took a pair of tweezers and peeled back the wound on his thumb. Maybe Jacob would be in there somewhere, just wanting to see what the rain might look like up close. Innocent little Jacob.

That's when it clicked for him. *Batman Returns* was *the* film. How had he not seen it? How could he have missed such a big detail? His head slumped to the side as he got up to pour himself another glass. The moment he sat back down, his phone started to buzz. He felt a chill run through his body, and his heart start to beat faster. His mind went straight to his thoughts earlier when he had been in his office. Could he take back his thoughts now? *Of course you had a reason for killing everyone but Noah*, Jake thought. *I don't believe you have your hand up my ass.* He knew the consequences for wronging God, why did he continue to do it? And at the same time, how could he fear a God he didn't believe in? He peered cautiously at his phone: Benny.

How long had it been? Years, at least. Why had they lost touch? Jake couldn't remember. It felt so easy to lose touch. A simple missed phone call here and there, an unanswered text, and suddenly years go by, and you wonder from time to time what they might be up to but don't have the energy or the guts to pick up the phone and ask.

"Hello?" he said, answering the phone. He tried his best to steady his voice and sound at least a little bit sober.

"Jakey?" His voice had deepened since they'd last talked.

Had Beth died? Jake couldn't see another reason for Benny to be calling. Is that why his voice sounded so deep? Jake felt himself start to cry.

"What's up?" he managed.

"God it's good to hear your voice," Benny said. "What's it been? A while, yeah?"

Jake wiped his eyes. Benny wouldn't be talking to him like this if someone had died. Why did his mind always jump to such dire conclusions?

"A while, yeah," Jake said.

"How you been? Can't seem to find you on Facebook."

"Oh. Yeah, I don't have one."

"Instagram?"

"No." Jake had had this conversation a thousand times with the ad(men)istration who wanted him to get on social media for outreach. Jake told them he wasn't comfortable with online outreach; he preferred to do it the old-fashioned way, in person. The truth was he wasn't sure he could handle the temptations. He already tried to limit his internet use. What happened when he opened Instagram and saw a picture of a nearly-naked woman on a beach? He saw that stuff enough on TV, he didn't need it at his fingertips.

"Well, what are you doing? You still a youth pastor in New York?" Jesus. It had been even longer than Jake thought. That or

Benny had forgotten that he'd gotten the head pastor gig nearly three years ago now.

"I lead the church now. In Tarrytown, not in the city."

"Tarrytown. Has a fun ring to it. Tarrytown."

"You still in L.A.?"

"Yep, still here. You wouldn't believe how much money there is in porn."

Corn flake cereal. Orange juice. Flour.

The TV said, "I'm Batman."

"I think I could believe it actually."

"You seen any of my latest?"

"No."

"Oh right," Benny laughed, "you're a pastor." He stopped a moment and then added, "Tell me again why a pastor can't watch porn?"

"2 Timothy 2:22," he started. 2T222. "Flee—"

"Don't quote scripture at me, tell me with your own words."

"It's a temptation. Temptations are bad. I avoid temptations."

"Looking at porn feels good. Masturbation feels good."

"I'm sure it does."

"Anyway, I was thinking about coming to visit, what do you think?"

Jake felt his face get hot. Benny? Here? In Tarrytown?

"In Tarrytown?" he managed.

"Thought you'd be happy. We haven't spoken in a long time, let alone seen each other. I have a goatee now."

"Isn't that a bit cliché for a porn producer?"

"Maybe in the '80s. Now I'm one of the few. Helps me stand out."

"Gross."

"Anyway, I'm coming whether you like it or not. I'd like to stay with you, but if I have to, I'll get a hotel. I have some business in the city."

Benny? In Tarrytown?

Jake's head was swimming; a combination of the vodka, the shock that had overcome him when he saw his brother's name pop up on his phone, and now this bombshell that Benny was dropping. Jake had come to Tarrytown to get away from his past, and now his past was coming to Tarrytown. He looked at the drink in his hand and wondered what he'd do if Benny found out about his drinking. Was he even being convincingly sober during this conversation?

"When?"

"July 28th."

"That's my birthday weekend."

"I know it is."

"You don't even send me a happy birthday text most years, and now you're flying in for it?"

"I told you, I have business in New York. It was a happy coincidence." Benny paused and sighed. Jake pictured him pinching the top of his nose on the other end of the phone. "Honestly didn't know I'd have to fight you on this. I thought you'd be excited to see me."

"I am," Jake said. It wasn't a lie, but it wasn't the truth either. He'd have to think more about this when he was sober and clear-headed, but he was rarely either of those things. "I'm just surprised is all. You caught me off guard."

"That's fair. Anyway, I've already got a ticket. Think about it and text me your address if you're cool with me staying. If you don't text it, I'll just assume that means you don't want me there. No pressure, just think about it."

"Ok."

"And Jake?"

"Yeah?"

"You can stop trying to act sober now." Jake could feel Benny's smile through the phone, and Jake smiled too, despite himself. Even after all this time, Benny could read right through him. Maybe it wouldn't be so bad after all, him being here. Maybe it would actually be nice.

"Love you man," Benny said. He hung up before Jake could respond. Jake wasn't sure what he would have said back anyway.

He finished the rest of his vodka in one large gulp. He didn't even notice the burn as it made its way down his throat. He was still drunk, but he felt more sober than he had before Benny had called. What had he and Beth talked about that made Benny so intent to make a trip out to him? Jake doubted the thing about having business in the city was true, but he couldn't be sure.

He decided he'd make it through tomorrow, let his nerves calm, try to stay sober for at least a while, and think hard about how he really felt about Benny coming to stay. Already, he was starting to miss Benny's voice and desperately wanted to see what he looked like with a goatee. Even the thought of it brought a smile to Jake's face. He remembered himself and Benny making fun of goatees when they were younger. Their father tried it out once, and they gave him hell for it. Funny how things work out in the end.

CHAPTER SEVEN

It was a cool Wednesday for a late New York spring. The sky was bright and blue with thin wispy clouds running quickly to the east. Jake had decided to go back to Sleepy Hollow Hospital to visit Philip. His aunt had said he'd been doing better, but they were still holding him in case something happened to him. Jake thought it might take his mind off of Lily's birthday party later that day. And somewhere, maybe in the back of his mind, maybe in the front of it, he'd hoped he might see Eve; he'd been thinking about the snake tattoo ever since their first encounter, about that spot it reached just below her neck.

When he got to the hospital, he was told that Philip had moved rooms. Jake smiled and thanked the man at the desk, but he felt his knees weaken knowing that a change in rooms probably meant a change in nurse. He'd have no reason to be around the boy's old room now and didn't want to look creepy lurking around the hall-way trying to spot that tattoo. He shook it off and made his way to Philip's new room. He'd brought a larger present with him this time, something that would get a much bigger reaction than the tiny army man.

He knocked on Philip's door and walked right in, careful not to look suspicious this time. Philip appeared to be sleeping. Jake could hear light snoring coming from the boy's bed. He sat down in an uncomfortable armchair beside Philip and felt a sigh escape him. The sound of the sigh made Philip stir and then he opened his eyes. When he saw Jake, he quickly sat up and smiled. Clearly Jake had made an impression on him. It had been weeks since their last meeting. Jake was surprised the boy had even recognized him.

Jake said, "Hey bud, how are you?"

"I'm good. Feeling a lot better."

"You've been here a long time, you sure are a trooper."

"The doctor says I should be able to leave soon."

"That's great."

"I played as Bowser," Philip said, nodding toward the Nintendo Switch at the side of his bed. "You were right. He handles way better."

"I'm always right." Jake smiled. "Anyway, I brought you something I think you'll really enjoy."

"Is it another parachute guy? Mine didn't work."

"Yeah, that's not surprising," Jake laughed. "No, this is way better." He pulled a Nintendo 64 out of his bag, along with a game cartridge and two controllers, one yellow, one blue. "I stole this from the youth group. I couldn't believe they still had one."

Philip's eyes widened. "Is that a Nintendo 64?"

"Sure is. This is what I used to play *Mario Kart* on."

"We can play?"

"Only if you let me win," Jake said. Philip nodded excitedly.

Jake went to the TV and plugged the Nintendo in. He hadn't thought through the fact that a modern TV may not even have the right plugs to hook the aged Nintendo into, but he got lucky. He blew into the cartridge and said to Philip, "It's tradition." He prayed, actually truly prayed, that the thing would still work, and sure enough it did. There was the familiar noise of the Nintendo starting up and the game loading.

He handed the blue controller to Philip and used the yellow one himself. It was odd, holding a controller like that again. Such a different experience from the more modern controllers. A thumb on a toggle and another thumb on the buttons, pointer fingers on the triggers on top and back. It was strange yet familiar. He hadn't played a game, let alone a Nintendo 64 game, for years.

"Hey!" Jake said when Philip chose Bowser, "that's my guy!"

"Too slow," Philip said, grinning.

"Fine," Jake conceded. He chose Princess Peach instead. Philip smirked, presumably finding it funny that Jake had chosen a girl.

It took Jake only a moment to get used to the controls again. It was—he hated the term, but it really worked here—like riding a bike; or a kart. Before he could start dominating Philip, he taught him what the controls were. Philip, a natural at video games, understood quickly and was a fair match against Jake. Philip won the first round, Jake the second. The third round, a computer-controlled Mario beat both of them, followed by Philip and then Jake. This put Philip in first and Jake in second for the final round.

As the round started, Jake looked over at Philip, who, despite a face of absolute determination, had a wild grin on his face. Jake thought back to when he was a kid, before his mother or father had died, and how happy he was when Benny would let him play games with him. He didn't care if he won or lost. He was just happy to be playing with his brother, who at the time was often cold to him; though, he would have preferred to have won. Jake put up a good round against Philip, but instead of throwing a red shell at him in the final lap he threw the shell behind him at Mario, who spun out and was overtaken by numerous other computer-controlled characters. And in the final moments of the race, Philip got a red shell of his own, which he threw back at Jake. Philip won the race; Jake came in fifth.

"I thought you were going to let me win," Jake groaned.

"That was me letting you win," Philip gloated. "That's what you get for playing as a girl."

Jake decided to ignore the misogyny—this wasn't his kid after all—and concede. "You're right. Told you Bowser was the best."

They played a few more games. Jake let him win some, beat him in some, and genuinely lost to him in others. Neither of them really cared who won, they just enjoyed the moment. They stopped playing when Philip's excitement turned to coughing and exhaustion. He looked like he might fall asleep sitting up in the bed with the controller in his lap.

"Alright, I think that's enough," Jake said. "I have to get going anyway."

"Oh. Okay," Philip said. He looked disappointed. "Maybe you could bring the Nintendo back another time?"

"Well, I hope I don't have to come back. You're going to be leaving soon."

"Oh, right."

"I'll tell you what," Jake said, "why don't I leave this here with you. It was in a storage closet anyway, I doubt the group will miss it."

His disappointment turned to elation. "Really? How will I get it back to you."

"We'll figure it out," Jake said.

"Thanks," Philip said.

Jake stood and said, "You take care, okay buddy."

"Wait," Philip said, "aren't you going to pray for me?"

That hadn't even crossed Jake's mind. He knew the excitement of a video game would do more for this kid than prayer had ever done for anyone. He walked over to Philip and put his hand on the boy's arm. They prayed together and then Jake left the room.

"Hey," someone said as he walked off. He turned around and saw Eve, the tattoo barely visible under her scrubs. Jake thought he might fall over. "You remember me?"

"Sure, hey, how are you?"

"I saw you playing with Philip. He looked happier than I've ever seen him."

"This time I didn't even have to mention butts." Eve smiled, but then her smile faded.

"He seemed to be getting better, but lately," she paused and shrugged her shoulders. "I'm trying to be here for him but he doesn't seem to care for me much."

"Where are his parents?"

"He hasn't told me anything about his dad. He might have passed. His mom works during the days. She comes in every night with a giant soda for him. I used to ask her not to, but he's been in here so long I figured it'd be kinder if I just let her do it. For both of them."

"People don't die from pneumonia, do they?"

Eve looked as if she might cry. "Not often. It's rare, even, but it can happen. Especially with children."

"God can be cruel that way," Jake said. What a stupid thing to say.

"That's an interesting thing to hear coming from a preacher."

"Yeah, I guess it is."

There was a silence long enough for Jake to think the conversation was over. He smiled at Eve and started to walk away when she said, "Can I have your number?" Jake felt his heart stop completely. He turned back toward Eve. "I know you have other things to do, but you're really good with him and he could use someone else in his life. I'd like to call you if things are seeming really bad. It's okay if you don't want to. I get that he's not your responsibility."

"No," Jake said, "no, please." Eve handed him her phone and he put his number in it. He texted himself, showed her it went through, smiled and said, "I look forward to hearing from you." And then, remembering the reason she'd asked for his number, he said, "Or, no, I guess I hope I don't hear from you?"

Eve laughed and said, "Don't worry, I get what you mean."

Jake smiled and left for real this time.

In less than a week, he'd gotten two girls' (non-coworkers) phone numbers. He wasn't sure if this was exciting or alarming. For so long he'd stayed far away from anything that could potentially get him in biblical trouble, and now he was about to head to the city for one woman's birthday party and had another number in his phone that belonged to the woman he had been quietly obsessing over for weeks. He'd let his guard down after all this time. And as he started up the engine of his car, the vibration felt like heaven on his groin, where he could again feel a hard-on. He was so out of his mind that he considered taking it out right there and stroking it until he came. Damn it all! Who cares what happens now! Leave me alone, O' vengeful one!

His head cleared just in time for him not to act. He thought of the call with Benny the night before and decided once and for all it would be good to have his brother here with him. If his brother was around, he'd be less likely to get himself into any sort of trouble. He pulled out his phone and texted Benny his address. He added 'excited to see you' and pressed send.

*****

The train on the way to the city was nearly empty. Jake once again sat so he could see the water on the Hudson. He took a flask, a cheap blackened metal thing he found at a thrift store, out of his pocket and unscrewed its cap. He tapped the flask on its reflection in the window, forced a smile at his own reflection, and took a swig. He wasn't drunk yet. In fact, this was only his second nip of the day. He'd spent the rest of the workday calling around to find a plumber to fix the toilets while their maintenance guy was on vacation, making some final changes to that Sunday's sermon, and trying to avoid talking to Kendall, who had just gotten back from her long vacation in Los Angeles. He didn't mind chatting with her, but he didn't think he could bear the post-vacation back and forth, at least not on that day when he'd had so much else on his mind.

Two seats ahead of him, there sat a kid no older than 16. He was watching something on his phone without headphones in, and Jake could make out words here and there. The phone said, 'Freeze!' Jake thought of the last scene in *The Shining* when Jack Nicholson is frozen solid. He wondered what it would be like to freeze to death. Would it come slowly and painfully, or would there be a moment when your body goes numb and quietens and lulls you to a merciful, long sleep? The phone said, 'Lily Scarlett.' Jake shuddered. Realistically, it must have said something like 'little starlet' or 'will he start yet' or anything other than what Jake had heard, but it shocked him nonetheless.

He looked at the back of the boy's head and wondered what his story was. Did he still have his parents? Or was he, like Jake, orphaned and alone at such a young age? Did he have a brother that he barely talked to? An aversion to sex? Jake took another sip of the whiskey and then closed his eyes to try to get some sleep. It wasn't a long ride to the city, but the vodka from the night before was really hitting him now. A little more whiskey would help, but for now, he felt like sleep. The phone said, 'Rest.' Or maybe it was 'Arrest.' Jake thought this as he drifted off.

He was only asleep a moment when the train pulled into Grand Central. He startled himself awake. Had he really been knocked out that whole ride? Where was the boy? What was the phone saying?

Jake left the train in a groggy haze. He blinked, what? A thousand times? Two thousand? Slowly, the train station came into view. Hurried New Yorkers pushed their way around him eager to get on their trains and home to their families.

He texted Lily: 'Where should I meet you?' and then stood motionless and waited for a response.

Almost immediately she texted: 'Peculiar Pub'. Just that, no 'excited to see you!' or 'can't wait!'.

He sent her a thumbs up emoji and made his way to the subway.

Another train ride, this one packed but quick, and he was in Greenwich Village, the sun still high up in the sky. It was warmer in the city than it was in Tarrytown. He knew it had something to do with all the high buildings and concrete, but he wasn't exactly sure what. Of all the neighborhoods in New York this was one of his favorites. It was busy but without the urgency of Midtown or the noise of the Lower East Side. It was near NYU, so it could be overcrowded with college kids at times, but this being summer, Jake was quite enjoying his half-ish mile walk to the bar. It was almost nice enough to take his mind off of the fact that he'd have to mingle with God knew how many people in the coming minutes; almost, not quite.

He saw the outside of the bar and stopped to take one last drink from his flask. He needed the extra bit of courage (and, let's face it, hangover cure) to take the evening on. Social anxiety be damned! He put the flask away, took a deep breath and entered the bar.

It was dark inside, and it took Jake's eyes a moment to adjust. There were only a handful of people inside, being a bit early for the bar scene in the city, and sitting at the bar, alone, was Lily. She had on a cornflower bodysuit and jean shorts—a bold choice for that time of year—white gym shoes, large-rimmed sunglasses perched atop her head. Her hair was in a messy bun that on anyone else might have looked lazy. On Lily, it looked meticulous, as if it had taken her an hour to perfect. She took a long drink from her beer and spotted Jake with her head nearly upside down. She put her head back into place and turned herself toward him in one swift movement. She was smiling at him.

"Jake!"

"Hey," Jake said walking toward her. He found himself wondering why had hadn't just finished off the flask or two or three of them. He tried to reassure himself this was just like their Sunday lunches, there was no reason to panic. But this felt different. He didn't know if it was being in the city—a place that he associated with paranoia and secrecy—the tiny straps on her bodysuit that were pulling at their shoulders, or the way the bar had that peculiar—yes, peculiar—bar smell.

Lily rose and gave him a hug. He'd realized in the weeks they'd known each other he hadn't so much as touched her. A boundary was being crossed that was making him more than just her pastor. A crossed boundary he liked very much. When they broke the hug, they looked at each other and smiled nervously; apparently, neither of them knew how to best start a conversation. Jake could picture Lily's brain trying to come up with some stupid joke or a bit that she could launch into to take up the space between now and whenever-thefuck. "H—" Jake started when the bartender saved them both.

"Can I get you anything?" she asked.

Lily sat back down in her seat as Jake looked at the beer options. Virtually the only time he drank beer was on Sundays at Ava's. He supposed he could go straight for a mixed drink, but something about the way Lily was holding her beer and the, again, peculiar, smell of the place made him want a beer.

"Guinness, please," Jake said.

"Make that two," Lily said, finishing the drink she'd been holding in one rather large gulp.

"How long have you been here?" Jake asked as the bartender

was pouring their drinks. He'd forgotten that there was a process to pouring a Guinness. Pour, pause, wait, wait, wait, wait, wait, wait, wait, pour, pause, serve. He wished he'd gotten something else so he could have something to do with his hands.

"Not long. Just for this beer." She tilted the empty glass. "I, uh," she toyed with the glass and didn't meet Jake's eyes. "Turns out my friends can't make it."

"Oh."

"Yeah. I know I should have told you but—"

"No, it's your birthday. I'm glad I'm here to celebrate."

"There are times I miss living here. I actually spend a lot of time thinking about it. But then it's my birthday, and my friends can't take time out of their day to come for a drink." She stopped a minute, perhaps waiting for Jake to say something, but he didn't know what to say. "Anyway, if I told any of them that the others had bailed, they would make time. But that's not the point."

The bartender set the drinks down in front of the two of them and Jake gave her his credit card.

"If I'm being honest, it's my fault they didn't come. I never come down to visit them, so why should they feel like they have to come out to see me? I haven't been the best friend lately. I guess, with you, I've been trying harder."

"And now," Jake said, turning to Lily, "you get to spend your birthday all alone with a pastor. What a treat."

He hadn't felt all that funny these days, but Lily laughed at his sarcasm. He was glad she did, because he'd been afraid she would start crying. Jake lifted up his Guinness and held it toward Lily.

"Happy, uh, twenty-ninth, birthday."

"Almost forgot, didn't you?"

Jake smiled and shrugged and they clinked glasses. He was glad he'd gotten a Guinness after all. He liked the way the foam felt on his upper lip when he took his first sip.

"You know I can pray that bad things happen to your friends, right? Even if you think it's your fault they didn't come, they should have made it out for your birthday. And I'm a pastor, God listens to me."

"I'm not even sure you listen to God." She'd meant it as a joke, but Jake felt like he'd gotten the wind knocked out of him. He had to take a long drink of the Guinness to appear normal. Possibly noticing his discomfort, she added, "Yeah, you know what, could you? Pray that they all get food poisoning or something?"

"That's the best you could come up with? Food poisoning?"

"What've you got?"

"I do this all day, do you really want to challenge me?"

"Uh huh."

"I could pray that they each lose one of each pair of shoe they own, forever."

"Diabolical."

"Now you go again," Jake said, "do better this time."

"You should pray that every time they get on a plane, there are babies in every single seat around them."

"I'll pray that they always get to the subway station just as the train doors close."

"That's the worst," Lily groaned. "You should pray that every time they go home with a guy, they are wearing the ugliest underwear they own."

"Can't top that," Jake said. Lily looked happy. Jake even felt happy, despite the anxiety rushing through him at Lily mentioning ladies' underwear. "What was your full plan for tonight anyway?"

"Drinks here. Food somewhere. Dancing at this fun Irish spot after that."

"You expected me to go dancing?"

Lily laughed and said, "No, I figured you'd dip out after dinner."

"Well, I can't do that now, can I?" Jake finished his drink and asked the bartender for another. Lily hadn't even finished half of her own. "Looks like I'll be dancing tonight."

In a matter of twenty minutes, he'd gone from needing sips from his glass to keep anxiety at bay to saying he'd go dancing. When was the last time he'd danced? He didn't go to prom in high school. He didn't recall ever dancing in college. Had he ever really danced?

"You really don't have to stay." Lily looked serious but hopeful that he'd stay anyway.

"I want to. Besides, now I'm scared of what you'll pray for against me if I ditch you."

"Yeah, probably a good call," she said. "Jake?" Her eyes met his. "Thank you. Really."

In perfect timing, the bartender set Jake's drink in front of him. He picked it up and clinked it into Lily's.

CHAPTER EIGHT

Jake awoke to the sound of his phone buzzing. The vibration rattled painfully inside his throbbing head. He was still fully clothed from the night before; he even still had his shoes on. He couldn't see the time, but he could tell from the low light outside that it was early morning. He'd been lying face-down on his bed, on top of the covers. He looked toward his side-table where he'd assumed his phone would be, but it wasn't there. It stopped buzzing and Jake thought he might go back to sleep. The moment he closed his eyes, the phone started buzzing again.

Jake shot out of bed and found his phone lying face down on the floor halfway across his bedroom. He was surprised he could even hear it, let alone that it felt as painful as it did within him. He picked it up and turned it over. Eve was calling, and he'd missed three other calls from her. He felt as if he'd been punched in the gut, even considered gasping for air. This was it. Philip had died. And it was Jake's fault.

He let his phone fall to the ground where it again landed face down. Bizzzz.... Bizzzz.... Bizzzz.... A giant wad of something vile gathered in his belly and was making its way up. Jake hardly noticed. He just stood there sweating, water welling in his eyes. He'd been good for so long. How could he have messed up? And why would God choose Philip? Take Benny take Beth take Eve take Lily take Kendall take Barry. Barry! Take Barry! No one cares for Barry! Take him! Only that wouldn't be the point would it. O', how confusing to not believe in a God who clearly does exist. O', how horrible that there is a God who's only purpose in life is to pick on you. Job would shrug it off and ask God for more punishment, but Jake wasn't Job, Jake was Jake, and Jake wanted out of it all. He fell to his knees.

The phone said: Bizzzz....

He picked it up again and, swallowing the steamy, gooey bile in his scratchy throat, he pressed the answer button.

"Hello?"

***

"I think I timed this wrong," Lily said. They were sitting in the dancing bar with a handful of other people. There was no band on the stage yet, and there was no one on the dance floor. "I've never been here on a weeknight."

Jake and Lily had stayed at the bar for a few more drinks and then walked west to Bleecker Street Pizza. Lily claimed it was the best in the city, and Jake didn't know enough about the pizza in the city to argue with her. They both ate too much pizza and were thankful for the walk back east to their next destination.

"That's okay," Jake said, rubbing his belly. "Hey, do you think there's a politically correct way to order an Irish Car Bomb?"

"A what?"

"An Irish Car Bomb. You know, like the shot?"

"Can't believe a pastor knows more about drinking than I do." Jake had had enough to drink that this comment didn't scare him as much as it should have.

"Well, we're in an Irish bar, it's your birthday, we're getting some Irish Car Bombs."

"Yes sir."

Jake got up to go and order the drinks. For how few people were in the bar at this point, it took quite a while to get them. He wondered how his bank account was doing and then decided it was a problem for tomorrow—tonight he would enjoy himself and help Lily enjoy herself. When he did order the drinks, the bartender smirked and got to work.

Jake remembered the first time he'd had an Irish Car Bomb. He hadn't had a drink since his senior year of high school. They weren't allowed to have alcohol anywhere on campus. This didn't stop a lot of the kids from having it anyway, but Jake was, mostly, a rule-follower. One weekend, a group of his friends were going off campus to some bars and Jake, for some reason he couldn't quite understand, had decided to tag along. The bar was packed edge to edge with drunken college kids, some from his school but most from the city college nearby. He was 21 and he gathered he might have been the oldest one there.

His friend brought him a glass filled about halfway with a dark beer and a shot filled with two different liquids, one brown and watery, the other opaque and coffee-colored.

"What do I do with these?" Jake asked.

"Easy. You drop the shot into the beer and chug. And don't forget to pray."

He was pretty sure his friend had meant the last part as a joke—bad Bible college humor—but Jake prayed anyway and then dropped the shot into the glass. He watched as the liquid inside swirled together beautifully. Then he took a breath and started to chug. Almost immediately he spit it out. It tasted sour and chunky. He thought he might vomit.

"You let it curdle!" His friend shouted having drained his own drink.

"What?" Jake said, still feeling sick to his stomach.

"That's Irish cream in there. If you let it sit too long, it'll curdle inside the beer. That's why I told you to chug!"

Jake didn't understand why you would want to have a drink of something that is at risk of curdling, but before he could protest, his friend was back up at the bar ordering them two more. This time, Jake downed the liquid right as the shot glass hit the bottom of the beer. The result was much better than his first go and he, in fact, found himself enjoying the taste of it. The mixture of liquor to cream to beer was just right.

"Here you go, hotshot," the bartender said, handing Jake his beers and shots. He paid her and brought them back over to Lily.

Jake brought the drinks back over to their table and set one down in front of Lily. Sitting down with his own drink he said, "So you're going to drop—"

"Yeah, that's enough, I get the idea."

"Just make sure you chug or it'll—"

Lily was already dropping the shot into the beer. Jake understood.   Women had been taking directions from men for centuries, the Bible itself basically forces women into submission to men, so she had every right not to want to listen to him. Except, in this case, it might have benefitted her.

Jake dropped his own shot and chugged quickly, savoring the mixture of sweet and spicy and bubbly. When he finished, he saw that Lily had only just started drinking. He didn't stop her. He watched as her eyes widened and she spit a large portion of the liquid back into the glass. Her face scrunched into a look of disgust.

"You let it curdle," Jake said.

Lily said, "Shut up," and wiped her mouth.

Jake smiled. Her stubbornness reminded Jake of Benny. Benny

always seemed to get his way. Even if his way was the wrong one, he made it seem like the right one. It's part of why he went so far away to college in the end. After opting not to attend Ohio University that year their mother died, he fixated on UCLA. No other school would work for him. He had to get far away, even if it meant leaving Jake behind.

"Let's just try that again."

Before Lily could say no, Jake got up to buy them two more drinks. This time Lily dropped the shot and chugged quickly. This being Jake's second, on top of the drinks they'd had before, he was feeling very drunk now.

Jake liked the way Lily made him laugh and the way he could make her laugh. He had experienced a severe lack of laughter over the last chunk of his life. He never found himself to be very funny—he often found himself wondering how comedians all seem to come from lives of pain and are able to come out on the other end and make people laugh—and he hadn't had enough real conversations with people to find them to be very funny. He'd forgotten how good laughter felt. How healing it could be.

A band was finally setting up on stage, and a few more people had trickled in. It wasn't crowded by any means, but it felt more bar-like. Lily bought them a few rounds, saying that Jake had way surpassed the amount she was comfortable with as a birthday present. Then she made a dig at his salary which he genuinely laughed at and said something like, 'I guess the payoff after death is supposed to make up for the shitty pay while we're alive.'

When they were good and drunk, and the music was playing loud enough for them to have to shout, Jake yelled, "Why are you really hanging out with a pastor on your birthday?"

Lily yelled seriously, "Why are you hanging out with a sinner on her birthday?"

And Jake felt an overwhelming sensation to kiss her. He'd been perfectly content just being friends with Lily. Anything more than that could mean absolute disaster. So, the moment this sensation washed over him, he washed it down with his drink and averted his attention to the band on the stage.

No one else was dancing, but at some point during the set, Lily took Jake's hand and started dancing with him. At first, he felt embarrassed to be the only ones dancing among the patrons in the bar, but it suddenly felt as if they were the only ones there and the music was just for them. Jake had no idea what he was doing—the most dancing he'd ever done was raising his hand into the air for the church band—but there, with the help of the drinks and the music, he felt like it was something he was an expert at. He just let his body move with the music without any care for what he looked like. And Lily continued dancing with him, so that was a good sign.

He wasn't sure when it happened, but suddenly, Lily's hips were in his hands, and she was turned away from him moving slowly back and forth. The gentle rub of her ass on his crotch made him stiff with excitement and mild confusion. And when she turned around, she pressed her whole self into him. He felt her breasts swelling against his chest, her crotch pressing harder, harder into his own.

O' God, how good, great, wonderful, breathtaking, amazing, perfect, mind-blowing it all was!

O' God, how he'd missed out on having his dick touched, rubbed, stroked, kissed!

O' God, how little he cared in that moment about his celibacy! To hell with it! Release him!

And then that feeling came. The one he felt watching Lily Scarlett in the computer room. The one that ended in a sticky mess. The one that ended in the death of his mother. His eyes widened and he tried to pull away, but Lily pressed harder into him, and he felt himself go.

His world flashed white. He'd seen heaven and this was it. The

Bible says, "Rejoice, for God has come!" and Jake knew now that he'd been interpreting that verse all wrong. How wrong Jake had been all this time. How much life he had missed out on!

And when the world rushed back to him, he realized with horror the mistake that he had made. He didn't want to believe it, but the evidence showed right there in a squishy blob seeping through his pants. He felt his heart sink and the alcohol and pizza in his belly try to make its way out. He left Lily and rushed to the bathroom. Inside, he threw up how many times? Three? Four? It didn't matter to him. All that mattered was the glob of stuff on his leg. He went to the sink and rubbed, scrubbed, polished the evidence away, only it left him looking even more guilty of his crime.

He rushed out of the bathroom, out of the bar, and into the streets of Manhattan.

***

"Jake?" Eve sounded frantic on the other end of the phone.

"Yeah?" Jake managed. It felt as if his hangover had disappeared. It was replaced with absolute dread. If only he'd been sober, he would have had self-restraint. Who was he to be out dancing in New York? Who was he to be spending time drinking with a woman that he hardly knew?

"Sorry I've called so many times it's just—"

It's just that a child has died. It's just that it's his, Jake's, fault.

"Philip got worse again. They had to put him into a coma. I just thought you'd want to know."

A medically induced coma? It may not be far from death, but death it was not. Jake felt his whole body relax. He hadn't even noticed he'd been clenching every muscle he had. He hadn't noticed the crushing grip he had on his phone.

"Anyway, I don't believe in God, and I certainly don't think anyone is listening to our prayers but—"

How often people of no faith asked Jake to pray for them in times of need. He understood that they needed to put their faith in *something*, but why they thought a pastor's prayer would be stronger than a neighbor's, aunt's, chiropractor's, dog walker's, Jake just didn't know. He didn't have God on speed dial, and God certainly didn't have Jake on his speed dial. God hadn't called Jake in a long time for anything but punishment. Punishment for what? Jake thought of the moment the night before when he'd decided he didn't care what happened. How good that moment felt. How freeing it was.

"You want me to pray over him?" Jake asked.

"Would you?" Jake pictured tears in Eve's eyes. He wondered how long she had been a nurse. Rule number 1: don't get attached. Rule number 2: don't get attached. Rule number 3: hand sanitizer. Rule number 4—Jake couldn't finish his thought. He pictured Eve breathing on the other end, her snake tattoo rising, falling. "His mom took some time off work to be with him more. It might be helpful for her."

Her or you? Jake thought.

The phone said: silence.

"Jake?"

"Yes. I can come pray for him. Of course."

"Thank you."

Jake asked, "How are you doing, Eve?"

The phone said: silence.

And then, "I'm," a pause. "I really hate this job sometimes."

"There's something we have in common," Jake said.

Eve laughed and said, "Thanks, Jake. I'll see you soon?"

"Yeah, see you soon."

They hung up and Jake realized he was still on his knees. If there was any time for prayer it was here, on his knees. He closed his eyes. Dear God? What God? A God that takes and doesn't give? Who wants a God like that? He opened his eyes and got to his feet. Suddenly, his hangover came rushing back to him. It went straight to his head, and he felt both dizzy and nauseous. He thought he'd thrown everything up the night before, but it was suddenly feeling as if he might need to have another go.

What stopped him was the thought of Lily. He'd left her alone in the bar. Just left. He had no way of knowing if she'd made it home. Someone could have drugged her, murdered her; worse, she could have gone home with someone (not Jake) willingly. He hated that that was what worried him most. Rule number 1: don't get attached. Rule number 2: don't get attached.

He pictured: dancing.

He pictured: two bodies on a pool chair, bouncing in the rain.

The release he'd felt was enough to make him go insane. In fact, he thought it was already making him go insane.

He went to send Lily a message and saw that she had messaged him the night before.

The phone said: 'Where are you?'

And then: 'Jake, where did you go?"

And then he saw that there were missed calls from her too. He hadn't seen them this morning, which meant that he'd seen them last night. He'd seen them and ignored them. Maybe he thought that ignoring her would make the act of it go away. Maybe it did. The coma could have meant death if he had answered.

Jake typed, 'Did you make it home okay?'. He pressed send.

Where was his apology? Would it have been so hard to say he was sorry? He knew he couldn't explain himself, but at least the simple act of apology could save their friendship. Was that what he was afraid of? How could he leave her all alone, drunk, in the dark streets of Manhattan and so casually ask her if she'd gotten home okay?

He forced himself to shower and change his clothes into something presentable. At first, he chose an outfit he thought Eve would like and then decided he should wear exactly the opposite of that. He texted Kendall that he would be in late and gave her a quick update on the situation. The truth was he was already late, so a small part of him was thankful for this very real excuse. He hated that part of him, but it was there; always there. He still hadn't talked to Kendall since her trip, and he truly didn't know why he had been avoiding her.

In the car on his way to the hospital, he thought about how he'd gotten home the night before. It was all very hazy, as was the bulk of the night. He remembered stumbling through the street, not a clue where he was heading. Home? A hotel? It was dark out but not that late. The streets were still full of people—young, old, in-between—and the weekday night life was really just beginning. He had a vague recollection of tears streaming down his face. The next thing he could remember was being in a subway station (he didn't know which) and badly needing to pee. He relieved himself on the tracks at the end of the platform as people pointed and stared. That's all he could remember. A cab wouldn't have taken him all the way to Tarrytown unless he offered a huge amount of money that he didn't have. He must have made it onto a train and walked home from the station, a reflex at this point from his bi-weekly liquor trips. He'd always considered his alcoholism under control. As long as he blacked out in his own home, he wasn't putting himself or others at any real harm. Knowing that he had been blacked out for his entire trip home unsettled him. He felt something like a basketball in his stomach bouncing up and down with the slight rise and fall of the road to Sleepy Hollow.

CHAPTER NINE

"Thanks for coming," Eve said when Jake got to the hospital. He'd texted her when he arrived, and she was waiting for him in the lobby. She was wearing normal clothes, a black tank top and faded blue jeans. Her snake tattoo was more visible than with her scrubs on and it took immense restraint not to stare.

"Of course. How's he doing?"

"Oh, you mean over the course of the last hour since I called?" Eve laughed nervously and then said, "Sorry. I was attempting a joke."

"It's okay," Jake said. He tried to smile but wasn't sure he was convincing. He had a horrible headache and still felt like he might throw up. "Are you supposed to be off today?"

"Yes. I just..."

"Let's go see him."

Eve walked Jake up to Philip's room. He could hear the ominous beeping even before they broke the threshold of the doorway. Beep. The sound of dying. Beep. The sound of life. Beep. The sound of somewhere in-between. Inside, Philip's mother was sitting in a chair next to Philip with her eyes closed. Philip was in bed connected to a countless number of tubes. If Eve hadn't told Jake that the boy was in a coma—or if not for the chilling cadence of the beep, beep, beeping—Jake would have thought Philip was dead. Only yesterday they had been playing Mario Kart and Philip had seemed nearly ready to leave the hospital.

"You must be Jake," Philip's mother said from the chair. "I'm Beth."

Of course her name is Beth, Jake thought. How frequently names seemed to be repeating themselves lately. Lily, and now Beth. Would he meet a Benny on the street? Would a Chet join his church?

"It's great to meet you," Jake said. He went to shake her hand, but Beth stood up and gave him a hug. They held each other a long time, both of them unsure who needed the hug more. When they broke it off, Jake wanted to say, 'I'm sorry.' He almost did. But Beth spoke before he had the chance.

"Philip couldn't stop talking about you. Not since you gave him that army man toy. And I think yesterday might have been the happiest I've seen him in… I guess I don't know how long." Jake noticed she'd said 'couldn't.' He knew it was just a slip of the tongue, but it made him feel even worse inside.

"He's a good kid. A really good kid. And he's a natural at *Mario Kart*." Beth laughed. Eve laughed too, behind them.

"I've never been very religious," Beth said, "and I'm regretting that now. Do you think maybe God is punishing me? I've been praying now but what good is re-taking a test that you've already failed?"

God is punishing me! Jake wanted to say. *This is my fault! Not yours!*

"Can I let you in on a little secret?" he said instead. Beth nodded. "Prayer is nothing more than putting out there the things that you want to happen. God doesn't have time to answer billions of prayers. If you believe He created our universe, isn't it crazy not to think He created it to answer our prayers for Him?"

"So, praying for Philip is useless?"

"Not at all. To me, it's much more comforting to believe that when we pray, we aren't praying to one being but instead to an entire universe that has nothing but time to answer our prayers."

"This is a bit alarming to hear coming from a preacher."

"That's why it's a secret. For your ears only." He remembered Eve was in the room with him. He pointed back at her, smiled and said, "And Eve's too."

Beth looked uneasy, and Jake wondered if it was a mistake to say what he had said. If people needed a God to comfort them, who was he to tell them that God was useless in time of need?

"Can we pray for him together?" Eve asked. She walked toward Philip's bed and put her hand on his arm.

Jake looked to Beth who said, "I'd really like that."

And so the three of them held hands and prayed over Philip. Jake spoke first, wishing Philip to health, praying that he would recover quickly and get back to his life. Beth spoke next, wishing for the universe to get him home. Eve spoke last and said that, while she loved seeing Philip, she hoped she didn't have to see him much longer, that he would stand up and walk himself out of the hospital with a smile on his face and that she would never see him there again.

Beth let go of their hands, but Jake's hand stayed clasped around Eve's. He hardly noticed it at first but then basked in this feeling of comfort that had come over him. Warmth radiated from Eve. He'd felt this way only when he had been dancing with Lily the night before. And then the thought of the night before made him shiver and he let go of Eve's hand and avoided her big eyes that he felt on him. O', if only Eve knew. O', if only Jake could tell one single person about his curse.

Beth left to get some coffee and Eve, perhaps uncomfortable with Jake's reticence to touch her, said she'd be back tomorrow and would stop in on her shift. If he, Jake, decided to come, he should text her.

Alone with Philip, Jake sat where Beth had been resting as he and Eve entered the room. He placed his hand on Philip's arm. There was warmth where he'd been expecting coldness. The boy still appeared dead, but the steady beeping and the warmth in his body proved to Jake that he was not quite dead. Jake knew, after all, what death felt like in a human being.

"I'm sorry," he whispered. He'd been expecting to say it silently in his head, but as soon as the words made their way out, he knew he wanted to say more.

"God, or whatever is out there, warned me long ago what would happen if I...

"I'm the reason you're lying here, and I'm sorry."

He sat with Philip a while, long enough to know he was going to get good and drunk again tonight. This time alone, safe in his own home with the TV on and no one around for him to hurt. When Beth came back in, she thanked him again, and Jake felt it was time for him to go. He said bye to Philip as he left the room and felt embarrassed as he walked to his car. What is the protocol on goodbyes to someone in a coma?

He drove to the church and sat in the parking lot for a long time. He closed his eyes and tried to clear his mind. Breathe in, breathe out. Thoughts came quickly. He let them slide in, considered them only a moment, and then swiped them away as with a broom in his lively brain. Soon there was nothing but waves on an empty beach ebbing with the filling of his lungs, flowing with the soft release of air. For those moments, nothing mattered. For those moments, it was only barren beach and setting sun.

When he opened his eyes, he felt relaxed. He knew it wouldn't last, but it was nice to feel that way, even fleetingly. He got out of the car, walked into the church, and basked in its emptiness. He even smiled. And then—

"Hey."

The room filled with all of the thoughts he had swatted away in the car. It all came rushing back to him with a force he couldn't have expected. It seemed to take his breath away all at once.

Lily was dressed in a red t-shirt and athletic shorts. Her hair was in a bun that looked more disheveled than like the organized mess it had been the night before. She had no makeup on and looked as tired as Jake felt. She appeared calm, but Jake wondered if that really could be. How could she be calm after what had happened? He'd been staring at her silently. Fear and embarrassment and shame filled him, seemed to make the room cloudy as with a smoke machine in a no-budget middle school musical. She was standing in the doorway to the chapel, possibly having been waiting for him there. How long had she had to wait? Now she was walking toward him as he stood stunned, not moving except for a shiver that made its way through his body.

"Can we talk?" Lily said. Jake nodded but said nothing. "I'm really sorry about last night."

Lily was *sorry*? *Lily* was sorry?

"I went too far. I was caught up in all of it. I was drunk. I guess I forgot who I was with."

Lily was *sorry*?

"From now on, we can just be friends. No dancing, no flirting. Friends. Would that be okay?"

Jake nodded. He still felt like he couldn't speak but he knew he needed to say something.

"I'm sorry too," he finally said. "I shouldn't have left you alone there. I have no idea what I was thinking."

"Forgotten. Friends?"

"Friends."

The word stung when he spoke it. Some part of him cried out: *Not friends! Remember the way she made you feel? She'll never make you feel that way again if you're just friends!* And another part of him said simply: *Remember Philip. Remember your mother. Remember your father.*

"I don't think I'm going to come to church anymore," Lily said. "I never really believed that stuff anyway I just... anyway I'd still like to get lunch with you on Sundays if that's okay."

"Of course. Someone has to be there to eat their hot dogs." Lily laughed.

She'll never make you feel that way again!

"I'll see you Sunday?" Jake said.

"See you Sunday."

Lily looked like she wanted to hug him but thought better of it. *Friends can hug!* Jake thought. She smiled at him as she walked out of the church. Jake was left alone again, but this time his solitude made him feel empty. He thought of his hug with Beth earlier. How nice that had felt. Part of him wanted to rush out to Lily and hold her. Or really what he wanted was for her to hold him, to pet his head like a cat's and tell him everything was okay. Would he purr? He thought he might. He felt capable of it.

The rest of the day passed slowly and painfully. He sat in his office for a long while and remembered his whiskey was almost gone. He had forgotten to replace it, a mistake he very rarely made. He sat in his chair and fingered the cross on his necklace. Why not finish the bottle? Even just a drop of the stuff would make him feel better. He knew he'd be getting drunk later, so why not start here, now? Something in him decided not to touch it, and it was a good thing, because Kendall walked in the room.

"Hey, you're here," Kendall said.

"Hey," Jake said.

Her hair was in thick braids, tied up into a tight bun at the back of her head. She had on a white button-up tucked into khaki slacks. Certainly the most dressed up Jake had ever seen her.

"Everything okay at the hospital?"

Kendall knew nothing of Philip, and Jake didn't feel like discussing it all with her. And the truth was he wasn't sure he could talk about it without bursting into tears.

"Yeah, sorry, just a last-minute thing." There was a silence. Jake guessed she was waiting on him to ask her how L.A. was. "How are things here?"

"Same as always. Place feels so empty during the week, even with people always in and out." She paused. "It's good to be back though," here she was really fishing, "two weeks is a long time in a single city."

It was unavoidable now. "How was your vacation?" Jake asked, and without knowing it started fingering his cross necklace again. Kendall smiled and entered the room further now. She took a seat at the other office chair and rolled it toward him.

"It was wonderful," she said. "Talia and I—"

Talia? Here? They were alone, but if she ever said Talia's real name in the church, she said it in a low whisper so that not even the Holy Ghost could hear. When she said it this time, it was said in her normal voice. She drew the 'a' out long, a little bit of L.A. having presumably rubbed off on her. Two weeks was a long time. Things could change in two weeks.

"—stayed at a friend's place. He's spending the summer in Europe, so we had the place all to ourselves. I don't think either of us could have afforded it if we'd had to put ourselves up somewhere. Have I ever told you what Talia does?"

There it was again. Taaaalia. Jake wasn't listening to Kendall explain Talia's occupation, only thinking how nice it would be to have his hand wrapped around the bottle of whiskey in his cabinet.

How nice it would be to tilt it back, for the blood of Christ to run down his throat like a swarm of perfect little honeybees.

"Anyway, have you ever been? You said your brother lives in L.A., right?"

Here it was, the reason Jake had been avoiding Kendall. He hadn't known it until she said it, but it was clear now. He'd made a mistake telling her about Benny in the first place. How strange that he called at the same time Kendall was over there. Why do things work out this way? Who is puppeteering this mess of a life?

"Yeah," Jake said, "I mean no. I haven't been. But yeah, my brother Benny lives there."

"You should visit him sometime."

"Sure. Maybe."

"What does he do?"

How do you answer that question to someone who wouldn't understand? Or maybe she would understand, but Jake didn't want to find out.

"I'm a little behind on my sermon this week: do you mind if I get back to work on it?"

"Oh," Kendall said, standing, "of course. Yes."

"Thank you."

Kendall started walking out of the office but turned in the doorway. Jake wasn't a fan of the dramatics. Just say what you need to say and leave a room. Or, better yet, don't say anything. Even better: don't come in the room.

"There's, um, something I wanted to tell you." She played with her fingers which were hanging down below her waist.

"What is it?" Jake tried not to sound annoyed. He felt he might have actually been convincing at it too, but there was no way to be sure.

Kendall walked back into the room and sat back in the office chair. This really must be something serious. Why all the formality from someone who hadn't been formal since the day they'd met.

"Talia and I went to a church when we were on vacation. It was a really beautiful place, and all of the members there were so kind and so accepting. We didn't get dirty stares. People actually wanted to talk to us. They wanted to know our names, where we were from, how long we'd been together.

"Well, then we got to the service and—Jake, it was wonderful— the pastor was a gay man. And it was clear he was a gay man, and he spoke freely about *being* a gay man. It fueled his sermon rather than filled in the subtext." Kendall's eyes seemed to be shining. "He interpreted the Bible in such a beautiful way. And the members were so engaged and excited to be there. And I just couldn't get over the fact that they all knew they were listening to a gay man.

"So, I went back during the week and found him there. He was up on a tall ladder changing a light bulb, and I swear to you in the moment the light flashed on, I thought he might have been Jesus come down from heaven. But then the ladder wobbled and I watched him cling on for dear life and mumble curses under his breath. I couldn't help but laugh. He saw me and smiled and said, 'Maintenance guy left for the day, I'm not much for fixing things.' He got down off of that ladder and I stuck out my hand for a shake, but he hugged me instead.

"He asked me what it was I needed. And at first, I didn't know. Why had I come to see him in the first place? I really hadn't come with a plan. And then I found myself telling him about my, uh, *situation* here. I spoke and he just listened. He listened well, but by the look on his face, I could tell he'd heard all this before. And when I was done speaking, he said some things I will never forget. He told me of his own challenge when he was younger. He told me he'd been to many churches that wouldn't accept him, but that he knew he'd found the right place when he went there. No one cared about him being gay, just as God wouldn't care if he was gay. God, after all, made us the way we are.

"I say all this to say, Jake, I'm done hiding who I am here."

Jake had been listening closely, and whatever part of him had been annoyed at her presence before had now wanted to reach out and touch her. He didn't want her to stop speaking. He found it all so beautiful and perfect. He hadn't even thought of the whiskey in his drawer all while she talked.

Jake took a deep breath and said, "You're aware of what could happen?" Kendall nodded. "And you're prepared to face whatever may come?"

"Yes."

Jake smiled. And then he frowned. "I was about to say this is brave of you, but I feel sad that it could still be considered something to *be* braved. All churches should be like the one you described. And here I am doing nothing to help that."

"You can always start now."

Jake nodded but then said, "How?" He was embarrassed because he thought the statement may have been rhetorical. People didn't always say things they had an answer to. But whether it had been or not she answered calmly.

"Preach love. Preach acceptance. It's all laid out so clearly for us in the Bible. God loves all of his creations. How the church became a place of hatred is beyond me, but that church has proven to me that things can be better."

"What are you going to do?"

"I'm going to bring Talia here one week. We're going to mingle like any other couple does. Maybe we'll make friends with the other gay couples here who have the privilege of not being seen as voices of the church like you and me. We'll just *be*."

Just be, Jake thought. He hoped to God, or whomever, that the members would just accept it and move on. After all, to Kendall's point, there were other gay couples here. Jake hadn't noticed any negative talk about them behind their backs, not that he spent enough time with the members for his noticing either way to be likely. He tried to allow himself to believe everything would be just fine, that things would go on as normal, as they should. He tried but couldn't. Not fully. He sensed danger ahead, but he couldn't let Kendall know that.

"I think that's wonderful," he said. "No more hiding who you are. That'll feel good." And he wished he, too, could reveal himself. Maybe if all of it was really out there, he could have a real life like everyone else.

"Thanks, Jake." Kendall said. She rose from the chair, smiled at him, and walked out of his office."

Jake was left alone thinking about Benny. Since Kendall had mentioned him, Jake couldn't quite get him off of his mind. He was due to come to Tarrytown in a little over a month and the thought of it made Jake terribly nervous. What did Benny even look like these days? Jake could only imagine him much taller than himself, though he knew it would be extremely unlikely that Benny had hit a late-30's growth spurt. He pictured a head full of hair, a greasy goatee, a girl on each arm. Was Benny into younger women? Older? Did he have a family? Jake thought he would at least know if Benny had a family. Beth would have told him. Or Benny would have said something himself.

Jake opened Facebook on his computer. How many of his questions could be answered by creating a simple login? He'd held off for so long, and why? Did people even use this thing anymore? Did he think he was better than everyone else? Did he simply enjoy being off the grid, whatever that even meant? What temptations would Facebook have that he hadn't faced recently? The past month had shown him that he didn't, in fact, enjoy his solitude as much as he had thought. It was necessary, but did he have to pretend to like it? Name. Jake? Jacob? Everyone in Tarrytown knew him as Jake, but his aunt Beth still called him Jacob. Benny called him Jakey or Jacob. Who was he planning to be friends with on here? Members had been asking him for years if he was on Facebook, and he had the absolute pleasure of telling them no. Would they be able to find him the minute he made an account? Jake decided to use his cross necklace after all. He finished the bottle and stowed it safely back inside where he could make an easy swap. He went with Jake as his name, figuring he could always change it later if he felt like it. Who cared if people found him on here? He didn't plan on being very active. He put in the rest of his information, used the picture he'd taken for his work ID many years before as his profile picture, and created his account. The interface was pretty straightforward. He found the place to search for friends and searched Benny's name. He scrolled through a handful of other accounts and then came across Benny's face. It appeared to be an older photo. Benny didn't have the goatee he'd told Jake he was sporting these days. He was clean-shaven, his hair was parted in the middle and feathered back at the sides. He looked straight out of an episode of *Boy Meets World*.

Jake clicked into Benny's profile to find it incredibly bare. He had three or four photos, all of them seemed to predate the creation of Facebook, or else Benny had a real early-2000's streak recently. There were a few posts on his page, mostly some event reminders and happy birthdays. Jake clicked the 'Friend' button and then, seeing that Beth was one of the people who'd posted a happy birth-day, Jake clicked on her profile. Beth's was brimming with activity. Jake scrolled through numerous event and vacation photo. He found online game scores and news articles and bad memes. Was this how Facebook was supposed to be used? If so, Jake didn't think he would like it much. He friended Beth and then went to close out of the browser only to stop and move his mouse to the search bar. He searched for Eve. He searched for Lily. He didn't take the time to look at their profiles—no good could come from that—he only clicked the 'Friend' button.

Jake licked his lips. There was still some whiskey residue on them, and he relished the flavor. It made him excited to get home and drink some more. He'd had a rough day, a rough two days, and he deserved to drink. He looked at the time. Four Time had flown by since the hospital, but he should be rehearsing his sermon for Sunday. He should be answering some of the emails he had from the church admin. There was probably something to be fixed or tinkered with or someone out there in need of a (useless) prayer or some other kid in the hospital or an organization to send donations to or letters to open or coffee to brew or a new A/V volunteer to interview or a new song to learn or—

Jake grabbed his car keys and made his way out of the church.

As he drove, he thought of nothing but the friends that were waiting for him at his apartment. He didn't think of Benny or of Eve or of what he'd done the night before. He didn't think of Philip or Philip's mother, Beth. He didn't think of Facebook or Kendall's impending doom—not doom, no, perhaps not doom—of Kendall's sure-fire doom. He thought only of what liquors he had left in his duffel. He was due for a refill soon, but he thought he remembered there still being a whiskey in there. Whiskey was what he really wanted. The stuff at the church hadn't satisfied him at all. He needed more.

The silence in his apartment was even greater than it had been in the church or in his car. He closed his eyes and breathed it in. Could you smell silence? Jake thought he could. He opened his eyes and felt something like a string around his waist tugging him toward the duffel bag. And now strings on his arms and legs and fingers sending him into the duffel and out with a bottle of. ah, yes, hello Mr. Williams sir. And then pulling him again to the kitchen to fetch a glass and some ice. God's little marionette. "I'm not a drunk," Jake said out loud to see if his nose would grow. There was no mirror in his kitchen, so he had to put his hand to his nose. He couldn't tell if anything had changed. Just to be sure he said, "I'm not attracted to Eve." His nose grew long and hard in his hand. "I'm not attracted to Lily." It grew long and harder still. "I'm happy." And now he had to stand back from the kitchen cabinet before his nose crashed into it. Luckily, his drink had already been poured, and the strings shrugged his shoulders for him and dragged him to the couch. So now he'd be the lying puppet with the long nose. So what? What did it matter?

With each drink, his nose shrunk until it was small and flaccid on his weathered face. *There*, he thought grabbing the half-empty bottle by its neck and throwing it back, *I'm a real boy again*. And before he passed out on the couch, he thought of his room full of dinosaurs. What had become of that room? Had the person who bought the house redecorated it? Maybe it was an office now. Or a teenager's room full of sports paraphernalia. Or a sex room. Or—

Jake passed out on the couch, the strings slackening as he slept.

CHAPTER TEN
2003

Teachers, student teachers, counselors, old people were constantly telling him that high school would be the best years of his life, and Jacob feared this more than anything. *This here? This shit?* He sometimes wondered if he shouldn't kill himself. He wasn't suicidal, not really, but if graduating meant life got even worse than it was for him now, what reason was there for moving on with his life? He hoped that these people were just projecting distaste for their own adult lives. Probably, if they had the chance to go back, they wouldn't do it. Classes suck, teachers suck, kids are shitty, the hours suck; most of all, the hormones suck. Suck. Lily Scarlett. Wow, could she suck. Sometimes he imagined his English teacher, Mrs. Felton, was Lily Scarlett. They looked alike except that Mrs. Felton was real and Lily was just a computer image burned forever in Jacob's mind. Sometimes, when Mrs. Felton was talking about Shakespeare or Holden Caulfield or, Gatsby? What Gatsby? Jacob would imagine her reaching around her back with one hand and slowly unzipping her dress. He imagined her breasts falling all at once out of the dress, the cool air making them tighten with goose pimples. Suddenly, the class would be gone, and she'd be making her way over to him in only her panties, and then on the way she'd slip those off too. And then she'd smile and open her mouth and move it toward his—

"Jacob, tell us what you think about our narrator's invisibility."

Jacob shifted in his seat to hide his erection. If this was her way of trying to catch him off guard for not paying attention, she'd asked him the wrong question. She should have asked him what he thought about what they'd been talking about. He hadn't heard a word she said in the last fifteen minutes. He was deep in his own Lily Scarlet/Mrs. Felton fantasy. Those breasts. That mouth.

"Jacob?"

Despite his sexual fantasies about her, Jacob despised Mrs. Felton. She knew he was the quiet kid in the class. No doubt she'd also heard what had happened to his parents, only where this made most teachers more likely to leave him be, Mrs. Felton seemed to be under the impression that participation in the class would somehow make him come out of his shell. To put it another way: it would make him more normal. More like the other kids. And so, all that semester she'd call on him to answer the stupidest questions. Sometimes he'd answer. Other times he would shrug his shoulders to Mrs. Felton's chagrin. This was the third time she'd called on him this class already. He looked at her and saw there was a smirk on her gorgeous face as if she could sense his annoyance and was proud to have been the annoyer.

"Well, he's not really invisible," Jacob said. She wanted him to talk, he would talk. "It's about us. White people. We don't see him, not really. Or at least that's the way he is perceiving it."

"Good, thank you. Now let's—"

"What I don't understand is his relationship with women."

"Go on."

"The book basically starts with him describing his dick getting hard over—"

"Jacob!" Mrs. Felton cried, "please don't—"

"Over a naked woman in a poorly made boxing ring. And then he's always shying away from women, even though he claims to support their cause. Then one woman throws herself at him, which, by the way, how is she going to do that if this guy is invisible, and then he fucks her and panics about it."

"Jacob!"

The class around him, which he had forgotten, gasped.

"He can't even bring himself to describe the act, as if it wasn't real but some sort of fantasy he only brought to life in his invisible brain. I say describe it. Did she give him head? Did he lick her pussy? Or, what is it they call it in the book? Her cunt?" Mrs. Felton was over at the phone talking rapidly to someone. "Tell us how it felt inside of her, not about how you're so paranoid about it afterward that you see some sort of apparition."

"Please go to the principal's office," Mrs. Felton said, but Jacob wasn't quite finished.

"You ask all the wrong questions about this book. Of course it's about race, isn't everything? But let's dig deeper and see what kind of insecurities this character has that go way beyond race. Let's see how this man does in 2003 with internet porn and magazines and sex workers advertising in newspapers. Let's see how much he can really get done in his movement with all of these distractions around."

The class and Mrs. Felton were completely silent. Jacob thought he'd made a semi-valid point. There were some holes, sure, he was making this up as he went, but in a real class discussion they could ignore his cursing and lewdness, and someone might counter with something he hadn't thought of before. How do they expect you to get something out of a discussion class when you're not really allowed to discuss? No sex. No profanity. Sex and profanity are all that exist in literature! What else is there? Love? Love is just a nicer way of saying sex.

Jacob grabbed his things off his desk and made his way out of the classroom, which remained quiet even as the door was closing behind him. The hallway was utterly empty and calm. He took a deep breath in. He hadn't intended to upset the class and certainly not Mrs. Felton. He wasn't sure what came over him. One minute he was hiding an erection and the next he was off on some tangent about the Invisible Man being the one who had weird sex issues. If only Mrs. Felton had let him continue his fantasy, he wouldn't be in this mess, and she wouldn't have to be doing damage control in the classroom right now. And she would be naked.

Jacob didn't go to the principal's office. Instead, he went to the one place he knew would get him out of the trouble he would most certainly be in otherwise. He walked to Mr. Nazari's office and knocked on the door.

Mr. Nazari opened the door, saw it was Jacob, and smiled warmly at him.

"Jacob. Come on in."

Jacob entered the office, and Mr. Nazari closed the door behind him. Jacob took a seat in front of Mr. Nazari's desk. Mr. Nazari sat on the corner of the desk, peering down at Jacob.

"What can I do for you?"

There was something pleasant about his office. In any other setting, it might be just a normal room, but amongst the other back-pain inducing office and desk chairs and the bad-poster-strewn classrooms, Mr. Nazari's room stood out as comfortable. The light inside was dim, always a relief from the fluorescents of the hallways. The chair in front of the desk was deep-cushioned and gave Jacob the sense of floating. There was a bobblehead of Mr. Nazari, a gift from a kid, no doubt, on his desk next to a picture that Jacob could never see but always assumed was of his family. Was it a wife and two girls? A husband and twins? Maybe it was just of his dog and cat, maybe not a traditional family, but someone to go home to nonetheless. Jacob had a sudden urge to tap the bobble-headed Mr. Nazari, to make his head bounce, bounce, bounce.

"I had an outburst in English. I'm supposed to be at the principal's office but I felt... I felt like I should come here first. To calm down."

Mr. Nazari frowned, perhaps understanding that Jacob had come here simply to get out of going to the principal's office, but he nodded kindly enough. Jacob swore he saw the bobble head nodding along with him.

"Tell me what happened."

"We were discussing *Invisible Man*—"

"Great book."

"Sure. Anyway, I got going about the narrator's relationship with women. I said some bad stuff. Bad words, bad acts."

"Which ones?"

Jacob looked at Mr. Nazari with confusion. Did he really want Jacob to say them out loud? Or was this a trick to get him in even more trouble?

"Well?"

"I said fuck."

"Sure."

"And I mentioned," Jacob cleared his throat, "sucking dick and eating pussy."

"Okay."

"And then I said cunt." Mr. Nazari winced at the word but remained calm. "But only because that's what the book called it."

"Let's not spread that. There are enough banned books here already, we don't need parents or teachers trying to ban this one because of a simple bad word."

"Yeah, sure." Jacob was looking down at the floor now. Having said all of these out loud right next to each other, he felt ashamed for having said them in the classroom. He understood why Mrs. Felton had to react the way she did. He would probably have done the same in her adult shoes.

"Let's talk about the real issue here," Mr. Nazari said, his face becoming very serious. He leaned forward, his hands resting on his knees. "This isn't your first outburst of this kind. Granted, you haven't had one in a while, but they aren't foreign to you."

Jacob couldn't look Mr. Nazari in the eyes. There was something wrong with him. He knew this. He just couldn't figure out what it was. He'd been seeing Mr. Nazari since he came to the high school, a counselor named Connie before that—Connie, call me Connie, none of this Mrs. business—and still he couldn't bring himself to tell them the real story of what happened the days his father and mother had died. Maybe if he did, they would be able to fix him, but he felt he'd rather die than tell even a single person what had happened. He had his daily—hourly—fantasies, but he never indulged them. He wasn't sure that would be worth what it could cost him. He thought of Benny in college. He thought of his Aunt Beth back at home. If he so much as touched himself, would Benny or Aunt Beth be stabbed, maimed, shot, hanged, drowned?

"Jacob?"

"Sorry. No, it's not."

Mr. Nazari jumped off of his desk and walked around to sit in his chair. He riffled around in a drawer that Jacob couldn't see and pulled out a file. This Jacob was familiar with. It was a light blue folder, his name typed from a label maker in the tab on the top. Mr. Nazari opened the folder and scanned its contents as Jacob sat silently wondering if he should have gone to the principal's office after all.

Mr. Nazari stopped looking through the folder, closed his eyes and sighed. He closed the folder and looked at Jacob with a look that was meant to be flat but betrayed a hint of pity.

"Look," Mr. Nazari said, putting the folder down and leaning his elbows on his desk. "I don't need to look in your folder to know what's going on. Hell, we've talked enough that I might know you better than anyone. I'm old as," here he paused, and then whispered, "fuck," and Jacob's heart leapt. Could he say that? Would he get in trouble? "And I haven't lost either of my parents, so I'm not going to sit here and pretend I know personally what you are going through. What I can tell you is I know other kids who have been in similar," a pause again, "situations. And I know all of them have acted differently but similarly."

Jacob must have looked confused because Mr. Nazari leaned back and made a sort of 'tsk' sound with his lips, as if he was trying to find the right words.

"What I mean is it's normal to act out. Inside, you feel something that no one can comprehend and having outbursts is your way of letting yourself be seen. What we need to do is try to put that energy elsewhere. It'll take time and patience, but we'll get there."

Jacob didn't know what to say. He just looked at the bobblehead and longed to tap it. In all his time in this office, he'd never done it. Why wouldn't he just reach his hand out and tap the thing? That's what they're for, right? Instead, he said, "Can I see that photo?" He pointed his finger at the photo he'd never seen.

Mr. Nazari looked disappointed. Had his message made it through to the boy? "Sure," he said, turning the photo around to Jacob. It was of Mr. Nazari with a woman and a boy and a girl. Having expected this, Jacob himself was quite disappointed at first. Only, Mr. Nazari looked happy and that made Jacob happy.

He reached out and tapped the top of the bobblehead. It bobbed and swayed, and Jacob felt himself holding back a laugh.

"Did one of them give this to you?" he said, pointing at the photo.

"My son," Mr. Nazari said with a smile, "his name is also Jacob. Our daughter's name is Ariana."

And then both Mr. Nazari and Jacob went silent a while, both watching the bobblehead with an intense curiosity. Mr. Nazari was, perhaps, thinking of the day the boy gave it to him. Jacob didn't know what the memory was, but he'd learned too much about Mr. Nazari in the past minute to ask him that too. Jacob was thinking about this boy who shared his name. He thought of how young the boy was and how young Jacob himself had been when his father died. He watched the bobblehead and thought of it toppling over. *Please, Jacob. Call 911.*

A bell rang, and suddenly, noise from the hallways filled the office. There was laughter and shuffling of feet and lockers opening and closing. Books filled bags and zippers zipped.

"Let's get you to lunch, yeah?" Mr. Nazari said, standing from his chair.

"Sure," Jacob said, also standing.

"I'll give the principal a call. Let him know it's all under control."

"Thanks."

Jacob started to walk out of the door when Mr. Nazari said, "And Jacob?" Jacob didn't turn, only placed his hand on the handle and waited. "Come back in next week on Tuesday."

Jacob nodded and left the office without looking back.

***

When their mother died, Jacob and Benny's aunt Beth scooped them up and took them to live with her in Akron. It wasn't all that far from Huber Heights, but somehow Beth had managed not to see much of either of them when they were younger, save for a few birthdays and Christmases. Now she was there for them every single day. She had never had children of her own. As far as Jacob knew she had never even been married. She was their mother's older sister, their age gap less than that of Jacob and Benny's but vast enough for Beth to take on an almost grandmotherly quality. Their own grandparents had died when they were young. Their parents around the time Benny was born.

Beth was there for them in ways their own mother had not been in the years between their father's death and her own. She promised to give Benny anything he needed for college. He denied his acceptance to Ohio University to spend more time with Jacob. He didn't know when or if he would start applying again, but he was grateful to Beth for promising to help. And within a year and a half, he had applied to film school in UCLA. By the time Jacob was entering his junior year of high school, Benny had left.

Benny had pretended to be strong during the months after their mother's death, but Jacob could tell it was a show. Maybe he was trying to protect Jacob, but it was more likely Benny was trying to protect himself. He didn't try to make any new friends in Akron and would instead drive out to Huber Heights most weekends and stay with friends. He'd often come home smelling like alcohol. Jacob could always tell, which meant that Beth could too, but she just let him be.

Jacob didn't try to make friends either, and he certainly wasn't making them by chance. His outbursts in school, though infrequent and harmless to anyone but the teachers they were directed at, and the fact that he was new to the school district going into Freshman year, gave him oddball status. Now in Junior year, he was still an outcast and he genuinely didn't mind. He read a lot in those days. Did his homework as he was asked. He and Beth developed a relatively close relationship, all things considered. They'd go to the movies together, out to dinners, and sometimes jazz shows, which Jacob didn't care for, but he knew Beth loved jazz.

"How was school today?" Beth asked from the kitchen when

Jacob walked through the door. Did she know? How much should he tell her?

"It was fine." He took off his shoes and put his backpack by the door.

"Anything exciting?" He couldn't see her from the foyer. Was she toying with him? She never gave him much hell for his outbursts, but Jacob still had an overwhelming feeling of guilt.

"Not really," Jacob said, rounding the corner. Beth was unloading the dishwasher with her back to him. "We discussed *Invisible Man*."

"Never made it through that one," Beth said, turning around with a mixing bowl in her hands. She reached up to a cabinet to put it away. "Way too long for me."

Beth was wearing one of Benny's old high school football t-shirts and high-waisted jeans. Her light brown hair was cut short in an Audrey Hepburn sort of way. She was tall and lanky, as if she'd never grown out of her high school body. Even the way she moved felt oddly adolescent.

She stopped moving and smiled wryly at Jacob. "I rather thought the women in it were all cunts."

Dread hit Jacob as if it were a train. One of those speedy ones in Japan. He sat down at the kitchen table and tried not to look ashamed. Beth went back to unloading the dishes, but Jacob could tell she was waiting for him to speak.

"Not my finest moment," Jacob said at last. "Though for the record, I didn't say it like that."

"I was going for shock value. Isn't that what you were doing in class?"

"I guess so."

Beth closed the dishwasher and peered at Jacob with a look mixed with disappointment and compassion. She walked over to the kitchen table and sat down with Jacob.

"Did you talk to Mr. Nazari?" She put her hand on his back and rubbed softly. Another day Jacob might have shrugged this off, but today it felt nice to be loved.

"Yeah. I went straight there."

"Good," she paused as if she wanted to say something more, and then said, again, "good."

It was silent for a moment. Jacob stared out of the sliding glass door that went from the kitchen to Beth's backyard. The wind was blowing the overgrown grass softly. Jacob wasn't asked to do many chores, but Beth did ask him to mow the lawn. Once every week or so, Jacob would grab the five-hundred-year-old push mower from the garage and cut haphazard lines into Beth's grass. He'd been too young when his father was around to learn how to do it. And when it was just their mother, Benny would cut the grass or ask a sympathetic neighbor to come over and do it for them.

"Jacob," Jacob looked back toward Beth, "did your parents ever talk to you about sex?"

Fireworks exploded in Jacob's belly. Not sparklers or those lame snake things; these were the kind that you couldn't find unless you knew where to go. The ones that amusement parks set off, the ones that the sketchy kid in school would try to sell you for $100. Was he sweating? Shouldn't he just say, *Yep, yep, yep Aunt Beth for sure I definitely had that talk already, say would you like to go see a movie?* Could he start running? He was going to throw up, he could feel it.

"We don't have to make this weird you know." Beth said. "I'm sure you know all of the juicy details. I can spare you that stuff."

Paralyzed! I'm Paralyzed! Help!!!!!!

"Benny was always very open with his... knowledge of sex. He thinks I don't know what he's pursuing in film school, but I know."

O', if only Benny could have been there.

O' sweet Jesus, please begin your rapture.

"Just let me say two things, and then I'll be done. Be respectful of whomever you're interested in."

Jacob wasn't listening, only he was listening. Did Beth think he was gay? Jacob didn't really care as long as they made it through this conversation.

"And don't put too much weight on the first time. This probably isn't the advice your mother would have given you—in fact, I know it isn't—but I think too many people get it in their heads that the first time is so incredibly special, and it takes away from the actual fun of it. Sex isn't everything, but it's a very good thing.

"That's it. Talk over. Oh, and wear a condom, but that's a given."

She smiled as if it had all been a big joke, but of course it hadn't been. Beth was nothing if not sincere. Jacob knew she thought this was all the right thing to say to him. Maybe if she'd known his real problem, she would have had something else to say. Maybe she'd slap him in the face and tell him God isn't punishing him for acting on disgusting impulses. Maybe if he told Mr. Nazari, his wonderful guidance counselor would tell him it's all in his head. Teenagers are touching themselves all the time—it's no real statistical anomaly that someone might die while you're doing it. Maybe if Mrs. Felton knew, she would have nodded at his expert analysis on *Invisible Man* and would have applauded him for his deep knowledge of the narrator.

What if Benny knew?

Beth stood up from the table, and Jacob knew he should thank her or at least acknowledge they'd had a chat. Instead, he felt as if he might still be paralyzed. His breathing was irregular, and he felt sweat beading on his forehead and the nape of his neck and the armpit part of his knees, the legpit, yes that must be it.

He gathered the strength to turn himself again toward the window. The tall grass now bothered him immensely. He decided it needed cut right then. It couldn't wait. It was sunny right now;

what if it started to rain? What if a monsoon came to Akron and the grass couldn't be cut for a week? What an absolute tragedy.

"I have to go cut the grass," Jacob said, forcing himself to stand. He heard Beth chuckle but say nothing further.

Jacob ran out to the garage and felt life returning to him. He relished in the heavy heat of the garage. He breathed in deeply and took in the smell of gasoline and plywood and hot rubber. He realized he still had his normal clothes and shoes on, but there was no way in hell he was going back into the house, not for a while, maybe not ever again. He opened the garage and wheeled out the mower that was heavier than he was. The breeze outside felt nice on his sweaty face. He took another deep breath and attempted to start the mower. One pull, two pulls, three pulls, four pulls, five pulls, *start motherfucker!*, six pulls, sev—

The mower boomed to life. No matter how many times Jacob used the thing, it always made him jump a little when it actually started up. He started mowing. Again, his lines were choppy. He missed chunks of grass here and there. His edges were garbage. And by no more than a quarter of the way through, he looked down at himself to see he'd been painted green. He thought of the giant on the green bean cans. Of Yoda. Of The Grinch. Of Kermit. Green with envy. Green lights.

Maybe he'd be green forever now. He didn't think he'd mind. It might be nice for people to just notice he was different instead of them finding out down the line. He could be 'that green guy'. 'Hey green guy, how are ya? Say, did you catch the game last night? Eagles vs. Jets. Green on green, how about that?'

This thought carried him through many wavy lines, into the garage, and back into the home.

CHAPTER ELEVEN

Jake sat on the train on the way into the city, his duffel secured closely beside him. On his walk to the train there was a strip mall, abandoned except for a lone hair salon with grainy pictures of celebrities out front meant to entice people to come in. Come in as yourself, come out as Brad Pitt and smelling of cigarettes and bad dry shampoo. Behind the hair salon were two dumpsters, one for trash, the other recycling. On these trips to the city Jake would gather up all of his old bottles of liquor, sneak up to the trash cans, careful to check for anyone who might be around, quickly unzip his duffel and turn it upside down over the one for recycling—you have to give back, you see, reduce, reuse, that kind of thing—and then wince before they crash at the bottom, a symphony of shattered gin and whiskey and vodka and tequila bottles. And before anyone may come back and wonder what all the racket is, Jake would jog away, the duffel bag still unzipped and slightly wet from left over droplets of delicious liquid. He sometimes pictured himself sucking the mixed liquid out of the bag. Wringing it out and into his parched throat.

The past week had gone by quickly and without any major issues. He'd given his sermon on Sunday with ease, though he still hadn't replaced the empty whiskey bottle in his desk. He wondered what Kendall was saying to the youth group. He hadn't seen her with anyone before or between services, at least not anyone that seemed like they could be Talia. Would she wait to say something until Talia joined her? Or would she let it slip early and let the vicious rumor mill pick it up from there?

Lily showed up at Ava's just as she always did. Though she wasn't very talkative, she still ordered her usual meal of hot dogs and beer; this Jake took as a good sign. They both pretended as if her birthday hadn't happened. Jake preferred this, only he wished things felt more normal than they did. He wondered how long it might be this way. Would they ever be able to truly be friends? Is that even what he wanted? In the bathroom of Ava's, he looked closely at himself in the mirror and wondered when he'd become such a misogynist. He didn't hate women by any means, but he certainly wasn't treating Lily or Eve the way he would be treating men. Maybe it was the animal instinct to mate, one that he'd been trying to ignore so long. Or maybe this was just another fucked-up thing to add to the extensive list of fucked-up things about him.

He hadn't been back to visit Philip or Beth or Eve, but he planned on going in the coming days. He wanted to get through the sermon he had planned for Kendall before having something else weigh on his mind. Besides, Eve hadn't texted him any updates, so he figured things were pretty much the same. What good would he be there? He'd just take up space.

And now, on a beautiful summer Saturday morning, Jake barely even felt his headache due to the excitement of a full duffel refill. He pulled out $300 from an ATM the previous day and wondered why they called money green. It looked more like gray to him. Bleak, almost. That is until the time came to give it to the liquor store cashier and turn it into bottle after bottle of sweet liquor. Yes, that would be more than green, that would be gold.

When he made it to the city, he started on his normal route. He didn't go far off of the train station, again a result of the paranoia that even here, still, he could run into someone who knew him. It was three blocks to the place he'd been going for a while. He was due to switch it up soon so that he didn't become a 'regular', but next time, maybe. After all, there are no shortage of liquor stores in Midtown. During his walk, he encountered hundreds of faces that were completely strange to him. Not strange in the sense that they looked weird or disfigured, strange in the glorious sense that he didn't know them from Adam. God, how he hated that term. Something he'd picked up in Bible college and had never quite shaken. Man with very long, greasy beard. Woman with baby. Man with baby. Woman with much older woman, perhaps a grandma or a wealthy lover. Man dressed in a Santa Claus coat and pants even though it was the middle of summer. Boy with dog. A lone pigeon. Woman in fire escape reading *Wuthering Heights* in large print. Girl in a black tank top with a snake tattoo on her ne—

Jake stopped in his tracks. Eve was coming directly toward him. She was looking down at her phone. There was a chance she'd pass right by him without so much as a glance. In a city of nearly 9 million people, so few of them actually look up anymore. Jake stood and prayed silently that she would remain one of the many passersby completely ignorant of their surroundings. *Dear God do this one thing for me. Dear God I'll start believing in you again. Dear God—*

Eve looked up. It was only for a moment. Only a flick of her eyes up and then back down to her phone. She'd looked right at Jake, but maybe she hadn't really seen. If he started walking now, maybe even a double-take wouldn't confirm his presence there. He could be a ghost, a doppelganger, a hallucination. But his feet wouldn't let him move. All these trips into the city and not once had he run into anyone he even remotely recognized, save for the time he thought he saw Barry but then realized it was a street performer putting on something like clown makeup. Why here and now? Was this a sign? *Please God don't let her look back.*

She looked back. Jake tried to turn his head away, but he was still frozen there in the street. Someone trying to get by shoved him hard, but still he could not get himself to move. It was like one of those nightmares where you try to scream but it seems to get caught in your throat and all you can do is sort of gurgle and twitch. *Dear God, please let this be a nightmare.*

"Jake?"

She was walking back toward him now, looking up from her phone, staring Jake straight in the eyes. Was there an out? Could he deny being Jake? Jake, who's Jake? I don't know a Jake. Could he shout fire! or tornado! or Ryan Gosling! to draw so much attention to the area that he had a chance to run away? He could deny it later. He'd been in Tarrytown all day. What happened in the city? Did you catch a glimpse of Ryan Gosling?

"Hey," she said, smiling, "what are you doing here?"

She was directly in front of him now. He must have looked like a scared dog, dripping wet, shivering from the wind and the rain; except it wasn't rainy or windy. Now he had to speak. If he didn't speak things would get much worse than they were now. Just speak goddamnit!

"Eve, hi," he managed. He hoped it didn't sound forced. He'd even tried to smile. Did it come off sincere or did it look like a Ted Bundy smile: all tooth no truth.

Her smile said: ohmygoditssogoodtoseeyouhowareyoutellmeeverything.

Her smile said: wanttograbacoffeeorabageloraglassofbeerwhocaresthatitsstillmorning.

Her voice said: "I haven't seen you around the hospital."

"Yeah, sorry. I've been busy. How's he doing?"

She was holding a large book in her hand. It looked collegiate, lots of colors and big lettering. She was saying something, but Jake was wondering why college textbooks are often so colorful. Children needed colorful stimuli. Adults only need it subconsciously—Coco-Cola red, bank or stockbroker or eco-friendly green, technology company blue—what are textbooks looking to convey with their colors? Or was it simply the cheapest patterns they could find to then upsell the books at 354% profit?

"...Anyway, he seems to be progressing. The doctors think they might try to take him out of his coma next week."

"I'll try to be there when they do."

Jake wanted to ask what she was doing here, but he knew that if he asked her, she would ask him again. This time, he couldn't use the surprise of the moment to get out of answering the question. He was trying to formulate something in his head in case she asked again, but the thought of the colorful textbooks was still rushing through his brain. He'd been doing these trips so long without running into anyone he knew that he'd forgotten the old excuses he used to have ready in case a run-in did happen.

"Do you want to grab a coffee?" Eve said. She had a hint of nervousness in her voice, something Jake hadn't heard from her before. She was always so cool. Even when Philip was put in a coma, she was worried but somehow cool, levelheaded. This was something Jake didn't relate to. He either felt things hard or not at all. Until lately, actually, it was mostly not at all.

Before he could talk himself out of it, he found his voice forming the word, "Yeah," and then the word, "Sure."

Eve took him to a coffee shop a few blocks away. Jake knew very little about coffee, but what he did know of it was typically from one of those green or orange and pink chain stores that sell hot water and lots of sugar. He had a cup of coffee at the church now and then on particularly bad mornings when his desk whiskey wasn't quite enough to get him out of his hangover funk, but whoever the coffee-making volunteer was either didn't know what they were doing or thoroughly enjoyed literal mud with clumps and all. He wished he had packed his flask in his pocket so he could at least spice the coffee up with something under the table.

They exchanged some niceties on the way, but Jake was still jarred at having been ripped from his routine and wasn't very talkative. He should be at the liquor store right now browsing this week's catch, and instead he was with this girl who smelled like the beach, sweet sweat and all, and whose Spotify-green eyes smiled even bigger than her mouth. And what do people put in a duffel bag? Gym clothes? Sex toys? Dozens of hot dogs? His brain wasn't functioning, and this gorgeous red-headed girl next to him was not hel—wait, red-headed? Wasn't she a blonde? *O' God, she is so pretty*—she was really not helping.

"Your hair," Jake said.

"Oh. Yeah," she brushed it softly behind her ear, "I just wanted a change. Blonde wasn't my natural color anyway."

"What's your natural color?"

"Maybe you'll find out someday," Eve said with a Cheshire Cat smile. Someday implies a future. What future was there here? Jake would end the coffee date early, go to a new liquor store a million blocks away from Eve, fill his duffel, and make his way home to dive into his new stash. He didn't have time for a future with Eve. He didn't—wait, did he say date? Was this a date?

They arrived at the coffee shop. It wasn't at all like the chains that Jake knew. It was quaint but packed with plushy chairs and intimate round tables. The walls were covered in beautiful wallpaper. Its smells swirled in Jake's head: freshly ground coffee brewed into a potent and creamy espresso, steamed milk of all varieties, croissants and scones and things with tart fillings. The baristas looked happy to be there. They poured milk into lattes and cappuccinos with intricate designs. They smiled and waved and worked with an ease that was both mechanical and artful.

Eve ordered an iced coffee with almond milk. Jake watched the small beads of sweat glisten on the back of her neck as she spoke. A single bead dropped and slid down her back, disappearing under the tank top into a world Jake knew nothing of. He suddenly found himself wanting to know that world. It must be quite wonderful down there. It must be—

No, there was that misogyny again. Or horniness. Either way, he needed to think about something, anything else. But his eyes stayed where the bead had fallen. And then they looked at the snake which seemed to say, *Are you jealousssss I get to be a part of her alwaysssss?*

"And whatever he's having," Eve said looking back at Jake.

Panic. "Oh," panic, panic, panic, "same." Did he like iced coffee? Did he like almond milk?

Eve paid for them both. Is it a date if one person pays for both of them? Should Jake have offered to pay? He was so out of his element here—and distracted by the thought of the unknown world of under-tank-top—that he hadn't even considered paying. How much did coffee even cost? He thought of being a kid, in the days before his father drank his weekly beer at Chet's. He'd order a cup of coffee, and Chet would come around three or four times to refill his mug. Jake asked if he could order it one week. His dad laughed and told him to go right ahead. He liked how it looked like the hot chocolate their mother would make them on cold winter nights. When he tasted it, he spit it back into the cup and his face wrinkled. It was very hot, and it tasted like gravel. His father laughed and laughed. Benny laughed too, perhaps having figured this out for himself as a young boy. Their mother looked concerned but couldn't help but laugh along with them.

Jake and Eve sat at an empty table and waited for their coffee.

Jake was still trying to find words to say. Nothing would come into his head. Was this really a date?

"I like how you look like any other person," Eve said.

Jake wondered if he'd heard her wrong. This seemed like an odd thing to say. He said, "Huh?"

"No one would suspect you're the pastor of a church. You look just like us. Sort of like how when you see a celebrity in public, they don't look like they do on a screen. I saw Mark Ruffalo on the subway once and he looked like he could be in a local East Village band and might have five roommates and a girlfriend pregnant by accident."

"So, you're saying I look like Mark Ruffalo?" Jake joked. He was coming back to himself.

"Yes, that's exactly what I was saying." Eve smiled and positioned herself across from Jake so that she was leaning her elbows on the table, looking slightly up at him. The red hair suited her. Jake wouldn't have thought her eyes could appear any bigger, but the red truly brought them out. A strand of hair hung down over her right eye and swayed back and forth.

"Anyway, I guess I just mean I like seeing you outside of the hospital. It's not the ideal place to keep meeting someone."

"No, I guess it isn't."

He knew it was coming before she said it. He knew he couldn't avoid it. No one sees someone randomly in a place they wouldn't expect to see them and *doesn't* ask the question.

"What are you doing in the city?"

Pilates class? Getting headshots? In an East Village band with five roommates and an accidentally pregnant girlfriend? Football tryouts? Church seminar? Piano lessons?

A barista came by with their drinks, giving Jake more time to think of his excuse. As he thought through it, he wondered what Eve would say if he told her the truth. Would she be disgusted?

Sympathetic?

"I thought I might go to some bookstores."

Bookstores! Really? Who carries an empty duffel bag around for their books? What book had Jake read in the past five years other than his Bible? He'd stopped reading books soon after he graduated college. He didn't get the point. Why fill your head with knowledge when you don't have an opportunity to use it?

"Any in particular?"

"I don't know. I'm not much of a reader."

Why that? Why just flat out tell her you're lying to her face?

"Trying to get into it?"

"Yeah, something like that. What's that book you're carrying with you?"

She'd placed it on the table and put her purse on top of it. Maybe she didn't want it to be seen.

"Oh," she looked nervous as she took the bag off of the book and turned it toward Jake. It was an MCAT study book. "I'm thinking about going to med school."

"Wow," Jake said with genuine surprise, "that's amazing. When is your test?"

"September," she took a sip of her coffee, Jake realized he hadn't even tried his yet. "I'm an idiot and signed up for the last one of the year. So if I don't do well, I can't try again until, like, January."

"You won't need to take it again." Jake took a sip of the coffee. He hid his wince. Somehow, iced coffee tasted even worse than the hot stuff.

"Oh yeah, how would you know? We barely even know each other."

"I just know." Jake smiled. "Anyway, why do you come out here to study?"

"I get my best studying done on the train and in coffee shops, so I try to come here on my days off."

The milk steamer screeched. Someone ordered an iced chai. Change in the tip jar rattled like a defensive snake. Someone ordered a cortado, whatever the hell that is. Liquids were poured into cups of ice. Lids clicked into place. Jake was forgetting he'd ever been nervous. He was forgetting about the empty duffel bag at his feet and about his lousy excuse of being in the city to go to bookstores.

"I think you'd be a great doctor."

"You think?"

"The best doctor."

"Yeah?"

"Yep." Jake took another horrible sip of his coffee. This one was somehow worse than the first. He wasn't sure where to take this conversation. He was worried it would turn to flirting. Or did he want it to turn to flirting?

The barista said: "Iced chai."

Eve said, "Well, I'm sure you're the best preacher ever."

Jake almost choked on his own spit. The best preacher ever wouldn't be in the city with a duffel bag right now. The best preacher ever would believe in his own words. The best preacher ever would have a healthy relationship with God.

"Now I know you're lying," Jake said with a forced smile.

"I bet you're so cute up there on stage with a Bible in one hand and a microphone in the other."

"I use a head mic."

"Asking people to close their eyes while you lead them in prayer. Do you know how sensual that is?"

And now it had turned to flirting, or too-casual banter, and Jake knew he should stop it right there. He thought of what had happened the last time he flirted with a girl. He thought of Philip, of Philip's mother. But, O' God, Eve was sipping her coffee, her lips puckered and sucking. And, O' God, O' God, he felt himself growing—why must he always be growing? Which mushroom was it that makes you smaller?

"Where's your first stop, anyway?"

"Huh?"

Eve had stopped sipping her coffee and Jake hadn't even noticed. He was busy trying to think of anything but the beautiful red-headed girl in front of him. What was the answer to that Jeopardy question last night? Did he leave the oven on? How do you spell resturant? Otters are cute, huh? What should be for lunch?

"You said you wanted to go to some bookstores. Did you have any in mind?"

Back to this again? Why couldn't he have thought of something, anything, else?

"Oh," he started, "I wanted to kind of play it by ear."

Play it by ear? What a stupid thing to say.

"I like that," Eve said. "I envy spontaneous people. Even as a kid, I had everything calculated out. If I were you, I would have scoped out not only the bookstores but the best route to go between each one, a lunch spot in-between, and what train I'd be taking home when I was done."

"So come with me," Jake said.

What! What!! Why on earth would he have said this? Was there something wrong with him? There were plenty of things wrong with him, but still, this?

She could still say no. She had to study, after all. One day of study gone is one day closer to doing poorly on the test. Eve couldn't have that, now could she? No. Of course she would say no, but thanks so much for the invite. A raincheck, that's all. Next time.

"I should say no," Eve started. Yes! No worries at all. Please have a nice study day. "But to be honest with you, I could use a day to get out of my head for once."

Jake's heart dropped and leapt at the same time. Was that possible? They're opposing movements but he felt them both very clearly.

Obviously, he should be upset. He couldn't put himself in situations like this. And what business did he have going to bookstores? But that dirty, deceptive, greedy part of him was excited to get to spend more time with Eve. He felt a small spot in the very back of his brain pulsing excitedly with activity. Possibilities rushed through his mind. Would they hold hands? No! He wouldn't allow it! Would they kiss in front of *War and Peace*? *Great Expectations*? *Cujo*? No! They couldn't! Would a morning turn into late-afternoon drinks? Would they spend the night in a cheap hotel that smelled of cigarettes and old hash-browns? No! Of course they wouldn't!

"That sounds great. You could use some spontaneity. I could use a little direction."

"I've already been planning a route in my head."

"Do you know a lot of bookstores in the city?" Jake asked. He was still battling with himself in his head. Was this good or was this bad? Bad. It was bad. And it was good. Fuck.

"I know a few. But there's one that is an obvious start."

"What's that?"

"Come on. You'll find out." Eve sucked down the last of her coffee and set it back on the table. Jake left his half full, sweating lightly. A puddle had formed where his coffee sat. Eve took Jake's hand and pulled him out of the store. To his delight and absolute despair, she let go of it as soon as they crossed the threshold of the door.

***

They started at The Strand. Jake had never heard of it, but Eve told him it was a New York institution. She said you have to visit The Strand at least once in your life. To Jake, it was just a bookstore. There were shelves and books and bookmarks and coffee mugs and tote bags. It seemed to be filled nearly to capacity. Everyone was frantic, hurried, as if they actually had things to do afterward except go to a bar with their friends. They seemed to know the exact layout of the place. Where Jake felt lost at every turn, others were bumping into him to get directly to an exact location where they would presumably find the exact author and exact work that they were looking for. Where Jake found the prices to be outrageous for a few pieces of paper, others seemed to be content, others even smiled to themselves as if they had found the best deal in town. Maybe they had. Jake didn't have a clue.

Eve moved through the store with a similar ease as the other patrons. Whether she was looking for anything in particular, Jake didn't know, but he sidled along with her. When she stopped to ask him about a particular book, Jake would nod and appear interested. He even threw a few of the ones she was most excited about into his duffel without looking at the price. She seemed so excited that he would read her suggestions which made him excited, even though he knew he wouldn't really read them.

They moved from The Strand over to some bookstores in The Village and then down to SoHo. Jake picked a few books at Eve's suggestion at each location. His duffel was filling and he wondered where the alcohol would fit. Would he even be able to stop off at a liquor store to fill it? He only had a half a bottle of vodka back home. Would that be enough to get him through the night?

But being with Eve made him happy. He loved watching her leaf through a book and tell him about what it meant to her or what she liked or hated about it. He liked watching her smile at him when he told her he'd like to buy the book. He liked the way she became shy when he said he'd like to buy her a book too. Her body said, *No you don't have to*, but her face said, *I'd love that so so so much*. He loved the way nurse Eve melted away and she became almost a child. Not in a creepy way. In that way that children see the world so differently than adults. In the way that Jake remembered himself feeling so excited when he got to make his bedroom into a dinosaur theme.

And when she asked him, after they had taken a cab to the upper east side to one last bookstore, if he would like to grab a drink afterward, there was no longer any regret. He'd wanted her to ask so badly. To have to leave her at that point would have been torture. His bag was nearly full of books now, and he didn't even care that it wouldn't hold any of the bottles he'd made the trip for. He could always come another day. He could pop into the city after church the next day. You could buy alcohol on Sundays in New York just like they were the same as any old day. They are, too, aren't they? It's all God's creation, isn't it?

They went to some Irish pub on 3rd Avenue. Why did he always seem to be ending up in Irish bars with girls? They sat at a small table in a little nook in the back, both of them essentially sharing a corner. Their knees knocked gently into each other any time one of them shifted in their seat. Jake's duffel was shoved carelessly under the table. There had been plenty of seats open. Why did she choose this one?

After a few beers and casual conversation, they moved, naturally, to the topic of Philip. Jake wished she hadn't brought it up. They'd been laughing only a moment ago. He'd gotten fully out of his earlier funk and was actually enjoying himself, now this?

"I don't normally get so emotional about patients. As a nurse, you can't. I see so much pain and death every day. So many tears, rarely any smiles. But when Philip came in, he just reminded me of my brother."

Of course there's a brother. There's always a brother or mother or father or aunt or uncle or boyfriend or wife or beloved pet or grandma or grandpa or that guy from that show that you really liked. Someone is always dying in your life; you can choose to move past it or you can choose to let it consume you. Jake wished he'd been able to do the former.

"Did he die?" Jake asked. What a stupid question. What a stupid way to ask a stupid question.

"Yeah. When we were kids. He loved life more than I did."

"What do you mean?"

"I mean he played every sport, did every after-school activity he could. He got good grades and had a million friends. He just loved living. I was never that way growing up. I was the quiet girl. I was the girl that would scoff if a teacher would try to ask me a question. I wasn't interested in sex or dating. I was sort of just... nothing.

"And then he died the summer before his junior year of high school. A car accident. No one was drunk or anything, nothing that dramatic, it was just a simple missed stop sign. His friend was driving but the other car went straight into the passenger seat."

Jake didn't say anything. He knew people were supposed to be comforting when others told sad stories like these. He could say a simple, 'I'm sorry,' or even just give her a simple, sad nod. But he just continued listening.

"Anyway, I don't know why you need to know all that. I just meant that when Philip came in, I was immediately reminded of my brother. Even on bad days, he just seemed like he was so excited to get back to life. He didn't laugh much, except when you came around, but you could tell he was in more pain than he'd let on. He's such a sweet boy. I just couldn't help but get attached to him, you know?"

She'd been playing with her glass of beer as she talked. She tilted it, swirled it, looked into it as if it held all of the answers she was looking for. Perhaps it did. It seemed to hold many answers for Jake; or at least muted the questions.

"He's a good kid," Jake said. "I have no doubt he'll get better."

If you don't screw this up, he thought.

"Yeah. I hope so."

It got silent then. Was she waiting for Jake to compensate with a sad story of his own? This wasn't something he wanted to do in the least. Instead, he thought of Benny.

"I have a brother, actually," Jake said. And then he felt like maybe he shouldn't have said anything. She just talked about how her brother died and how much she missed him, and here he was gloating about having one of his own.

"Oh yeah? Tell me about him," she said, sitting up straight. She looked happy to hear about it. Maybe she'd just wanted to talk about something else.

"Benny. He lives out in L.A. I haven't seen him in a very long time, but he says he's coming to visit soon."

"Older, younger?"

"Older. Actually, quite a bit older. Our parents die—" Was he really going to do this? He never talked to people about their parents dying. Why would he tell her now? It didn't even need to be said.

"Our parents died when I was young. Maybe Benny was old enough to experience it differently. When my mom died, we went to live with our aunt, but he was pretty much off to college at that point. I lived with her through high school."

How had a story about Benny turned into this tragic story about the loss of two parents and brothers who never talked? Jake had to admit, behind the anxiety and anguish he felt having said all this, there was something else entirely: relief.

There was a TV over the bar that said: "Home run!"

"Can I ask what happened to your parents?"

Jake must have been mistaken. There couldn't be TVs in this bar. There was nothing in this bar. It was completely silent. There wasn't a single sound. Not of beer flowing from the tap into a glass. Not the empty chatter of the college football fans. Not the footfalls and unnecessary honking of the busy avenue outside.

My dad died when I looked outside of a window and saw two people having sex in the rain. He died because I kept looking. I wanted to see more, more, more.

"My dad died suddenly of some heart thing. An aortic aneurism, I think."

My mom died because I went onto the internet and masturbated to Lily Scarlett.

"My mom... took too many meds and passed out in the bathtub."

He could have put the latter differently. He could have told her that she'd killed herself, as he and Benny had always known. But these stories were dramatic enough without needing that extra color. This conversation had turned very morose, and Jake didn't like it. If he drained his glass now, he could get at least one more refill before they left.

Jake drained his glass.

"That couldn't have been easy, being so young and having your parents die."

And being the killer, Jake thought. Just then, the waitress came around and asked if he would like a refill. Yes please. Absolutely. In fact, bring five more. Six, even.

When the waitress walked off with his empty glass, Jake wished she'd left it so he'd have something to do with his hands. Eve was taking a sip of her own beer. She brought it up to her lips slowly, drank slowly, lingered. Jake just sat and tried not to scream or laugh or some animal mixture of the two. How do you get back into fun conversation after one as sad and tragic as the one they'd just finished? Do you make a joke? Do you take off your pants and dance on the table like a Rockette?

"We turned out okay though, huh?" Eve said.

"I guess so," Jake said. He thought of the extra drink coming, he thought of the reason he was really there. "More so on your end. I pretend to save lives; you actually save them."

"You think what you do is pretend?"

Jake had said too much. He was thankful when the waitress sat his fresh drink back down. He thanked her and took a long pull. All of this gave him time to think of a response.

"I guess I mean it's not tangible. I can pray for people all I want, but in the end of the day, either the prayers are answered and they thank God, not me, or the prayers aren't answered and they get mad at God and mad at me. Maybe I didn't pray hard enough. I didn't focus on their prayer over the other prayers I've been asked to give."

"Giving people hope isn't nothing."

"All I mean is I think it's great what you do. And incredibly brave."

"Thank you," Eve said. She was trying to hide her smile, and it came off bashful. And cute. A smile Jake wouldn't mind kissing. He wished the hand she had around her beer was in his own hand. He wondered what it would feel like to touch her waist. Her back. He wondered what it would be like to kiss that spot where her neck meets her shoulder, where the snake tattoo lay tempting him, always tempting him.

"What are you thinking?" Eve asked.

Jake was used to getting lost in some fantasy or another. He was not used to others noticing.

"Oh. It's just been a really fun day, that's all," Jake said. "Thanks for joining me."

"Jake, I had such a good time." Eve was grinning. It seemed like she really meant it.

"Sorry you missed out on studying today."

"Are you kidding? I needed an excuse to get out of it today. I needed...this," she gestured to the space all around her. She twirled the straw inside her drink and looked intensely at Jake. It was an intense look, wasn't it? He felt his heart beating quickly. This was that moment, that one in movies, when the two leads were supposed to kiss. Maybe they do and you cheer. Maybe they don't and it leaves you depressed and angry with the characters for missing their moment. She took a sip of her drink. He watched her neck move as she swallowed. When she saw he was studying her, she tilted her head in a question.

Jake reached out pulled Eve toward him, his hand gently tugging at her neck. He ignored the fear rushing through his body. He ignored the cacophony of his heartbeat. The audience would cheer for the leads in this film. There would be no anger, no depression, only smiles, maybe even happy tears.

Jake felt her neck pulling back at his hand. His mouth felt only air. A member of the audience booed, absolutely appalled.

"I'm sorry," Eve said, her voice betraying her discomfort. "I didn't mean to—"

"I'm sorry," Jake interrupted. He downed the remainder of his drink in one gulp and made to leave, only he realized he still needed to close his tab. What could he say to her? What had gone wrong? The signs had all been there, hadn't they? Hadn't they?

"To be honest, I just got out of a long relationship, and I'm not ready for anything serious. I'm sorry if it seemed like I was flirting with you. Or maybe I was flirting with you. I'm just trying to work through the pain I'm feeling, and maybe it's not coming out in the healthiest way.

"I just think it's better if we stay friends," Eve said. "We are friends, right?"

Friends! Friends! O' God, how could Jake go on?

O' God, O' cruel God, what on earth had happened?

"Yeah. Sorry, I. I got carried away I guess." He lifted his empty drink, its previous contents the blame of his behavior. Of course he would blame the alcohol. How boring.

"It doesn't have to be weird," Eve consoled, unconvincingly. "Forgotten," she said, flicking her hands open in a 'poof' motion. She smiled.

Forgotten. That word again, from the voice of a woman, again.

No one really forgets.

"Forgotten," Jake agreed. He tried to smile back but hated to think about what it looked like on her end. How could he ever forget this moment? He wished he could just 'poof' out his hands and make it go away.

***

Jake had paid for the drinks and said he was heading back to Grand Central Station. To his dismay, Eve said she'd take the train back with him. It was the longest trip of his life. They tried to maintain conversation, but it only seemed to increase the awkwardness to the point that Jake started taking books out of his duffel one by one and reading the backs. Anything to distract his hands, his eyes, his brain.

When they got off the train, Eve gave Jake a ride home. He told her he was fine with walking, that's how he got there after all, and she wouldn't take no for an answer. They sat in her car out front of his apartment, and Jake had to stop himself from asking her up. An alternate future flashed in his mind, a future of how things might have gone if she had kissed him back in the bar. He pictured her in bed next to him. He pictured running a finger softly down her neck and back as she fell into a light sleep. Instead, he thanked her for the ride and told her he'd go to see Philip soon.

Inside, Jake was drinking the last of his liquor and doing everything he could to wash down the aching need to touch himself. And when the last drops hit his throat, he pulled out a pair of scissors and tugged his pants off. He stood in front of his bathroom mirror with his half-hard dick in one hand and the pair of scissors in the other. Tears were streaming down his face. The TV in the other room said: 'We've got a winner!' He opened the scissors and moved them to his penis. Jake recoiled a little bit at the chill of the metal on himself.

He felt the strings pulling against him as he worked. He could see them going taut in the mirror. All it would take is a snip. One swift squeeze of his hand and all of this could be over. He pictured it falling to the floor, blood spraying the mirror, the sink, the towels. He pictured himself laughing manically, laughing at God, *I bested you! You didn't think I would go this far, did you!* He pressed his fingers together and the scissors began to pinch. It didn't hurt. He moved his hand, the one around his penis, forward and back, forward and back. It grew, pushing the scissors open wider. He thought the scissors might make a cleaner cut if he was hard. A moan escaped him, and then a sob, a sniffle. He continued to touch himself, the scissors pressing harder and harder until he couldn't take it any longer. The strings were pulling as tight as they could go. He thought of his mother telling Benny she would cut it off if she caught him with a girl again. That look in her eyes.

Jake screamed.

He threw the scissors on the ground and collapsed, prostrate, next to them. Even this he couldn't follow through on. There was no blood, only tears and a deflating penis. Jake curled into a ball and felt himself rocking back and forth. All he needed was to put his thumb in his mouth to complete the picture. This thought made him laugh. It was a sad laugh. A crazy laugh. But it brought him into sleep on the cold bathroom tile next to the half-open scissors.

CHAPTER TWELVE

The time had come to preach acceptance, and Jake wasn't sure he could go through with it. He'd avoided topics like this for so long. He'd prepared, hadn't he? So why was he standing on the stage in front of all these people feeling himself shiver continuously? Would words come to him, or would he need to flee? He certainly felt the need to flee. In all his time as a pastor, he'd never felt stage fright. Even in the early days as a youth pastor, or when he would stand in for the head pastor, he never felt nervous. The stakes felt low. He had a Bible in his hands with a page of talking points. Even if he forgot something he could just pretend the urge to pray came over him and lead the group in meaningless prayer. He could even bring someone on stage for a demonstration, something he'd employed before during a particularly heavy week of drinking where all he'd written for his sermon was a single line: Is God Real? These were the days where he was still hanging on to his last threads of belief. This sentence was a revelation for him. He had the graphics guy blow the words up big for the screen behind him. IS GOD REAL? He chose three people from the audience, people he knew would help him support his case, his case being that, yes, certainly God is real. Obviously. And one by one he asked the people on stage to share a story, any story, that made them believe God was real. People still talk to Jake about that 'sermon'. They say it was the most powerful thing they'd ever seen. And Jake feels laughter bubble up in his throat when they do.

So why did the Bible in his hand this morning not bring him comfort? Why did his script seem far away and unreadable? He felt sweat building on his forehead, on the nape of his neck, in the dark recesses of his armpits. He'd used up the last of his liquor the night before and still hadn't replaced the empty bottle in his office. Was he simply in withdrawal? His body needed alcohol like the Church needed to steal tithes. His mind seemed to be pulled in two directions. One side was thinking of the sermon he was about to give, the other was wondering, always wondering, how the hell was he going to get his hands on some alcohol? There was always Ava's after church, but a beer or two wasn't going to get him where he needed to be. He could take the train into the city, but he thought if he had to wait that long he might pass out, perhaps go into cardiac arrest. And there were all of these people staring at him, waiting for him to speak. But how could he? That morning, Kendall came up to him holding the hand of a woman. She introduced them—Jake, Talia, Talia, Jake—but he'd hardly been able to smile in response. What were the rest of the members saying?

Jake's vision blurred and then unblurred as he began.

"Welcome," he started. He cleared his throat. "Good morning, everyone. It's a beautiful day, isn't it?" There were some audible agreements among the congregation. Jake forced a smile.

"I'd like to talk to you all about perhaps the most important thing we've talked about all year. Love. Love is patient, love is kind. You all know that verse. Weddings, movies, songs all use this line as the perfect description of love. Only, I'm not sure it's really true."

He paused a long time for effect. He was getting in the groove, feeling himself loosen, no matter how hazy everything was.

"Love is not always patient, and it certainly isn't always kind. Envious? Who here has someone they love?" Almost every hand in the room shot to the sky. He pointed, "You, you, you, you, have any of you ever once been jealous toward the person you love?" Chuckles throughout. "Love does boast! Boast about love! Love does not always protect even when we may think that we are protecting. But who cares?

"Love is the most beautiful thing in the world." Jake almost let out a laugh as he said this. What was love to him? Did he love Beth? Benny? He couldn't even get the courage to pick up the phone and call them. "Jesus died for His love of us. We were so dirty, so filthy and icky and mucky and He felt so sad, for He loved us so much that He died for our dirty, filthy souls, so that we could be with Him in heaven. Love changes us, no matter how stubborn we may be. Love wakes us up in the morning and lies in bed with us at night." Some chatter. These sensitive, sheltered children. Was that too risqué? Wait until you find out what your actual children are watching on their phones and tablets and laptop screens.

"Galatians 5:22 speaks of the fruit of the spirit. It says that the fruit is joy, peace, goodness, faithfulness and *love*. I could pull out a hundred, a thousand Bible verses about love. You could stop listening and open your Bible to any random page, and I bet you find a verse that mentions it. Go on, try."

Jake stopped speaking as people opened their Bibles. There was pointing and laughter. How much longer would they be smiling and laughing? This was all meaningless. It was a lead-in to his grand finale. He'd establish how great love is and how important it is in the Bible, then the big reveal: even gay love is important.

He continued his sermon. Love is this, love is that. He referenced passages from all over the Bible. And when the time came to make his point, he realized he was stalling. The sweat and shakes were returning. His vision was again blurring. But then he heard himself say it, the first words to the big moment.

"Please turn your Bibles to 1 John 4 verse 7." He paused as pages turned. "It reads, 'Dear friends, let us love one another, for love comes from God. Everyone who loves has been born of God and knows God. Whoever does not love does not know God, because God is love.' Let's read that again. 'Dear friends, let us love one another, for love comes from God. *Everyone* who loves has been born of God and knows God.' *Everyone.*

"There is a theme across the Bible, especially in the New Testament where old rules were being changed or challenged, that *everyone* should be treated with love and respect, that *everyone* belongs, *everyone* was made in His image. Some Christians choose to ignore this. Some Christians choose to believe that certain people are disgusting, unnatural, perverse. How can this be the case when God's love encompasses *everyone*?"

There was a cacophony of silence. Had silence ever been so loud before? Jake's heart was pounding as he wrapped up his sermon.

"Always remember that love is for *everyone*. Let us pray."

As he prayed, Jake got the sense that no one was praying along with him. His eyes stayed shut, so he couldn't be for sure, but he thought he could hear movement and whispers. He pictured wide eyes and disgust. He pictured members standing up and leaving the chapel. Only, when he finished the prayer and opened his eyes, it looked like nothing had changed at all. No one had moved an inch. And as they got up to leave people seemed normal, perhaps even happier than normal.

Conversation after the service was normal, too. Jake remembered that day he'd been half-listening to his mother's conversation after church with Mrs. Whiting. He remembered the way she whispered 'gay' as if it was the most nauseating word she knew, as if just by saying it above a whisper she might get moved over God's list of people going to hell. There was none of that here. In fact, Jake got the impression that if Kendall re-entered with Talia right now, she would be bombarded with love and smiles and embraces. Jake almost felt like embracing her himself.

As the first service shuffled out and the new service shuffled in Jake's mind was awhirl. Over time, he'd come to hate the people that he'd been preaching to. He hated the way they shouted 'amen' and interrupted his sermons. He hated the way they glowed when he told them that they were loved by God. He hated the smell of them, the look of them, the way they breathed. But could he have been so mistaken? Was it simply his waning, and then dead, faith that made him hate them? *They get to have faith; why don't I?*

The second service went very much like the first, only Jake's spirits were much higher, his hangover much more controlled. He felt the passion in his voice when he spoke of love. He felt the word 'everyone' boom out of his mouth. And when he wrapped up, the silence felt somehow stronger than before, more powerful. And again, after the service, people seemed in high spirits.

When the last few stragglers left the building, Jake went to his office and sat down at his computer. He opened Facebook. All of his friend requests had been accepted. He had even received a handful of requests from some members of the church and some old college friends. Before he could stop himself, he clicked onto Lily's profile. Lily with her big grin. Lily with her amber hair. Lily with—

"Hey," Kendall said from the doorway. She was poking her head in as if she couldn't bring herself to fully enter. She was alone. "Talia caught your sermon. She said it was beautiful."

"Thanks," Jake said. He didn't know what else to say.

Kendall entered further and said, "Thanks. Maybe it seemed like a normal sermon but it means a lot to me. It's funny, no one at all seemed to care when I introduced them to Talia. I was so nervous about this, and it turns out I had nothing to be nervous about."

"I'm glad you can be yourself here. I wasn't so sure myself."

Kendall shot herself at Jake and wrapped him in a hug. After a moment, she released him, smiled, and ran out of the office.

As Jake prepared to leave the church and head to Ava's, his office phone started ringing. Even before he answered, he knew who would be calling. After all, when was the last time someone called him on his office phone? This is really what he suspected all along, wasn't it?

"Hello," Jake said into the phone. He wanted to throw it. Maybe he should.

***

Jake sat again on the train to Manhattan. He didn't understand how it was still such a beautiful day. Everything felt so ugly. Shouldn't it be storming? He'd texted Lily that he couldn't make it to Ava's. He didn't give a reason. Maybe he should have just come out and said it. *I can't handle the things that life throws at me without a belly full of poison.* But then she would ask what life had thrown at him, and he was sure that it would all fall out of him like a river of blood. No. Better to be on this train alone, headed toward a duffel full of temporary bliss.

They told Jake they'd wished he'd come to them first. Maybe they could have helped. They said that there was nothing they could do. The members simply wouldn't allow it. They would boycott. They would lose more people than they could afford to. If she wasn't preaching to their children, maybe this could be handled differently. How long had he known? Did he know how much damage he was doing? They'd even had to consider removing him as well. He'd have to issue an apology next Sunday. Was he on Facebook? Maybe he should apologize there as well. And Jake asked which members were complaining. They can't tell him that. Yes, but everyone seemed so normal, like they didn't care. There is no place for... that in this church. So, what will happen to her? That's up to her, maybe she can find a church more fit for someone of her *kind*. When will you tell her? Oh, we won't be telling her, we want that to come from you. You both are friends, right? Okay take care.

He understood now that no matter how accepting of (or more likely ambivalent about) Kendall's sexual orientation his members might be, it would never be enough for the wrinkly old men who run things. They were the real enemy and always would be. But what could he do now? He could quit, too, he supposed. A she-goes-I-go sort of thing. In fact, it would probably be the right thing to do. But then he would be out of a job too. Where would he go? He'd never worked a high school job. The inheritance he received from his parents covered most of his college tuition, and his aunt Beth had helped him with the rest of his expenses so that he could focus on school (and on God, of course) without the distraction of a job. He was skilled in only one thing, and over time, he was becoming less good at that thing. Bad at that thing is closer to the truth. And so how could he quit, and how could he not quit?

The train sped south, and Jake felt himself go stiff at the thought of having to break the news to Kendall. Part of him wanted to just leave a note on her desk or send her a text or email.

Hey it's your pal Jake! Remember how I told you everything might turn out okay? Well, I was wrong! Haha. Nope I've been told to tell you that you're out. Pack your shit. You're making the members 'uncomfortable'. Lol. A teacher of God just can't be gay, I guess.

Love,
Jake.

He knew he couldn't do this, yet it somehow didn't seem possible to tell her to her face. How do you look someone in the face and tell them they aren't enough? How do you tell them that you can't accept them for the way that they are, especially when that someone is good? And what if he just didn't tell her at all? How long would they let that go on before telling her themselves? Would they fire him or just roll their snake-like eyes and send him off to spread their version of the gospel?

The train stopped in Grand Central before Jake could finish these thoughts. A drink would help. Many drinks would help. That's when he could do his real thinking, when his brain really turned on. With each sip of whiskey, he knew, he'd find one piece of the answer, then another, then another, then...

He changed routes lest he somehow run into Eve again. Instead of going straight for the liquor store, he stopped at a bar. He needed immediate nourishment. He was in such a hurry he didn't even look at the name on the place. He just followed his nose toward the smell of his salvation. It was large and dingy for a Midtown bar. It reminded him of a small-town watering hole, except he knew the prices would be outrageous. He didn't mind. He asked for a glass of whiskey, sucked it down before the bartender could put it back on the shelf and asked for another, just like you see in the movies. The bartender rolled his eyes but poured the drink.

"Hey," Jake heard beside him. His stomach sank. Was it Eve again? Lily? What were the chances of this happening two days in a row? This was it. He'd tell them everything, whoever they were. He looked beside him to see a complete stranger. It was a woman who looked maybe a decade older than himself. She had dark hair and bright eyes. She wore too much makeup, but Jake got the impression that she'd look prettier without it. Then he noticed her hand was on his leg.

"Looking for some fun?" she asked him.

It crossed his mind to say yes. Pay her some money and this could all be done with. What would he ask for? Handjob? Blowjob? Or should he go all in?

"I'm a pastor," he said instead. He smiled at her, trying to appear friendly.

"Most of them are," the woman said, taking her hand off of his leg. "They always make me get on my knees."

"We're all hypocrites," Jake said and downed his whiskey as if to prove his point.

"All you people do is fuck people out of their money, why not fuck someone for money too?"

"Strangely enough, I agree with you. Clearly, you're better at your job than I am."

She laughed and said, "If I was good at my job, I wouldn't be here chatting with you. I would have moved on by now."

"So why don't you?"

"You look like you need a friend."

"You're not wrong," Jake said, and then motioned for another drink. "Would you like a drink?"

"Thank you, but I don't drink," the woman said.

"How people get through life, through even a day, without alcohol is beyond me."

The bartender set down another whiskey and eyed the pair with suspicion.

"It never did me any good," the woman replied. "And the most good it does for men is make their dicks soft. They'll pay me for an hour only to go soft in five minutes or sometimes not get hard at all."

"Ironic."

"What is?"

"They call alcohol 'hard' and all it does is make you soft."

"You're funny," the woman said. Her face was stolid. "My dad died of cirrhosis. Ugly way to go. His started with the legs. Blew up like balloons. His toes looked like Vienna sausages, especially when he tried to cram them into his sandals, the only shoes he owned they could fit in because of their adjustable strap."

"Why are you—"

"His stomach followed," she continued, miming the inflation of a stomach. "Then I remember these purple bumps appearing. They looked like grapes or blueberries. Hernias. At some point I noticed he was all yellow. I don't know if he was that way all along or if it happened later on but you couldn't tell him apart from a bundle of warty lemons. Funny thing is he kept drinking through it all. Said it was to 'manage the pain'. Imagine my confusion when I wondered if he meant the pain of the disease or the pain of having me as a daughter."

When Jake was sure she was done, he went to take a sip of the whiskey in front of him but then thought better of it. He knew he'd still drink it the moment she left, but what kind of psychopath would drink alcohol in front of this woman after that ugly story? He'd heard of such diseases of course. He hadn't heard them described in such detail, but he knew the risk he was taking every time the good Lord's juice hit his lips.

"Just take the drink," the woman said, "I can tell you're just like him."

Jake sipped the drink.

"You sure you don't want to fuck?"

No, at this point Jake wasn't sure of much of anything.

"I'm sure," Jake lied.

The woman shrugged and left him alone at the bar. He looked at what was left of the whiskey and swirled it in the glass. Of all the things to love in the world, why did this have to be what he loved most? He loved the way it seemed to singe the hair in his nostrils when he breathed it in. He loved its color, like caramel or butterscotch. He loved the way it made him feel. The way all whiskey, vodka, champagne, beer made him feel. He even found himself enjoying hangovers sometimes because then the next drink he took would be like medicine. He never understood the idiom 'hair of the dog that bit him' until one morning when he was so ferociously hungover that he literally tried to bite the liquid that flowed into his mouth. You bite me, I bite you back. It's all love, brother.

He raised his glass to no one or nothing in particular and drank the last of the whiskey.

Feeling revived, Jake paid for his drinks and then made his way to a liquor store. He filled his duffel and left feeling like Santa carrying a sack full of gifts. He even laughed at the thought of Santa sliding down chimneys to leave bottles of liquor for children. One bottle of Jameson for little Cindy Lou for being a very good girl. Drink up, Cindy. You never know who could die on you tomorrow, might as well live it up now little one.

Jake was feeling so jolly on his train ride home that he nearly forgot about what had happened that morning. He'd leave that problem for sober Jake, if he ever appeared again. Sober Jake can handle the problems, and drunk Jake can ignore them. That's how this has always worked, right? This was the way it had to be. The way things were.

CHAPTER THIRTEEN

"Jake."

"Yes?"

"We couldn't help but notice that Kendall was still preaching the to youth group today."

Jake had been just about to leave his office to head to Ava's when his phone rang again. All week, he'd attempted to get up the courage to talk to Kendall, although he still wasn't sure that was the 'courageous' thing to do. Every day he found some excuse not to tell her. He used Philip as an excuse to get away from the church. He visited the hospital a few times that week to sit with Philip and his mother. He texted Eve, who stopped by as well. Philip was still in his coma, but the doctors said he was improving, and they should be able to wake him up soon. This was good news, Jake knew, but there was a part of him that didn't want Philip to improve. If he could stay this way forever, Jake would always have an excuse to visit Eve. Jake hated himself for having this thought but could never quite shake it.

On Thursday, Eve asked him if he had started reading any of the books they'd bought together. He thought about lying and saying that he had but then he was afraid she'd ask him about it and he decided it would be better to just tell her no. He hadn't even taken the time to put them on a shelf or even pile them neatly somewhere. He'd grabbed his duffel, turned it upside down and emptied its contents in the middle of the floor. He had to make room in the bag for the stuff that really mattered.

And suddenly it was Sunday again, and Kendall continued on as if nothing was wrong. Nothing *was* wrong, to her. But Jake knew he couldn't put it off any longer.

"Yes," he answered. There was a long pause.

"We're having members threaten to leave," the voice on the other end lied, "if you don't get rid of her, we may have to rethink your employment here as well."

"Why can't you ju—"

"Goodbye, Jake."

The voice had been calling on a cell phone. Jake could tell because there was no satisfying click at the other end of the line. No conclusion. The voice had said goodbye, and then everything just went silent, as if no one had really been there at all. Maybe it was all a figment of his imagination. Maybe no one was on the other line after all. But when he checked his recent calls, sure enough, someone had called him, and the numbers on the screen could not be a figment of his imagination.

***

Lily was already there when Jake walked into Ava's. She was talking excitedly to Thomas who was, as always, in a white t-shirt and a dirty apron. As if trying to embody some cliché about cooks in a diner, Thomas had a spatula in his hand and was waving it around as he talked to Lily. Apparently, neither of them had heard the bell ding as Jake walked in, because when he made it to the table, they both looked up at him with surprise.

Thomas smiled at Lily and then said to Jake, "We've been a such a wreck without you."

Lily snickered, clearly catching some inside joke they had together. When had Lily become close enough with Thomas to have inside jokes?

"An absolute mess," Lily said. Thomas snickered.

"Well, I'll leave you two alone," Thomas said, and then, "Beer?"

Jake nodded and sat across from Lily.

"What was all that about," he asked.

"Oh, Thomas and I are just in love. It's not a big deal."

"Ava might have something to say about that."

"She knows all about it. Encourages it, even."

"Where is Ava anyway?"

"She's super busy today."

Jake looked around the diner. The only other people in the diner were a family of four eating silently in a corner booth. Jake thought of Chet's. He thought of the days after their mother died, when sometimes they'd eat an entire meal there without saying a word to each other.

"Looks like it," Jake said, still looking over at the family.

Lily said, "Hey." Jake looked back at her. "Aren't you going to ask me how I've been?"

"How have yo—"

"I mean you keep bailing on me, you think you'd be more excited to see me."

"I know I—"

"But on the bright side, it allowed mine and Thomas' love to flourish."

As always Jake found it hard to keep up with Lily and her ability to keep going with a bit. It made him smile to think that in just a few minutes she'd be ordering her hot dogs with ketchup.

When she paused long enough for Jake to finally speak, he said, "It's been a crazy few weeks. It's good to see you."

Lily smiled. "It's good to see you too."

"Any more late nights in the city?" Lily looked upset for a moment, and Jake wondered why those words came out of his mouth. He started to think through ways to take it back or else change the subject entirely.

Before he could, Lily said, "Leave any more girls all alone at a bar in the middle of the night?" She said it with a small grin, clearly proud of this retort.

"That would mean me hanging out with other women."

"You don't?"

Jake thought of Eve. Hadn't they hung out? Did it count if it was impromptu? And what about his visits to the hospital—hadn't a big part of those visits been the excitement of getting to see her? Would he ever even be able to face her again after that denied kiss?

"What do you think?" Jake was proud of this question. He didn't lie, even if by asking the question he was insinuating that no, he did not hang out with any other girls or women or anyone he could potentially attracted to.

"Avoiding the question, that's interesting," Lily said. "Who is she?"

His plan having backfired, Jake decided to lie. "I don't see other women. I'm cel—"

"Celibate. Yeah, I remember." Lily studied Jake a while and then said, "Can I ask you something?"

"I guess," Jake said.

"Did you... when we were dancing, did you... finish?" She pointed to her crotch.

Jake felt his face flush. His heart started racing. Was he going to faint?

"What can I get you two?" Thomas said from beside them, setting down their beers. Jake hadn't noticed him come up. He wasn't sure he was going to be able to speak. The beer would help. He picked it up and took a sip, hoping that Lily would order first.

"Hot dogs for me," Lily said. Jake smiled despite himself.

"Of course," Thomas laughed. "Jake?"

"I forget where I left off," Jake said, the beer having loosened his enclosed throat.

"I believe you had the quiche. Ava came back and said you were giving her hard time again like you did with the clams."

"I didn't—ok, then I'll have whatever is next on the menu."

"That'd be my famous chicken pot pie," he said, pointing to the menu item and looking pleased.

Lily and Jake thanked him and he returned to the kitchen. Jake wondered again where Ava might be. He'd met Thomas many times, but very rarely did he actually come out and serve. And then, suddenly, Jake's attention was diverted to the family of four in the corner booth. They had finished their meals and were still sitting silently. The two kids and the woman were on their phones. The man just sat there looking off into space.

"So?"

Jake looked back to Lily and felt courage well up within him. He brought himself to nod. He couldn't speak the words but, sure, he could move his head. As embarrassed as he was to admit it, he also felt a sense of relief. And the feeling made him wonder what it would feel like to tell her everything. Before he could think too much longer on it, he took another drink of his beer as Lily was deciding what she should respond.

"Sorry. I didn't... how did it feel?"

Jake hadn't expected this question. And he was surprised when he found himself answering honestly: "Really fucking good."

Lily's face filled with emotions. Jake couldn't tell which.

"Did it break your covenant with God or whatever?"

Jake thought of Philip. He'd breached a line and was put in his place. But then Philip hadn't died. He seemed to be improving.

"I don't know," he said. "My celibacy vow is my own. I'm not bound by the rules of the church. But I haven't... finished... since I was a teenager."

"And since that night have you done it again?"

"No."

"Have you wanted to?"

"Yes. Of course, yes."

The tension between them was immense. Jake felt as if a string was tugging on his insides. As if very soon they were going to be pulled out of him and spill onto the floor. Poor, poor Thomas. This would be too big a job for a mop bucket and a rag.

"Do you think God really wants to deprive you of things that feel good?"

Jake wanted to scream, then. *Yes! My whole life God has been proving to me that he does not want me to feel even an ounce of plea-sure! And how can that be when God doesn't even exist!?* Instead, he opted for silence. He knew Lily would take this as an admission that yes, he, Jake, might be wrong, but he didn't really care.

"Truth?" Jake said, already trying to come up with his next lie.

"Yes," Lily said. Her face was serious. Where was her sarcasm? Why was she choosing now to bring this all up?

"I don't know." An actual truth. It wasn't anything big. In fact, she was probably disappointed at the answer. But he couldn't have put it any more succinctly. He *didn't* know. How could he?

"Fair enough," Lily said. "Better than the answer I thought you were going to give me."

"Which was?"

"Yes. Another pastor might have."

"Sometimes I wish I was more like other pastors."

"I don't," Lily said. She smiled. Jake sensed the conversation was about to shift, and he was grateful for it. He took another drink of his beer. "How many of those do you drink a day?"

Jake looked up at Lily with pure terror in his eyes. He wondered if they were red and Mephistophelian. He felt like fleeing. Anything would be better than having to answer her question. In a flash, he saw a car coming through the wall of the diner and striking him. In another flash, his phone and Lily's phone start buzzing: nuclear missile to hit Tarrytown in minutes.

"Would you like another?"

Thomas was hovering over them, setting their food down on the table. Jake wondered how long he had been silent. Had it been long enough that Lily knew the real answer? That, once again, it was: 'I don't know.' He usually lost count after four or five. And how did Lily know this in the first place? Had she seen him in the city? Was she there when he talked to the sex worker in the bar? Did she follow him when he filled his duffel with goodies?

Jake shook his head and said, "No, I'm okay," but in fact he was not. He wanted two more. Three more. More.

"I'll have another," Lily said. Jake couldn't be sure, but this felt like a deliberate act to taunt him. She knew he wanted another, probably knew that he would go home and have plenty more.

When Thomas left, Lily just stared at Jake, her face a question. It wasn't quite flippant, but it wasn't all serious either. It was as if she knew he wasn't going to answer but wanted to get her point across nonetheless, her point being: *I know everything*.

"My brother is coming to visit next week," Jake said, digging into his pot pie. He was desperate to change the subject, even to something he didn't necessarily want to talk about either.

"Ah, the infamous brother that you literally never talk about." She dropped the quizzical look from her face and started eating a hot dog. Her mouth full, she said, "You have any plans?"

Jake had tried to come up with plans for he and Benny to do while Benny was in town but hadn't been able to think of anything. He knew one thing for sure: he didn't want his brother to come anywhere near his church or especially to hear him preach.

"Not really. Maybe I'll bring him here."

"We're like twenty miles from the greatest city on earth and you're going to bring him *here*?"

As she said this, Thomas came out of the back to bring her a beer. It was clear he heard what she said.

"Sorry," Lily said to Thomas.

Thomas smiled and said, "I don't know who you're talking about, but she's right." He walked over to the family of four who was getting up to leave and told them to come again.

"Do I get to meet him?" Lily asked.

"Do you want to meet him?"

"Obviously I do."

"We'll see. Maybe."

"Oh, maybe *and* we'll see. Seems promising."

Jake shrugged.

"What's his name again?"

"Benny."

"Great. I'll find him on your Facebook and tell him I'm looking forward to seeing him."

Jake had forgotten about having friended Lily on Facebook. He'd been private for so long it pained him to think that someone could just go on his page and look into his life like that. It was only his brother, but what else could they find if they really went looking? There was his aunt Beth for one, who knew what people could find out about him through her. Lily could find Eve. Would she just shrug and move on? Or would she wonder if this was *the girl*.

"Relax," Lily said, sensing his dread, "I'm just kidding. You're really wound tight today. Is everything okay?"

In all the time he'd been talking to Lily, he'd almost forgotten about the call he'd gotten earlier.

"It's... I'm..." And then he told her everything that had gone on with Kendall. He hadn't planned to tell Lily any of it, but once he started talking, it poured out of him. Lily listened and didn't even try to crack a joke. In fact, by the end of the story she looked angry. Jake had seen her upset before but not angry, not like this.

"Fucking assholes," she said when he finished. "Fucking assholes," she repeated. "What are you going to do."

Jake shrugged.

"Don't sit there and shrug. Tell me what you're going to do about it."

Jake started to regret having told her about it. He should have dealt with it on his own. But then hadn't he turned to alcohol every time he tried to work it all out? O' God, why didn't he ask for that second beer?

"I don't know what to do. The way I see it, I have three options: fire her, wait it out and see what happens, or quit. Two of those options leave me jobless. One of those options is unthinkable."

"Don't sit there and act like you don't know what the right answer is."

He did know the right answer. But he was weak. He'd always been weak.

"I don't know," he said again. To this Lily scowled.

"There's only *one* option," she corrected. "You wait it out, they'll fire both of you and you live in shame. You fire her, you keep your job and you live in shame. This isn't some straight white-savior bullshit, this is your friend we're talking about. Don't be like them. You aren't like them. You're good, Jake."

Was he good? What does it mean to be good anyway? Good to others or good to yourself? He certainly wasn't the latter, and he wasn't sure he was the former either. He preferred to be passive.

Forgotten. He liked to be the guy you saw on the street and couldn't quite place. *Do I know you from somewhere?* And to be passive, you couldn't be bad or good or impactful in any way. Lately, things had gotten out of hand, and he was afraid they may never get back on track.

Jake's pot pie was nearly untouched, something he knew he had to fix or else Thomas would pretend to be insulted and he and Lily would start cracking jokes about it. He ate some as Lily sat looking concerned. The food was cool now and not particularly special in the way of taste, but he ate it nonetheless. He didn't want to talk about the situation with Kendall anymore and so he wouldn't. He would eat, and Lily could watch him.

"Ava is home sick," Lily said after a long silence. Jake's mouth was full, so he just looked up at Lily. "Thomas didn't want me to say anything. He says it's no big deal, but I'm not so sure."

Ava too? Would things get so bad that she would have to go to the hospital, too? Would Jake start spending more time there than at his own church? What would happen to the diner if Ava was gone? Thomas certainly couldn't run the place all on his own despite its lack of customers.

When he finished his bite, Jake asked, "Do they know what it is?"

"Thomas says it's just a little cold, but like I said, I don't know."

"Well, maybe that's all it is. Don't worry. Ava's tough, you know that."

"I don't know if I can handle anot—"

"Jake, my boy, how'd you like that famous pot pie?" Somehow yet again Thomas had snuck up on them. Jake looked down at his feet to see if he was barefoot or wearing only thick socks. He was not.

"Delicious, thank you."

"There was something off with the hot dogs today," Lily said.

"There's always something off with the hot dogs," Thomas said with a laugh, "You should stop ordering them."

"Oh, I couldn't do that," Lily said with a glance at Jake.

"Anything else I can get you today? I gotta' close up early on account of... well we have no other customers, and I could use the day off."

"Jake," Lily said with a faux-incredulous look on her face, "I think Thomas here is kicking us out."

"Lily," Jake said, playing along, "I think you might be right. How rude."

"If you two weren't such poor customers, I'd reconsider. You tip like shit. And Lily's always smelling like hot dogs."

"Now don't make this personal, Thomas," Lily said.

Jake said, "She does smell like hot dogs, doesn't she?" Lily kicked him under the table. "Anyway, sure we'll get on out of here. You should get home to Ava."

Jake realized as soon as he said this that he shouldn't have.

"She'll be alright. Here's your check." Thomas walked off.

As Lily and Jake left the diner, Lily turned and said, "I want to meet your brother when he's in town. I mean it."

"Ok," Jake said, because he couldn't think of anything else to say.

"Ok," Lily said. "Bye, Jake."

Jake found himself wanting to hug her goodbye. What was it with him and hugs lately? He thought of her arms wrapping around his torso, his around her neck and back. How warm it would be. How soft she would feel.

"Later," Jake said, walking off.

Inside his car he checked around to make sure no one was looking and wrapped his own arms around himself. He nestled his head into them, took a deep breath, and cried. He didn't know exactly what he was crying about—it could have been a large number of things—but O' God, was it a relief.

When he finished, he wiped his eyes, turned his car on and headed home with thoughts of whiskey and vodka and tequila dancing in his head.

CHAPTER FOURTEEN
2004

Jacob had been excited for college. Everything he read or heard or saw about it said it was the time when you got to become your true self. Before college, you're under someone else's roof. For him, that roof had changed at an inopportune time, but that had just been a minor setback. College would be his time to really find out who he was. Was he this kid that had nothing to do but read books and go to movies with his aunt? Was he going to be this kid that was afraid of anything to do with sex? Or was he going to go to college and become someone completely different? At night, in that last year of high school, he would come up with possibility after possibility for what he might become. He imagined his first college party, one of those toga parties like from *Animal House*, and he imagined drinking beer straight out of a keg, upside down with someone holding his legs up. He pictured himself walking straight up to a pretty girl, maybe someone older, a Junior, and asking her if she'd like a drink. She wouldn't even need to say yes, the smile would say it for her. And then before he knew it, they'd be in a stranger's bedroom kissing. Maybe she'd let him feel her breasts. He could almost feel the condom in his back pocket, *just in case, just in case*.

Patrick, a friend from school—Jacob's only friend, if he could even really call him that—had invited him over to his house to play video games with some of their other classmates. Patrick was someone who already had his entire future figured out. He'd submitted early applications to three schools and got into all of them. He announced he'd be going to Penn State to study to be an engineer. Given Jacob hadn't even decided which school he liked, this was something of a sore subject between them. Would he just sit there and brag the whole time? Worse, would he ask Jacob, again, if he'd made any decisions on his future? Jacob had hoped his aunt would find some reason to tell him he couldn't go to Patrick's house, but when he brought it up, she looked delighted.

"Is it a sleepover?" she asked, sitting next to Jacob on the couch where he'd been sitting.

"I don't know. I think so. He said to bring a sleeping bag."

"He said to bring a sleeping bag, and you don't know if it's a sleepover?"

Beth certainly was in good spirits about this. Probably because she hadn't had a night to herself since Jacob and Benny had moved in with her. Or possibly because she'd been telling Jacob for years that he should try to make more friends. Go out. Experience things. And all this time he'd just been going out with her, if at all.

"I don't think I have a sleeping bag," Jacob said, trying to get out of going.

"There's one in the basement."

"I'm not feeling very well."

"You stop that, what time are you going?"

That was that. Jacob would be going to his first ever sleepover in his senior year of high school. Did kids even do sleepovers that late in life? It felt a little funny, but at this point, he knew there was no getting out of it.

Patrick lived only a few streets away, so he told Beth he would walk. Beth offered to drive him, but he said he'd like the fresh air. This was true. He wanted to the time to think through what he would say if Patrick brought up the infamous college question again. Jacob had spent so much time fantasizing about what it might turn him into that he truly had no idea what he would do. He'd thought about a number of things—marketing, writing, social work—but nothing really stood out to him more than the others. He could start with an unidentified major, but that would mean his struggle would no longer be internal, everyone would see that he had nothing figured out. And even in that case, he'd need to pick a school. He'd been to visit a few Ohio schools: Ohio University, Ohio State University, Miami University, The University of Akron. They all felt more or less the same to him. There was some grass, some buildings with desks inside, tiny dorm rooms where you were forced to live with a stranger for at least a year.

Dorm rooms. Dorm rooms always mean sex. Sock on the door, the squeaking of cheap bedframes, light moaning for thirty to forty blissful seconds. On each tour, this was all he could picture. He liked the idea of co-ed buildings. Only one flight of stairs would separate him from a world of young women taking lukewarm showers, putting on ridiculous amounts of makeup, perhaps walking around in blue satin robes.

As he made it to the front door of Patrick's house, he realized his mind had once again drifted away from what he might want to do for college. Patrick would once again ask him what he had planned and once again Jacob would either have to make something up or tell him that he had absolutely no idea. Patrick would smirk either way and tell Jacob, again, about the entire future he had planned for himself. Jacob put his hand up to the door to knock and then put it back down by his side. He could still leave. He could tell his aunt he threw up or that Patrick threw up or that he was attacked by a stray dog. And just as he turned to leave, a girl appeared behind him or, rather, in front of him.

Sara. A girl he'd had a crush on since his first day of school after moving in with his aunt. A girl he'd never once spoken a word to, at least not outside of his own head. Inside his head, they'd had full conversations. That they should meet here now, like this, was absolutely terrifying and wonderful and horrible and sublime. He noticed she didn't have a sleeping bag with her and felt self-conscious about the one he had under his arm.

"Hey Jacob," she said, her voice so cool. The car that had presumably brought her to him was pulling out of the driveway, the person inside was waving goodbye.

Jacob? That's Jacob's name. It was beyond comprehensible that Sara would know his name. They'd had about a million classes together, but how on earth would Sara remember his name? He was the kid who spent a quarter of his time in a guidance counselor's office. The kid who liked to freak out on teachers. The kid who had no idea what he was going to do with his life.

"He—hi—hey the—" Did he just piss himself? His legs didn't feel particularly wet, but he wasn't sure how it was possible that he had maintained control of his bladder in a moment like this.

She had on jeans and a winter coat. The coat was blue and poofy. Jacob found himself wondering what she was wearing beneath it.

"Are you going to knock?"

O' God, if only I could move my legs.

O' God, if only I could move my lips into a smile.

O' God, O' God.

Sara squinted at Jacob with an air of cool confusion and, with immense patience, made her way past him and knocked on the door, which was still at Jacob's back. They stood this way, her side to his side and facing in opposite directions, until the door opened and Jacob heard Patrick give Sara a delighted, "Hello".

His body returning to him, Jacob managed to turn around and give a polite smile to Patrick. Patrick welcomed him in and told him he could leave his shoes, coat, and sleeping bag by the door. He said they'd be down in the basement and walked off. This left Jacob alone with Sara again, this time sharing the intimacy of taking off clothes together. She took off her coat first, revealing a self-cropped Gap sweater. As she stretched herself to hang the coat the sweater came up, revealing the entirety of her perfect stomach. Jacob took off his own coat but couldn't keep his eyes off of Sara. She was unlacing her black Converse All Stars—of course she had those shoes—and Jacob was kicking off his old Nikes, loose enough so that he didn't even have to bend over to do it. Because of this, he was finished before Sara had even gotten one shoe off. This left him with a dire conundrum. He had two options: turn around and leave Sara alone in the foyer, one shoe still on her perfect feet, or stay with her and face the sheer awkwardness that was his interaction with her so far. This decision took him too long to make. He'd been standing in place long enough that he'd passed the point of no return. He had to stay. It wouldn't be long, but it would be long enough he could make an absolute fool of himself. So, he decided to make small talk and was surprised to find he was able to manage saying a full sentence: "Do you live far from here?"

It was such a simple question, but its response held such intimacy. In only a second, he could find out if Sara lived close to here and, in effect, close to him. Or otherwise that she lived far away, and even then, he'd still get to know something about this girl he'd been thinking about for years. He knew that whichever answer he gave, he'd be imagining what it might be like inside of her house, inside of her bedroom. Already, before she'd even opened her mouth to answer, he was picturing what it might feel like under the covers of her bedspread. Somehow warmer and cozier than his own.

"Not too far," she responded, the remaining shoe sliding off of her foot. "I live over by the Castle Diner."

How many times had Jacob's aunt taken him to Castle Diner for their breakfast buffet? At least once a month, probably more. And to know now that he'd been within a whisper of Sara sent a chill of excitement from the top of his neck to the little tailbone in his butt.

"What about you?" Sara asked. Was she lingering? Her shoes were off now, and she was just standing there, her back to the door, asking Jacob an equally intimate question; although Jacob didn't think his answer would excite her as much as hers had excited him.

"I live just down the street," Jacob said. He pointed in the direction of his house but realized too late that he'd been turned around; his house was in the exact opposite direction. He decided not to correct himself. There'd been enough awkwardness at the door already. "I walked over here."

There was silence for a moment. Jacob was about to start moving toward the basement door when Sara looked him directly in the eyes and squinted quizzically. Jacob's heart dropped. Did he have food on his face? A pulsing zit near to bursting? Had a unibrow magically appeared above his nose?

"You have really pretty eyes," Sara said with a smile. And then she turned to walk to the basement.

Jacob stood motionless as the gravity of what she had just said hit him. This meant two things: that she hadn't noticed his eyes before and that she had noticed them now. This also meant she was trying to flatter him. He'd only heard the word pretty to describe girls before, but it didn't bother him. It made him feel good, actually.

He followed Sara down into the basement where there was a faint but growing sound of music playing. Also growing were the voices he heard, not just of other boys but of girls too. And as he broke the threshold of the stairwell, he saw that there were nearly twenty people in the basement. Some of them had plastic cups in their hands, and Jacob's eyes slid toward a table in the corner that had a few large bottles of liquor and some various types of soda. Before he could even look around at who was at the party, he felt a wave of anxious nausea pass over him. This wasn't any sort of video game night at all. Why had Patrick told him that? Did he know that Jacob wouldn't have come if he'd told him the truth? If so, Patrick knew Jacob better than Jacob thought he had, because he absolutely would not have come if he'd known that there would be alcohol and girls. Had there been that many shoes next to the door? That many coats? He'd been so distracted by his conversation with Sara that he hadn't even noticed. This was much worse than having to spend the night discussing his future plans, or lack thereof, with Patrick.

Patrick came toward Jacob with a smile and said, "Everyone, this is Jacob. I think most of you know him, but he's not very talkative in school, are you Jacob?" He patted Jacob on the shoulder as if they were grown men seeing each other for the first time in twenty-five years. "Help yourself to a drink, bud."

Patrick stood there waiting for Jacob to say something. Jacob didn't know what on earth to say, so he motioned to where the music was playing and said, "What is this? I don't think I've heard it before."

"This is My Chemical Romance. The album isn't out yet, it comes out this summer, but my dad does distribution for the label and got us an early copy. It's fucking incredible."

The music conveyed lots of emotions. There was anger, sadness, rebelliousness. These thoughts came and went because all Jacob could really think about was how Patrick-like it was to throw a party and play music no one else could have.

"Sounds cool," Jacob said. Patrick again stood staring. "I'm going to grab a drink," Jacob said, though he didn't really want one. He walked over to the liquor table and looked at his options. He'd had beer with Benny before, but he'd never tried liquor. He'd seen plenty of it in movies—whiskey in westerns, gin in BBC programming, vodka and tequila in party films—but had never been around any to try. He closed his eyes and put his hand out, hoping that no one was watching him. Duck, he thought, putting his hand on one of the bottles, duck, duck, duck, goose. He opened his eyes to see that his hand had landed on the bottle of whiskey. He poured some in a cup with ice and added a splash of Coke. As he went to take a sip, he noticed that Sara was standing at arm's length to his right, staring directly at him with an inquisitive smile on her face.

"You've never drank before, have you?"

"I have," Jacob said, holding his cup down by his waist.

"Whiskey?"

"Sure."

"Uh huh," Sara said. She rolled her eyes, but her smile remained. "Let's see you drink it then."

Jacob lifted the cup coolly to his lips and tipped it back. As it went into his mouth his first reaction was to spit it out. Knowing this wasn't an option, he tried to swallow, only his throat wouldn't let him. The outcome of this was that the burning, foul liquid stayed sloshing around his mouth as he tried his absolute best not to look panicked. When he finally managed to swallow, it was clear to him that Sara saw right through him, based on the I-told-you-so smile spread across her pretty face.

"See," Jacob said sarcastically, "told you so."

"Yeah, you totally didn't look panicked."

"Right. Can I make you one?"

"Sure, but add way more Coke to mine, heavyweight."

And suddenly Jacob found himself making a drink for his crush, something he never could have believed would be a possibility. He was careful not to spill as he made the drink and did it as slowly as he could without seeming suspicious. He wanted to drag this moment out as long as it could possibly go. Who knows where she would be off to once he put the drink in her hand?

"A perfectionist, huh?" Sara said. She had moved closer to Jacob so that he could feel her breath kiss the side of his cheek.

"I guess so," Jacob said. He hadn't been able to think of a response because all of his energy was being put into trying to make his hands stay still. If he lost focus for even a moment, he thought they would start shaking so violently that whiskey and Coke would go everywhere. Only once this thought occurred, he thought of it getting all over Sara. He pictured her wet shirt sticking tightly to her body. And suddenly he noticed the Coke he was pouring was missing the cup and wetting the table below it.

"I guess not," Sara said with a snicker. She looked around to see if anyone was watching, and when she saw no one was, she said, "Don't worry, I won't tell. Let's just walk away." She grabbed the drink out of Jacob's hand and then turned and grabbed his free hand with her free hand. She brought them over to the couch where two other classmates Jacob recognized were sitting.

"Janet, Bobby, you know Jacob, right?" Janet and Bobby nodded and said hi. Jacob smiled and nodded back. "Anyway, I bet you didn't know Jacob is a real bartender." She sat down on the couch pulling Jacob with her. They squeezed in, four of them in a couch built for three.

"Really?" Bobby said. Bobby had been in a few classes with Jacob, and while Jacob didn't know him that well, he did know that he took everything literally. Once, in English class, he asked if he had a different version of *To Kill a Mockingbird*, because in his version, no one killed a mockingbird. This elicited numerous laughs around that classroom, making Bobby himself laugh, though he had no idea why.

"Yep. Best bartender in Akron." Sara nudged Jacob's arm, and he had to take another drink from his cup to hide that he was blushing.

"You're quiet in school," Janet said. Jacob knew Janet well. Not because they were close, but because she was the most talkative girl in the school. It bordered on annoying, though she had a billion friends and teachers loved her, so clearly it worked for her. "I thought it was hilarious when you went off on Mrs. Felton about *Invisible Man*, though. The classroom is no place to discuss race in the first place. I mean it's practically offensive." Jacob did not know until that moment that Janet was a racist.

"That's not what I—"

"Anyway, it's cool that you're here. I wouldn't have guessed you'd show up to a party."

"Yeah, it's cool," Bobby said. Clearly, he wasn't understanding the dig that Janet had just delivered.

"I think it's cute how quiet Jacob is," Sara said. "There's something bothersome about someone who doesn't shut up."

Jacob snorted despite the fact that he was still internally processing yet another comment from Sara about his virtues.

"Right?" Janet said. "I hate that. Jacob, Bobby told me you have an older brother, is that true?"

"Yeah, Benn—"

"I wonder if he'd know my older sister. How old is he? My sister started college last year, she's at Bowling Green. Where did your brother go? I applied to Bowling Green but it's not my first..."

Jacob took a long... a very long drink from his cup. For the first time since he made himself the drink, he found himself enjoying its fiery sting. He found himself wanting more. And when he looked back into his cup, Janet still going on about something or another, he noticed that he'd already finished the drink. A moment ago, it had been nearly full and he'd only been able to take tiny sips; now, he was sitting on the crowded couch with an empty cup longing for it to be full again. He looked over at Sara, who seemed to have regretted sitting down at the couch. She looked back at him, down at his cup, and then down at hers. She still had about half a cup left, but she lifted it to her lips, tilted it back, and downed the entire remainder. When she finished, she winced and said, "Jacob and I are going to get another drink."

She stood up from the couch and once again grabbed Jacob's hand. She pulled him up and dragged him over to the drink table where the puddle of Coke still sat gently rippling on the table to the beat of the music. They were alone again. Jacob still wasn't sure all of this was real. It felt like a dream, especially now that the alcohol had started to make its way to his head. He knew his feet were on the ground, but it felt as if he were floating. He didn't feel drunk, whatever that meant, but he did feel very good and knew that he wanted to feel more of that. Before Sara even asked him to, he started making them both another whiskey and Coke. He did it quickly now, less concerned about drawing things out with Sara and more concerned with having his next sip.

"God, Janet is even worse when she's been drinking," Sara said as Jacob was pouring Coke into the whiskey he'd just poured.

"Is she a racist?"

"Oh, that thing about the book? I don't know. Probably. I shouldn't have dragged you over there."

"It's okay. I don't really talk to anyone at school, so it's probably good to get to know some of these people."

"Like me?"

Jacob had forgotten to be nervous around Sara since they'd sat on the couch. The nervousness came rushing back to him when she said this. He quickly finished pouring the Coke in their drinks for fear that he would spill on the table again. He put the bottle down, handed Sara her drink, and said, "Yeah, I guess. It's not personal."

"I know it's not," she said with a smile. The smile fell, and her face became very serious and sad. "I know about your... well, I know why you had to move to our school."

"Hey, can you make me one of those?" someone said from

beside Jacob. It was someone he didn't recognize. Jacob nodded and started making his drink.

"I guess I always figured everyone knew," Jacob said to Sara.

"I'm really sorry tha—"

"Don't." Jacob looked up at Sara to show her he was serious. "All I've wanted since moving here was to feel normal, and it's impossible to feel normal when everyone pities you. I know you're trying to be nice, and I do appreciate it, but let's just pretend I'm as normal as the rest of you."

"You are nor—"

"Hey, so can I get that drink or...?"

Jacob poured about half a cup of whiskey and put in a single splash of Coke. He threw in some ice and thrust it toward the kid. "Enjoy," he said, "now go on."

"Wow, that was hot," Sara said. "I like assertive Jacob."

"That was more like pissed-off Jacob."

"Either way, it was pretty hot."

Maybe it was the alcohol, or maybe it was the anger rising and subsiding within him like an ocean's tide; whatever it was, Jacob no longer felt nervous or anxious when Sara complimented him like this. He found himself acting as if she'd just told him she liked his socks. He did a sort of shrug and a little smile. He felt like James Dean, or like Sean Connery effortlessly picking up yet another beautiful woman with a martini in one hand and a gun in the other. He also felt enormously hard. Normally, this would embarrass him, but now he almost wanted Sara to see it. He pictured going to the room in the back corner and lying down on the bed while she pulled off his pants. He imagined her lips kissing his naval and then his pubic hair and then wrapping around his pulsing penis. He imagined—

"You okay there?" Sara said. At first, Jacob thought she'd noticed his boner but then realized she was looking at his eyes. "Where did you go?"

Jacob took a long drink from his cup, its contents already getting low, and said he was fine. He asked her if she wanted to go play foosball with him. The foosball table was the first thing he saw when he'd come back to reality, and he didn't have time to think of anything else. When she agreed, Jacob hoped to God that she had never played before, because he himself had never touched a foosball table. Sara walked over to the table, and Jacob said he'd be right there. He finished the rest of his drink and quickly poured himself a new one. He noticed as he poured it that he had gone even lighter on the Coke. Could it be that he actually liked the taste of whiskey? He didn't know how that could be possible given how bad it had tasted on his first sip, but when he finished pouring the drink, he felt his mouth watering for more, more, more.

It turned out that Sara had indeed played foosball before. In fact, she told Jacob, after winning the second game 10-2, she had a table at home. She played with her younger brothers and was undefeated. As the games went on, Jacob got the hang of things, and by the final game, he'd actually taken the lead 5-4 until Sara came back to beat him 10-5. He didn't mind losing. He liked to watch Sara when she scored a goal or blocked a particularly tricky shot. Her face would light up as if she'd just found out she got into college, or like she'd just opened that gift she'd wanted so badly for her birthday. Other partygoers would come to cheer her on and make fun of Jacob for losing to a girl, but to Jacob, it felt like he and Sara were the only two people at the party. Or, rather, he, Sara, and his drink were the only ones at the party. Sometime during the third or fourth game, his drink had once again run out, and he asked someone to make him another one. They came back with a cup of Coke with a splash of whiskey. He was disappointed but said nothing.

When they finished playing, Jacob was feeling drunk and bold. He said good game to Sara, and instead of the courteous handshake or high five he'd been giving her throughout the games, he went around to her side and gave her a hug. She leaned into the hug and wrapped her arms tightly around his waist. He wasn't sure he ever would have let go had it not been for Patrick.

"Everyone," Patrick shouted. The party went quiet. Sara released Jacob to listen to what Patrick had to announce. "We're going to play spin the bottle."

Jacob felt himself go tense with dread. He looked over at Sara, who was rolling her eyes. "Of course," Sara said. The party was situating themselves into a large circle. As this commotion was going on, Sara smiled at Jacob and said, "Hey, you want to sneak out of here?" Jacob nodded. He'd intended to do it coolly, but his head felt limp as he did so, and he found he had to put in some effort to pull it back up. Sara grabbed his hand again, led him up the steps, and back to the foyer.

Sara started putting her shoes on. Jacob started trying to slip back into his own and was having a hard time of it. He sat down, finding it easier to balance on his ass than on his own feet.

"Patrick always cheats at spin the bottle," Sara said, tying on her second shoe. "He likes to spin it, and then if it's going to land on someone he doesn't want to kiss, he fakes a sneeze and moves it to someone he does want to kiss. He thinks it's funny." Jacob's left foot felt stuck in the shoe, which was only halfway on his foot. "Here, let me help you," Sara said. She knelt down and put his shoe on with ease. Jacob still didn't feel the way he thought being drunk would feel, though he thought he must have been drunk because why else couldn't he perform a menial task like putting on a shoe, and why did it take effort to keep his head up?

Sara handed Jacob his coat, which meant she'd taken notice of the coat he'd been wearing when they walked in. They put their coats on together, and Sara pulled Jacob outside. It had gotten chillier than when Jacob had walked over. The sun was gone, and the only illumination was from the streetlights in Patrick's neighborhood.

Jacob could see his breath. More importantly, he could see Sara's. She pulled him to the sidewalk and then slowed to be beside him as they walked hand in hand.

"Sorry," she said, "I hate those parties sometimes. Seemed like it might be more fun to hang out with just you."

"No. You're—it's—"

"You drank a lot, huh?" Jacob shrugged. This felt safer than trying to answer again. "That's okay. Last party I went to—do you know Lisey? Well, her parents came home and busted us. While they were yelling at Lisey, I tried to make it past them to the bathroom, but I couldn't. I threw up all over her mom." Jacob laughed, and Sara laughed with him. "Yeah. So I decided to take it easy tonight."

"I lied before," Jacob said. "This was my first time drinking."

"Yeah, I know. You aren't exactly a good liar."

"I didn't even know that about myself. I don't lie very often." Was an omission the same as a lie? And if so, how long is a lie a lie before it becomes the new truth? Jacob certainly felt as if the version of the story he told the police and the doctors and the school counselors was the true version. When he reflected on that day, he rarely pictured himself at the computer. He didn't think of the confusion that happened when the water touched his feet at the same time as he'd finished.

"You don't lie to your aunt?"

"I don't really have anything to lie to her about."

"You've never said you did your homework when you really didn't? You've never told her you were going to bed only to stay up late eating bad food and watching TV?" Jacob smiled and shook his head. "What about tonight? Did she know there would be alcohol at this party?"

"I didn't even know there would be alcohol at this party. Or girls. Patrick told me we were playing video games."

"Would you have come if you'd known it was a party?"

"Yeah, I wou—"

"I told you. You're not a good liar," Sara said. Jacob shrugged.

He said, "I certainly wouldn't have come if I'd known you would be here."

"What? Why?" Sara said. She looked genuinely concerned. Sad, even.

"I would have been too nervous."

"What do you mean?"

It must have been the whiskey pulling the strings to make his mouth move, because sober Jacob wouldn't have said this to Sara with a gun to his skull. Sober Jacob probably wouldn't have any words to say at all, or else if he tried to speak, it would come out in stutters. This was Jack speaking. If anything good happened tonight he had only Jack to thank.

"I guess I've had a... a crush on you. For a while."

Sara stopped walking. Was she blushing, or were her cheeks red from the cold air? "You have?" She looked serious but in a kind of way that was intentional, like she was forcing back a smile too large to be fully contained.

Jacob shrugged again and tried to keep them moving. Sara stood still.

"How come you never talk to me?" Jacob shrugged once more. "No, tell me," Sara insisted.

Jacob thought about this and then said, "I've never really fit in since I moved schools. I guess I never really fit in at my old school either. I find it easier to live in my own head than in the actual world."

"So do you fantasize about me?"

"Sure."

"And?"

"And what?"

"What do we do in these fantasies?"

Even with the alcohol, Jacob didn't feel he would be able to answer this question. If he lied, he was sure she would see right through him. If he told the truth, she might be disgusted. Worse, she might like hearing about them. The only other option was to dodge the question completely. This option would prove to him and to Sara that he, Jacob, was a coward. Here, Jacob had the girl of his dreams asking him, seriously, what she does with him in his fantasies. Here, there was a chance that she would perform whatever he said in order to make his dreams come true. He should tell her of the one where she takes off all of her clothes, wraps her panties around his dick and jerks him off with them. Or the one where she pretends to be a robot and follows every command he gives her. Or maybe the one where she uses her breasts to make him finish.

"We should head back," Jacob said. Sara nodded and started walking back without a word. Jacob could tell from her face that she was disappointed. It felt like this was a test that he had failed. If he had played this right, he could have seen a boob, maybe even touched it, or at least gotten a kiss from her. All the way back, he fantasized about what they could have done together, only the fantasies were interrupted with the thought that now that's all they would ever be. Just fantasies. Unless...

When they got to the door, Sara reached her hand out to open it. Before she could, Jacob blurted out: "Sometimes we just kiss." Sara turned to face him with an interested smile. "Sometimes I just talk to you as if you were my girlfriend."

"And other times?" Sara asked.

"Sometimes we have sex."

"How?"

"All kinds of ways."

"Tell me one." She moved close to Jacob so that he could feel the heat from her body. He felt himself growing hard again. He hadn't touched himself since that day at the computer, but the fantasies never went away, and it was growing increasingly more frustrating that he couldn't bring himself to masturbate.

Jacob swallowed. "There's one where you strip for me. Slowly. You strip everything below your waist off first, and then you strip off your shirt. And then you take a maddeningly long time to strip off your bra."

"Teasing you."

"But then you finally take it off."

"And then?"

"Sometimes that's it." She looked at him questioningly. "Sometimes you go down on me, or I go down on you."

She moved closer to him, pressing herself into him. She looked like she might kiss him. But instead, she grabbed his shirt and pulled him along with her as she opened the door, entered the house, found an empty bedroom, and shut the door. She threw him on the bed and stood in the middle of the room. She said, "Watch me," in a sexy whisper.

She stripped, moving her body slowly as she did it. She stripped the way Jacob had described to her, bottom half first. She slipped out of her shoes and then her socks. She worked her way up to her jeans. And then when those were off, she played with herself over her panties before pulling those off too. She looked a little silly completely naked on her bottom half with her big coat still on her upper half, but Jacob was far too distracted to notice this completely. When her coat and cropped sweater came off, she continued swaying but didn't remove her bra. She traced her body with her fingers and lingered when they reached her vagina. Finally, she moved her arms back to unsnap her bra. Jacob's heart was pounding. She moved them away and smiled; she was having fun with him. She moved toward the bed and put her face close to Jacob's. She moved to kiss him and then pulled away from that, too. And when she unsnapped her bra and slipped her arms out of the straps, she held it in place with her hands.

O' God, please let her drop her hands!

O' God, please let me see them!

And then she dropped her hands and revealed what Jacob wanted so badly to see. Only when he saw them, he felt fear shoot through his body. As she took off his shoes and pants, he felt himself shaking and sweating. He felt like he couldn't breathe. His chest was rising up and down quickly so he must have been breathing, but he felt like the air wasn't truly making it into his body; he felt like a fish that had just been yanked out of the water.

When she pulled down his underwear, Lily Scarlett flashed in his brain. Lily Scarlett with her satin robe. Lily Scarlett with a penis in her mouth in the kitchen. And then he saw rain. Two naked bodies dancing—no, fucking—in the rain. Two bodies writhing in the pain that is pleasure.

Jacob. Sweetheart. Call 911.

Sara moved her mouth so close to Jacob's penis that he could feel her breath on it. She licked it softly. He thought of Benny. Would he be next? If he went through with this, would he return home to his aunt sitting at the table waiting for him with a phone in her hand and a look of horror on her face?

Jacob. Please, honey. Please call 911.

And as Sara went to wrap her lips around it, Jacob screamed, "Stop!" Sara pulled back. Jacob still couldn't find his breath. He felt like he was going to die. What a way to go. Naked on the bottom half and fully clothed on the top.

Sara, hunched over and naked, had a look on her face like she'd just been punched. Through the pain of whatever was killing him, Jacob still wondered how he could fix this. He wanted this so badly. His fantasy had come true, or almost had, and now here he laid halfway-to-weeping on a strange bed. And why couldn't he catch his breath?

"Are you okay?" Sara asked. Her voice was soft. She'd gone from being hurt to being a nurturer. She was Mary, and Jacob was a little lamb who'd wandered away. "Jacob?" Now concern. Sara became a big spoon, sliding in beside Jacob and holding him to herself. "Just breathe," she said. "Breathe. Just breathe."

After a while, Jacob caught his breath and was able to calm down. But as he did so, he realized he'd rather have actually died to spare him this absolute humiliation. What would he say to her? What would she tell her friends? Would she ask him what had happened? Could he bring himself to tell her? And instead of sticking around to find the answers to any of these questions, Jacob shot up from the bed. Sarah protested as he put on his pants and shoes, but he was too focused on getting out of there to really hear what she was saying. He didn't even bother to steal a last glance at her, still naked and glowing in the moonlight coming through the blinds, he just ran out of the room and then out of the house. It felt a hundred degrees colder out than it had only 15 minutes before. This seemed impossible, but could something be impossible if you were actually feeling it?

Jacob walked himself home, intent on never speaking to anyone from school again. He would graduate. Maybe he would do college, maybe he would go immediately into a job. Wherever he ended up, he would have to be careful. He couldn't lose anyone else. The pain of it would likely kill him. Though maybe death wouldn't be so bad.

CHAPTER FIFTEEN

Jake sat waiting in his car at the train station. Benny had texted him that he was supposed to arrive at JFK that afternoon. From there, he would get on the train and head up to Tarrytown. Jake didn't bother to tell him how long of a trip that would be because he knew there weren't many other options. A cab would be outrageously expensive, and the drive would probably take over an hour anyway. So, Jake sat waiting. He'd brought along one of the books that he'd picked out with Eve to give him a distraction and ease his nerves. It was *The Brothers Karamazov,* which he'd picked that morning simply because it had the word brother in the title and thought it would be fitting. He hadn't expected to truly read, only to have something to hold onto and look at, but he suddenly found himself 20 pages in and already invested in the characters. For years, the only reading he'd done had been out of the Bible. That, too, was fiction, but it was much less interesting.

A train pulled up to the station. Jacob watched as its passengers shuffled out onto the platform with their loved ones, children, suitcases, backpacks. And then he saw Benny. He still had the goatee he'd talked about on the phone. It wasn't like Jake had pictured. It looked good. It suited his face. His hair was medium length and slicked back, but it wasn't greasy. It was still thick and dark, though there were specks of white peppered throughout. This, again, suited him. It was as if aging actually made him more attractive. As if all his life he'd been waiting to grow into this body right here. The wind blew a large wisp of hair in front of his eyes and he had to use his hand to smooth it back. When he did this, he spotted Jake, smiled, and waved enthusiastically. Jake took a deep breath, checked himself out in the mirror, was mildly disappointed in what he saw, and then got out of the car to greet his brother after who-knew-how-many years apart.

"Jakey," Benny said as he walked up for a hug. Jake felt himself being squeezed under Benny's muscular upper body. He'd remembered Benny being strong when they were younger but was surprised to see this was still the case. He wondered how much time Benny spent in the gym. "How are ya?" he said when they stopped embracing. "God, it's good to see you. Can I say God in front of you? Oh, hell, might as well tell you upfront I'm going to say it anyway. And Jesus. And fuck. All those words." He smiled at Jake like he was supposed to be in on some sort of joke.

"That's fine," Jake said. He gestured to the trunk of his car, which he had popped for Benny. As Benny was putting his bags inside, Jake sat back in the front seat and took another deep breath. One more moment of silence. One more moment of peace. And then Benny opened the passenger door and sat in the car.

"This is what you're driving these days?" He looked around the inside of the car, holding back disgust. Jake wondered what Benny was driving. Probably something new and expensive.

"Pastor's salary," Jake said. He thought that maybe in being curt Benny would catch on that he didn't want to talk about his job or how little he made doing it. Maybe they could avoid the topic of jobs altogether. Jake certainly didn't want to hear about Benny's job either.

"Right. Makes sense."

Jake started up the car and pulled out of the parking lot.

"I'm starving," Benny said, patting his flat stomach. Jake could have sworn he heard a clink, as if he'd hit a hammer on an anvil instead of his own hand on his stomach. "They have food here in Tarrytown?" He said the word Tarrytown sarcastically, as if it was a fictional place. Jake was used to this. Anything in New York but not in the city was practically not really there, at least according to anyone who didn't live in one of those places.

"You don't want to drop your bags off at my place first? I'm just around the corner."

"Nah. There's nothing all that important in there, just clothes. I could use a burger."

Jake smiled at the thought of Benny eating his cheeseburgers every Sunday at Chet's. Jake hadn't planned on taking Benny to any of his regular spots. It wasn't that he was to be kept a secret, he just didn't want people asking what his brother did for a living. He didn't want to see the shock in their eyes when they heard that the pastor's brother proudly works in porn. But the pull of memories of Chet's from so long ago made him change his mind. He turned in the direction of Ava's, hoping that Lily wouldn't be there. As far as he knew, she only went on Sundays, but based on the friendliness between her and Thomas, he wouldn't have been surprised to learn she was going more often. He had promised her he would invite her out to meet his brother, but he wanted it to happen on his terms.

It wasn't far to Ava's, but Jake was finding it hard to make conversation with his brother. How strange to not have anything to talk about with someone who you used to talk to every single day. How strange to have not seen each other for years and still have so little to say. As they drove, Jake pondered the last few years of his life.

What had he done worth noting to his brother? He thought of the alcohol he'd stored out of sight in his apartment. He thought of his near-total loss of faith. He thought of Lily's birthday. Lily grinding against him on the dance floor. Of Eve's snake tattoo.

Benny must have been thinking about what he could share from his own life because he, too, was silent. He was staring out the window taking in Tarrytown brick by brick by sidewalk by traffic light. Jake couldn't see Benny's face without turning to look directly at him, but he imagined it was filled with ambivalence. Jake thought about voicing over a sort of tour of the town, but then he realized he knew very little about the town he inhabited.

"So how have you been?" Jake said, resorting to small talk. *Small talk*, he thought, *is better than no talk*.

"I've been great. I just signed a lease on a new place on Venice Beach. Commute'll be a bitch, but it's a fuckin' gorgeous spot." He stopped talking a second but then added, "you'll have to come visit sometime."

"Pastor's salary, remember?"

"Yeah, yeah. Well, maybe that'll be my birthday present to you."

"When have we ever bought each other birthday presents?"

"We could start now," Benny said. Jake looked at him to see if he was serious and saw that he was. Jake just nodded and smiled as if to say maybe, but even a vocal 'maybe' was too close to a yes.

Jake drove into the parking lot of Ava's only to find that it was closed. There was no sign on the door, just darkness within. Jake got out of the car to peer inside and realized that Benny had followed him out of the car and was peering in with him. "Reminds me of Chet's," Benny said, looking at Jake. "You remember Chet's?" Jake nodded and tried to hide his disappointment. "Been to that sports bar across the street?" Benny asked. Jake looked and shook his head. "Well let's go there then." Benny started walking there, and Jake followed without objection, leaving his car in the parking lot of Ava's.

The sports bar was quaint and dimly lit. It smelled of urine and chicken wings and Miller Light. There were a handful of people scattered around the bar, some at the bar itself and a few at the rickety tables around it. There wasn't much chatter happening. Most of the patrons had their eyes glued to the TV, an afternoon beer sweating in their hands. Jake and Benny took a seat at the bar a few seats away from anyone else.

"What's your stance on drinking?" Benny asked. "You seemed pretty loaded when I called you a while back."

"I drink," Jake responded casually, or with what he hoped was casual.

"Beer, whiskey, wine?" Jake just shrugged. "I'm a Scotch guy myself. But I think I'll have a beer. How about you?" Jake just nodded. Benny ordered two beers from the bartender and asked for a food menu. Jake pretended to scan it over as Benny talked on. "So, a priest who drinks. You're not a drunk, are you? No, that would be too cliché."

"Pastor."

"Right. Potato potahto. Tell me Jacob, do you like what you do?" The bartender set a beer in front of each of them and asked if they'd like to order any food. Benny told her politely that they'd like a minute. "So?"

"Sure," Jake said. "It's okay."

"Lying to your own brother. Isn't that, like, a sin?"

"I'm not lying," Jake lied.

"Well, I don't know why you're doing it if you don't like it. You're like ten feet from one of the greatest cities on the planet!" He put his arms out as he said this. "You could do anything you want there."

"Well, I'm not there. I'm in Tarrytown. And I like it here."

Benny snorted and took a drink from his beer. Jake picked his own up and took a long drink. Benny must have seen this as some sort of competition because he picked his glass back up and drank it down to where Jake's was before setting it down again.

"You talked to Beth lately?" Benny asked. Jake was still pretending to scan the menu.

Jake said, "Sure," and shrugged his shoulders.

"Look at me, Jacob." Jake looked up from the menu. Benny's face looked very serious. Stern. Like a father about to yell at his child. "Do not lie to me. I didn't come all this way to have you spout a bunch of bullshit."

"Why did you come all this way?" Jake asked. "I know it wasn't for a meeting."

Benny sat back in his chair and sighed. "Beth told me she was worried about you. Used to be me that never called. Now... anyway, I thought about how we've seen each other less and less over the years. How little we know about each other anymore. And I decided to come and see you. Thought it might be nice to spend some time together, especially on your birthday."

Jake took another drink of his beer. If he hadn't, he was sure tears would have spilled down his face, and it mortified him to think of doing that in front of Benny. He hadn't cried in front of Benny since they were kids, and he certainly didn't want to break that streak now. He nodded as he drank. It was one of those nods that said: I hear you, just give me a second. And when he put it back down, he knew he had to speak, but wasn't sure what he was going to say. Sure, they'd grown apart. But isn't that what brothers do? Especially brothers whose parents had died when they were young? Brothers that lived on opposite coasts?

"Thank you," Jake said. "I appreciate you coming out here. You don't need to worry about me, but it'll be nice to spend some time together. Get to know each other again."

"Damn right it will." Benny picked up his glass and motioned for Jake to do the same. "The bubble winked at me and said, you'll miss me, brother, when you're dead." Benny winked and smashed his glass into Jake's.

"What's that from?" Jake asked.

"No idea. An old cheers I heard once. Fitting though, right?" Both drank their beers until they were empty and then ordered another round.

Jake felt in higher spirits then, and he and Benny chatted over their beers and some burgers they had ordered. Benny caught Jake up on his own job. He'd moved around some big-time studios for a while before opening his own independent production company. He said the money now was in the stuff that looked amateur. The trick was to make it seem like the girl is posting from her own account when really, his company owns the account. Jake listened but didn't really understand. What was the difference between amateur porn and normal porn? What did it matter to viewers whose account the content was coming from? But he enjoyed seeing Benny's face as he talked about his job. It sounded like he was doing well, which is really all Jake cared about.

Jake told Benny as little as he could about his own job. He didn't tell him about Kendall or that he still had yet to fire her despite a final warning from the administrators. He didn't tell Benny that he often preached without actually believing in what he preached. Or that he prayed without truly believing anyone was listening. He didn't tell Benny about his vow of celibacy or about his over-consumption of alcohol. Never in the course of their conversation did he technically lie; he just left little truths out here and there. It was harmless. They were still catching up and getting along nonetheless.

When they had finished their burgers and had about half a beer left each, Jake's phone buzzed inside his pocket. He took it out to find a text from Eve. She said they'd woken Philip up and he was weak but doing okay. She asked if Jake would be able to come by to see him. He wondered if she really meant Philip or if Eve really wanted him to come and see her.

"What is it?" Benny asked, nodding toward the phone.

"Oh, its no—"

Benny gave him a look that said: no lies.

Jake sighed. He told Benny about Philip, starting from the first time he went to pray over him. He left out the parts about Eve.

"We have to go see him," Benny said when Jake was done.

"I can see him after you leave."

"Absolutely not. I'll get the check. Let's go."

The last thing in the world Jake wanted to do was bring his brother with him to a hospital to see a boy that he hardly even knew, but now that Benny's mind was made up, Jake didn't think he would be able to change it. He nodded and texted Eve that he would come right away.

***

The hospital was busy, and Jake and Benny found themselves being shoved around by people walking quickly to various hospital rooms or the cafeteria or out to their cars for a moment alone. They made their way through the crowd slowly, Jake getting increasingly more nervous the closer they made it to the room Eve had told him to go to. It was one thing to talk about his career and a whole other thing to actually show it to Benny in action. He would undoubtedly have to pray over Philip in front of Benny. What would Benny think? Would he laugh? He probably hadn't prayed since they were kids. Worse, would he see right through the façade? Jake imagined him asking afterward why he prays when he doesn't believe anyone is listening. What would he respond?

The door to Philip's room was closed, and Jake knocked. He was reminded of that first time he visited Philip when he'd stood at the door and started to knock when Eve pushed past him. That smile she smiled. The door opened, and Jake's heart leapt, hoping it would be Eve that answered. But it was Philip's mother, Beth.

"Oh, Jake," she said, joyfully. She had tears in her eyes, but she was smiling. Jake could tell she wanted to hug him, but was feeling shy about it, so he decided to hug her there in the doorway. When she did, she noticed Benny, whom she had failed to see before. "And who is this?" She let go of Jake and stared at Benny.

Benny started to speak, but Jake jumped in before he could. "This is my brother. Benny." Again, Benny started to speak, but Beth hugged him too, no longer shy about it. "He just got into town today, and he doesn't have a car or anything, so I brought him along."

"Well, it's wonderful you're both here. Please come on in." Beth opened the door wide for them, and Jake and Benny entered.

When he saw Jake, Philip's eyes lit up with joy. He looked pale and weak. But he was moving. He was breathing on his own. This was good. This was better. Jake moved toward Philip and put on what he hoped was a relaxed smile. "Took a long nap, huh?" he said. He hated himself for making this bad joke, but it made Philip laugh anyway. And then Jake found himself not knowing what to say next. What do you say to someone who has just woken up from a coma?

Benny saved him by moving closer and saying, "Hey, kid. I've heard a lot about you. Heard you kicked my brother's booty at *Mario Kart*." He stuck his fist out for a bump. Philip bumped it and gave them a cocky smile. "I used to beat him all the time at video games. Course, I'd let him win some every once in a while." He winked at Philip, who was really enjoying this. Had color returned to his pale, sunken face? When they walked in, Jake had been taken aback by Philip's look of exhaustion, but now, after the exchange of only a few words, he seemed to be returning to himself. Here was this boy that couldn't hold back a giggle at the word butt. Here was this boy who fought through his sickness with apparent ease. Jake couldn't help but smile at him.

There was another knock on the door, followed by the quiet entrance of Eve. Jake's heart started pounding. It took her a moment to register who was in the room. It was Benny she saw first. She looked confused. Her eyes looked him quickly up and down as if wondering why this stranger looked so familiar. And then she saw Jake and the dots had been connected. Jake smiled nervously at her. Eve smiled back. She moved in to give him a hug. Did she feel no awkwardness after the attempted kiss? Had it really been forgotten? Could people truly forget things like that? As they hugged, Jake looked at Benny, who raised his eyebrows and darted his eyes between Jake and Eve. This was a silent question, and Jake didn't have any intention of answering, at least not at that moment.

"How are you feeling?" Eve asked Philip.

"I'm okay," Philip said. Jake guessed that he didn't feel okay at all but was being strong for the present company. Eve checked the monitor next to his bed. She only looked at it a moment, as if she knew nothing would be out of place. Jake wondered if she'd only popped in the room hoping to run into him.

"Any pain? Do you need water or anything?" Philip shook his head and Eve nodded. Beth moved to Philip's bedside and put her hand on his shoulder. Eve looked back at the rest of the room, where Benny was waiting patiently to be introduced.

"This is my brother. Benny. Benny, this is Eve."

"Pleasure," Benny said. Jake didn't like the way he said it. How could a single word sound so flirty? And was he crazy or did Eve respond positively to it?

"Great to meet you," Eve said. "Jake talks about you all the time." Jake wasn't sure why she lied about this. Was it for his sake or for Benny's?

"That's odd. He hasn't told me about you yet. A shame."

Jake cleared his throat. He motioned with his eyes for Benny to leave the room. This was not the place to flirt. Maybe it was hypocritical, since Jake had been coming to the hospital often for the chance of seeing Eve, but it felt shameless to flirt like this in front of a sick kid. Benny got the message and excused himself from the room. As he was closing the door, Jake noticed Benny's eyes meet Eve's. They both lingered for only a moment, but to Jake it felt much longer.

"He was lying by the way," Jake said, turning to Philip, "I always let him win."

"Uh huh," Philip said with a smile.

"Besides, he's an old man—no way he could beat me now."

"You're an old man too."

"Hey. Watch it." He'd almost forgotten the next day was his thirty-third birthday.

Everyone in the room was enjoying their exchange. Beth looked happy to see Philip smiling and joking again. Eve seemed relieved that things were improving. Jake wondered how long it would be until Philip finally recovered and what the chances were that the sickness could strengthen again, but he didn't ask. To ask would bring them all back to the reality of the situation, and that's something no one in that room needed.

Jake promised he'd be back if Philip was still in the hospital for a few more days, but he hoped that soon the boy would be able to go home and live his life again. How lonely it must be to have only a nurse a mom and a pastor for company. Where were his friends? Had they been to visit? Did Philip have any friends? So strange to feel like you know someone so well when you really don't know them at all. He left Beth and Philip in the room and followed Eve out of it. He was eager to have a moment of alone time with Eve but then realized that his brother would be waiting outside. Sure enough, the moment they emerged, his brother pushed himself off of the wall on which he'd been leaning and went straight for Eve.

"You this nice with all your patients?" he asked.

"You this pushy with all women?" Eve retorted. Jake noticed she was smiling slightly, clearly enjoying this game that his brother was a pro at playing.

"Just beautiful ones."

Eve snorted, and Jake felt like he should say something before Benny took over the entire conversation. "Do they think he'll be able to leave soon?"

"I don't know," Eve said with a shrug, "I'm just glad he's awake. He seems weak but better."

"What is that?" Benny asked, pointing to the tattoo sticking out of Eve's scrubs. She looked at him and shrugged again, this time with a smile.

"I have to go check in on some other patients," she said. "But maybe I'll see you both soon?"

Before Jake could tell her they'd be busy, Benny said: "Absolutely. Are you free tomorrow night? It's Jakey's birthday and we intend to celebrate."

Eve looked at Jake, puzzled, as if she couldn't grasp why he wouldn't have told her his birthday was coming up. But then she looked back at Benny and said she'd be there. Before she walked off, Benny asked her if he could get her number, and without looking back, she told him he could get it from Jake. They both watched her go.

***

Jake and Benny went to Jake's apartment so Benny could drop his bags off and get settled in. Jake had laid a pillow and a large blanket on the couch that he so often passed out on. He'd cleaned his apartment in anticipation of Benny's arrival, not something he did very often, and hid his cache of alcohol under the bed in the duffel bag. He didn't know how much Benny might go around snooping, but he wanted to make absolutely sure Benny wouldn't stumble across the bevy of bottles and start asking questions that Jake surely didn't want to answer. The problem was this: right now, Jake wanted a drink more than anything, and he couldn't even do it properly in the comfort of his own home. His brother's flirtatious attitude with Eve had bothered him immensely. He was barely able to speak to Benny on the ride back into Tarrytown, and with every passing second of silence, he only became more distressed. Benny had been pestering him to invite another girl to the birthday celebration. He didn't say it out loud, but Jake knew he wanted it to be like a double date. That would mean Eve would be Benny's date. How could Jake allow that to happen? What would he do if he had to be in that situation? And who would he invite? Certainly not Lily. He'd promised Lily that she could meet his brother, but how could he be around Eve and Lily at the same time? He thought he would explode.

When Benny went to the bathroom, Jake slipped into his room and pawed under the bed. He came out with a bottle of vodka, screwed the cap off, and took a long drink. He barely noticed the sting or the bitter flavor. He felt as if he'd been stuck in a desert and come across an oasis. He heard the toilet flush and took one more drink before screwing the cap back on and shoving the bottle back into the bag. Still on his knees next to his bed, Jake suddenly felt like weeping. What would his brother do if he walked out of the bathroom and heard him weeping in his bedroom? What questions would that prompt? Worse, would he come in and try to reassure him like he did the day their mother died? Would Benny wrap his arms around Jake from behind and hold him like a child?

He met Benny back in the living room, and Benny again inquired about Jake inviting another girl to meet up with them the next day. Jake sighed. "There's this girl, Lily. She invited me out for her birthday, so I should probably invite her tomorrow."

"Lily. Sounds hot." Benny winked at Jake. He was in very good spirits. "Now. How about another drink?"

Jake didn't decline. They went to another bar in the area and then to dinner somewhere unmemorable. He texted Lily and Eve to meet them tomorrow at a nice Italian restaurant. He even told Lily it was for his birthday. Both were excited to come; Jake was just happy to be drunk when they texted him back. He lay in his bed that night, the ceiling spinning, and fell asleep to the sound of his brother snoring in the next room.

CHAPTER SIXTEEN

Jake woke early to the sound of the TV playing in the other room. It said: 'Good morning.' The sun was low in the sky and licked his face through the open blinds. He felt the familiar ache in his head that he often felt in the mornings. He felt the bubbling in his stomach that often preceded a long sit on the toilet. He welcomed these feelings. This meant that even with the arrival of his brother, nothing had drastically changed as he had feared it would. He felt anxious about the dinner later that night, but anxiety was a feeling he could deal with as long as he had a few drinks on hand. He needed badly to pee, but he didn't feel like facing his brother yet. Instead, he held it in, rolled over, and went back to sleep for a while.

The day went smoothly after that. Ava's was still closed, so they found another place to grab some breakfast. Benny sure could eat. Jake's appetite was small, but Benny made up for it with an order of three pancakes, three eggs, three pieces of bacon, sausage, and hash browns. Just as he had as a kid, he ate without regard to order, stuffing his face with bites of each, never quite fully chewing before adding something new. He talked with his mouth full of food and coffee. He expressed his excitement for later that night. He asked about Lily. Who was she? Was Jake dating her? Were they fucking? To all of these questions, Jake just shook his head and shrugged, picking at his plate of scrambled eggs with his fork. Benny also asked about Eve. He didn't ask the same questions, as if he couldn't imagine a girl like Eve being with a guy like Jake. Jake told Benny she was trying to get into medical school, and Benny nodded, already planning on a way to bring that up in their conversation later. He certainly hadn't lost his ability to flatter women.

While Jake was in the bathroom, Benny must have done some Googling, because when he sat back down, Benny asked if they could go back into Sleepy Hollow to see a lighthouse. Jake had heard about the lighthouse but had never made the trek out there himself. He didn't really see the point of going to see it in person when he could just Google it and see it right there on his phone or computer. But he was also glad for the suggestion because he had no idea what he and his brother would do before they had to get ready for dinner, and he badly needed a distraction or a strong drink.

Jake drove them to Kingsland Point Park, where you could sit on benches or under gazebos and stare mindlessly at the Hudson River views. They walked along the river, stopping to look at the lighthouse. "You remember that movie *Sleepy Hollow*?" Benny asked. "Guess you might have been too young to watch that when it came out."

"I saw it with Beth," Jake said. "We used to go to the movies a lot. They had a Tim Burton weekend at the theater."

There wasn't a lot that made him happy in those days, so when Beth discovered that going to the movies was something he enjoyed, she started taking him often. She wasn't much of a movie-lover herself, but suddenly she was seeing multiple movies a week. Thinking of it by the water with Benny, the wind blew the scent of popcorn into his nose. He could taste Sprite on his tongue.

"See, I don't get it. You two were close. Now it seems like you couldn't care less about her."

The sun was still rising, but it was already hot. Both brothers were sweating through their t-shirts. Jake had been wrong. The lighthouse was a better view in person. It was peaceful.

"I do care. I just can't bring myself to call. I... I don't ever have any updates to share. We used to talk a lot in college, but then I moved out here and every day is the same."

Jake hadn't expected the conversation to get so serious. It seemed to have happened out of nowhere, and it caught him off guard. For years, he'd felt so prepared for every outcome or else avoided anything that could find him in a precarious situation. And then came Lily and Eve and Philip, and now Benny. Some part of him wanted to go back to the way things had been. Wouldn't that be easier?

"So, tell her about that girl Lily. Send her a picture of this lighthouse and tell her how beautiful it looks. Go into the city and buy her a souvenir. You know where she lives. It's about making an effort."

"So just because you make an effort now, you think you can lecture me on making an effort?" Benny turned to look at Jake. Understanding dawned in his eyes, but he stayed silent, perhaps wanting to confirm what Jake was going to say next. "You left for college and barely ever called. Even when you'd fly back in for a visit, you'd find every excuse you could to get out of the house. So don't talk to me about making an effort."

Benny considered this a moment, but seemed to have already thought out an answer. Perhaps he was deciding how to deliver the answer. Would he be calm? Angry? Upset?

"I'm not saying mom's death didn't affect you," he started, calmly, "but maybe it was easier for you to find someone else to take her place because you were younger. You remember the days I lived with you and Beth? Neither of us did much of anything except lay around. Maybe when I left, you realized you needed someone and so you warmed to Beth. Me? I did a lot of bad shit in my first few years of college. It was tough for me, being older than everyone else in my class. Did I ever tell you I almost died?"

Jake shook his head. He'd been angry with Benny for talking about Beth replacing their mother, but he was too curious about what he was saying now to interrupt.

"I was so fucked up on pills I couldn't make out my own hands. I stumbled into the street just as a big van was flying by. It was this close," he touched his left finger to his right elbow, "it scraped my elbow. If I'd gone only a few inches further in that street, I'd probably be dead."

And surely you'd be dead if I had slipped up, Jake thought.

"Anyway, I calmed down after that. I'm not sober or anything, as you saw last night, but I can handle my intake. And when I started working in the industry, I became lonely. You can know everyone there is to know in porn and still somehow wind up a lonely son of a bitch. I called Beth one day to ask about you, and we talked for, hell, like two hours. And then I just kept calling. And one day she tells me you haven't called her in ages, and I start thinking maybe you're lonely too, only a different kind of lonely."

For a quiet moment, they stared together at the lighthouse. It really was beautiful, wasn't it? Until you considered its loneliness. Out there in the water, alone, its only job to guide others to safety, all the while taking the beat of the rain, the slap of the wind, the burn of the sun. Jake imagined another lighthouse only feet away. Two beautiful things, no longer lonely, their lights touching every few rotations to form a burst of bright white.

Jake moved to continue walking along the Hudson. This wasn't the kind of thing you had to respond to. His silence could simply mean he heard what was being said and was reflecting. But he felt like saying one more thing and then hoped the subject would change and they wouldn't come back to it.

"Thanks for looking out for me, but I'm okay. Sure, I get lonely sometimes, but so does everyone. I'll call Beth more. I've been meaning to anyway, really. Maybe I just needed a kick in the ass."

"If there's one thing you can count on me for, it's kicking your ass," Benny said with a smile.

Jake smiled and then went serious and said, "Don't talk about this kind of stuff tonight. With Lily and Eve."

"Of course not, this is brother talk."

"Thank you."

"I've missed you, you know?"

"I know," Jake said. "Me too." And he meant it. He'd known he missed his brother, but he hadn't known until that moment how much he missed him. It was nice to have someone to really talk to. He wasn't honest about his drinking or his vow of celibacy, but he'd never really talked about his loneliness out loud. He'd never talked to anyone about his inability to pick up the phone and call his aunt. These things felt good, and it felt good to hear his brother be open about some of the same stuff. It scared him to hear Benny had almost died. He wondered what day it had been. What if, at the exact moment Sara had moved her mouth toward his penis, Benny had stepped near-blind out into the street? And the moment that Jake told her to stop, the van in the road moved ever-so-slightly away from Benny so that all he was left with was a scraped elbow? He could ask Benny, but that might bring up more questions that Jake still wasn't ready to answer. They continued walking along the Hudson until both of their stomachs started to growl and their mouths started to water for something bubbly. They snuck one last look at the lighthouse, now top-lit instead of front-lit, and they both smiled without knowing why or that the other was doing it. Passersby who saw them smiled too.

***

Sweaty from the terrible heat—and lightly buzzed from lunch and post-lunch drinks—Jake and Benny both showered and readied themselves for Jake's birthday dinner. Jake felt surprisingly calm. Their talk earlier had made him feel better about their night to come. If anything went wrong, he had the feeling Benny could fix it. What else were big brothers for? And besides, what could go wrong? He vaguely remembered his earlier anxiety, but for the life of him, he couldn't figure out now what it was he'd been so anxious about. It felt like when you start to tell someone a dream only to find that you can only remember the grander details. The story you were so excited to tell becomes just another boring dream with little meaning.

They both finished getting ready with some time to kill. They decided to leave for the restaurant early to have a drink at the bar, since Jake still pretended not to have any alcohol around the house. It was a lie that was becoming harder to keep, knowing now that Benny would be the last person to judge him for overindulging from time to time. But now that the lie had been made, Jake couldn't see any way to un-make it. He'd thought about sneaking some into a cabinet and then putting on a show of making it look like he'd just found it by chance, but Benny would see through that even quicker than he'd seen through Jake's bullshit about having talked to Beth recently.

"You know what the worst part about producing porn is?" Benny asked Jake over a drink at the restaurant bar. Jake gave Benny a look that said, *Obviously not.* Benny smiled and continued, "Every time I look at a person, any person, I know immediately if they'd be good in porn or not. It's a curse. I'm always doing it whether I want to or not."

"Do one," Jake said, amused.

"Bartender." Benny pointed at the bartender. He was around Benny's age with a full beard and a bald head. "Perfect for porn. Bet he's got a *Boogie Nights* cock too." Jake winced at the word cock but asked him to do another. "Woman to your right, Louis Vuitton bag, she'd be awful on screen."

"She's beautiful," Jake said after taking a glance at her. She'd seen him looking and gave him a dismissive smile.

"Oh, sure, gorgeous. Probably great in bed even. But not on camera. The bag is a dead giveaway."

"What does it matter who would be good in porn or not? How many people in this room do you think would be willing to do a scene?"

Benny looked at Jake like he was crazy, and then went ahead and asked, "Are you crazy? Remember when we were kids and we'd put on little plays for mom and dad? We told them we wanted to be movie stars. That's what everyone wanted in those days. It's changed now. Everyone wants to be in porn."

"I don't think that's tr—"

"Miss?" Benny said, leaning in front of Jake to talk to the woman with the Louis bag. "Hi, I'm Benny." He stuck out his hand.

"Mary." Benny gave Jake a look that said, *Mary! See, I told you she'd be bad in porn*. Mary shook Benny's hand.

"Look. I'm in from L.A. I run a production company where we mainly produce adult films. I think you're gorgeous and thought you might be interested in screen testing for us sometime." Mary blushed. She was flattered and flustered.

"Oh, I—"

"It's no pressure, just take my card and think about it." Benny reached in his back pocket and pulled out his wallet.

"I don't think I should—"

"Here. Take the card. You can throw it away if you want, burn it. I've got hundreds."

She took the card with a smile and a nod and then went back to her drink.

"See?" Benny said to Jake.

"She took your card, so what?"

"You don't take someone's card if you're not interested."

"Sure you do."

"How about a bet?"

"On what?"

"The card is still sitting there by her drink," he pointed casually at the card, which was indeed by her drink, "I bet you a hundred bucks when she stands up, she tucks it into her purse."

"I'm not betting you a hundred bucks."

"Okay, fine. Just wait and you'll see."

Jake couldn't help but laugh. He tipped his glass toward Benny and took a drink.

Eve arrived first, to Benny's delight. She wore a black midi dress with thin straps. There was a slit in the bottom where her bare leg slipped in and out. She smiled first at Benny who tipped his drink at her. Then she turned to Jake and told him happy birthday. She hugged him. The fabric of her dress felt nice under his fingertips. He found himself wanting to bite the tattoo on her neck. Not hard. Like a playful cat nip. But he restrained himself and pulled out of the hug.

"You look like," Benny paused, taking Eve in, "a martini girl. Can I get you one?"

"Shouldn't we go to a table?" she said.

"Jake's got a lady friend coming." It came out playful, like a father poking fun at his child's first date, but it made Jake freeze. He looked warily at Eve.

"Oh?" she said. She was still smiling, but her eyebrows fluttered. "And who is this?"

Jake stayed silent. Surely, she wouldn't be upset to hear that there was another girl in his life. Until they ran into each other in the city, they'd only had a few conversations, in a hospital no less. And, of course, there was that kiss. That attempt at a kiss. But then why did he get a weird vibe from her? Was it all in his head?

"Elaina," Benny said. Did he get it wrong on purpose so Jake would have to speak?

"Lily," Jake corrected, taking the potential bait. "She used to go to my church."

"Oooh, a church girl," Eve said. She was looking at Benny when she said this, as if it was an inside joke they both had. "Can't wait to meet her." This again seemed genuine, but Jake felt uncomfortable. "And I'm more of a tequila drinker," she said to Benny.

Before Benny could get the attention of the bartender, Lily entered the restaurant. She had on a red dress with white flowers sprinkled about. Her hair was perfectly straight and tickled her half-exposed shoulders. She wore red lipstick and a touch of dark blue eye shadow. Jake turned to face the bar before she could spot him. He finished what was left of his drink and wished there was more. He turned back around to see Lily looking right at him, smiling.

"Happy birthday," she said, and came in for a hug. Her dress, too, felt nice. Her neck, too, he wanted to playfully bite. And when she let go, Benny was ready with his hand out, leaving no time for Jake to introduce Benny himself.

"Benny," he said, "Jake's older brother."

"Lily." She shook Benny's hand but looked at him with much less enthusiasm than Eve had in the hospital. It wasn't a look of indignation, only of indifference. Instead, she grinned at Jake, this time as if it were he and her that had the inside joke. Jake tried to remember what all he had told her about Benny. Could it be that she already didn't care for him despite having just met him? Or was he again misreading everything? He almost choked when Lily spotted

Eve beside Benny with her hand up in a half-wave.

"I'm Eve," she said.

"Lily," Lily said politely.

"Lily," Benny said, "you look like a martini girl to me." Eve laughed and shook her head. "Can I get you a martini?"

"I'll take a beer," Lily said.

Eve said, "Zero for two," and Benny rolled his eyes. "We should get our table anyway, unless Jake is expecting any other girls?"

Lily looked at Jake and then at Eve. He could see it dawn on her that Eve wasn't necessarily here with Benny. Here were two girls that Jake wasn't romantically involved with—at least not outside of his sick head—wondering why, how, who, what. Or, as he'd been wondering all night, was this all in his mind? Mere months ago, he didn't have even one woman in his life, and now here he was wondering if these two beautiful women were interested in him. He didn't even want one woman to be interested in him. He wanted to leave the restaurant and go home and curl up into a little ball in his living room with a glass in one hand and an endless bottle of whiskey in the other hand. He wanted to call Kendall and tell her she was fired and go back to preaching things he didn't believe in. He wanted his life back. His life before Lily, before Eve; before Benny came back into it.

He also wondered why Benny had put it that way. He'd said it like a joke, but hadn't he known it was out of line? Benny was the one that had begged Jake to invite women, and now here they were, presumably uncomfortable because of the implication that Jake was interested in both of them. Was he just being an asshole? Or was it his weird way of becoming the center of attention. If it was the latter, Jake didn't mind, given he'd rather the attention be away from himself.

"Excuse me," Benny said to the hostess, interrupting Jake's internal panic attack, "we're ready to be seated."

They were brought to a corner table where Jake and Benny slid into the center seats, Eve beside Benny and Lily beside Jake. Benny ordered their drinks. He didn't bother to ask what kind of tequila or what kind of beer Eve or Lily wanted. He didn't ask Jake if he'd like the scotch that he ordered the both of them. He was confident in his choices and no one corrected him. Jake noticed that Lily was sitting close to him. So close he could feel her leg bouncing softly next to his. And then an image of Lily Scarlett flashed in his head. A blue satin robe. Water and semen and vomit.

"Excuse me," Jake said to Lily. He thought he might throw up, so he couldn't elaborate as to why he needed to get out of the booth. As she was rising, he nearly shoved her over trying to get past her. He ran to the bathroom and into a stall, getting immediately onto his knees. He retched and nothing came out. He could feel hot bile in his stomach trying to shove itself out of him, and yet still nothing came.

When he returned to the table, he tried to smile as if everything was normal. Just a normal booth exit. Just a normal trip to the bathroom. Nothing weird here. Lily rose again and Jake slid back into the booth. Benny was talking animatedly about something that happened on his flight in. Eve was listening intently; Lily was sipping her beer. Jake knew he should say something. If he was silent long enough, someone was bound to notice and ask him about it. He looked at Lily. She smiled at him behind her beer glass. He tried to think of a bit to get her started on since it would get him talking, and then she would take it away from there. He was thinking through options in his head when Lily spoke.

She said, "You think they have hot dogs here?"

Now Eve was talking to Benny animatedly about something that happened to her at work.

"I don't think this place is nice enough for hot dogs," Jake said. He had to get out of his head, and joking around felt like the only escape.

"Good thing I brought my own." She gestured to her purse. "That thing is stuffed full of loose hot dogs."

"That's smart. I have to keep them in my pockets, and they usually end up smushed."

"If you're nice, maybe I'll sneak you one later."

"It is my birthday after all," Jake said.

"Right. So, I should probably just run off without saying goodbye."

This stung a little, but Jake knew it was all in good fun. He said, "Yeah, exactly. It's an expert move, really."

Joking with Lily always seemed to calm Jake down. He liked seeing her smile. He liked the sound of her laugh. He also liked that their conversations typically didn't make it far past hot dogs.

"So, Lily, what do you do?" Eve said from across the table. It surprised Jake and Lily, both having assumed Eve and Benny were still chatting away over on their side. Jake was also surprised to realize he had no idea what Lily did. All this time they'd been getting to know each other, and he hadn't bothered to ask her what she did for a job.

"I'm in advertising," Lily said, then immediately asked, "What do you do?"

"I'm a nurse. I—"

"And you?" Lily interrupted, looking at Benny. Jake lifted his glass for a drink.

"I," he paused, eyeing his attentive listeners, "produce adult entertainment."

The table was silent for a moment. Eve and Lily seemed to share a look. Jake took another drink.

"So, porn," Lily said. It wasn't a question, more a clarification, as if to say, *Just because we're women doesn't mean you need to sugarcoat it.*

"Sure, porn."

"Full-length films? Eight-minute blow jobs?"

Benny smiled at her and said, "Well, when I started out, I was doing longer films. Internet porn was around but very different from the stuff on today."

"How so?" Eve asked. Were the ladies ganging up on him?

"Well, now producers have to compete with the self-released content. Makes our job harder, but the industry safer. I won't lie to you when I say I saw some fucked-up stuff, but things are getting a whole lot better now. Any big production house, at least any I've been involved with lately, has people on staff dedicated to making the sets a safe place for all involved. Anyone becomes uncomfortable, we assess the situation and shut it down if need be."

"And what was the fucked-up stuff you saw?" Lily asked.

Benny looked down at his hands. It was the first time since his visit that Jake had seen him lose his air of confidence. There was something like fear or regret in his eyes. He sighed, looked back up, and smiled again, "I'd rather not talk about that. A person is not the industry they work in. I've always put the people before the money, and that's what I attribute any success I have to."

"Fair enough," Lily said. She seemed bored, as if she'd heard that story many times before. Jake looked at Eve, who was smiling softly at Benny.

"Wonder if I've seen anything you've done," Eve said.

"I don't know. I'll have to sit you down and show you some of my work sometime."

The flirtatiousness in his voice made the bile rise again in Jake's belly. Their interaction had gone far past polite chatter. How could he have misread things so badly that day in the city? Seeing her flirting now made him realize how wrong he had been to assume she was flirting with him that day. She had said she wasn't looking for anything serious, and maybe, with Benny, she didn't see anything serious at all.

"How about you, Jake?" Lily said. "Have you seen anything your brother has made?" Benny laughed loudly at this question and tried to hide it behind a drink.

"Ha ha, let's all make fun of the guy that can't watch porn."

"Can't or won't?" Benny said.

"Won't," Lily answered. It surprised Jake that Lily was siding with Benny, given the way she had just scrutinized his career choice. "Jake's celibate?" she said to Eve, who looked mildly confused. Lily herself looked confused, as if she'd thought Benny and Eve would both have known this. Jake closed his eyes. He hadn't told Benny about his vow of celibacy. He hadn't planned on ever telling him.

"Celibate?" Benny asked. "Like you've never…"

"You've never…" Eve repeated.

"Oh, I…" Lily stopped. She looked apologetically at Jake.

"Are you waiting for marriage or something?" Benny asked.

In this moment, Jake wanted to be dead more than anything. That moment of release he would feel if someone another table over stood up and shot him directly in the head. How nice to be filleted with the branzino in the kitchen. Or for the rapture to come and suck him up into the heaven, the existence of which he'd so frequently denied. Even hell might be better than here.

Benny, sensing his discomfort, said, "Ah, it doesn't matter. It's your birthday, let's celebrate." He hailed the waiter over and asked for a shot for each of them. This excited Eve and elicited a sound of disgust from Lily. When they were delivered to the table, however, all four of them did the shot without complaint. At some point, their food came, and everyone ate and talked with their mouths full. There was no more talk of Jake's vow or his profession. Benny must have broken the seal when he'd told them what he did for work, because suddenly he had story after story of various shoots and parties and awards shows he'd been to over the years. He had the whole table—yes, even Jake and Lily—laughing and cringing and wide-eyed.

At some point, after they had ordered a bottle of what Benny called dessert wine but was really just a bottle of wine opened after dinner, Benny kicked Jake under the table. At first, he thought it had been Lily, but she was looking off into the distance, in her own world for a moment. He looked to Benny who was jerking his head back toward the bar. Jake shifted his gaze to the bar where he saw the woman they had spoken to earlier getting up from her seat. They watched in anticipation as she gathered her things, the card sitting unmoved by her napkin. Jake had no doubt she would take it. Benny knew things about the world that Jake had never even begun to understand. Jake knew how to engage a crowd of proud Christians, how to order from a menu at a diner, and how to drink. He did not know how to interact with women, not really. He did not know what the inside of an airplane looked like. Or what the inside of a woman felt like. The woman at the bar started to walk away, hesitated, reached toward the card, and then pulled her arm back. She shook her head softly and smiled to herself. Then she turned and walked out of the restaurant, leaving the card sitting next to the napkin. Jake looked to Benny, confused. Benny just smiled, shrugged, and raised his eyebrows in a way that said: *You should have taken the bet.*

"What are you two staring at?" Lily asked.

"Jake doesn't believe most people want to be desired."

"That's not true at all."

"I could've told you that," Lily said to Benny. Again, she'd meant this as a joke, but she'd never brought another person into a joke like this. Was she drunk? Would Benny ask her to elaborate? Jake knew he needed to change the subject quickly.

"It's Friday night," he said, "should we go out to another bar?"

"We're in," Benny said, speaking for himself and Eve. Eve

nodded.

"You sure you can handle it?" Lily said in a whisper. Jake nodded, though he wasn't really sure about anything anymore. She shrugged and said, louder, "Let's do it."

***

They ended up at a pub in Sleepy Hollow. Eve said they made the strongest drinks in the area. How Jake and Benny had ended up in Sleepy Hollow a third time this trip Jake had no idea. And as drunk as he had become, it hadn't slipped his mind that they were there at night. Although the town was close by and it was certainly possible some of his congregation lived there, he was grateful to have gone somewhere out of town. He didn't mind drinking at Ava's or another restaurant where he could be seen, but he did mind being *drunk* where his members could see. He would have preferred drinking at home alone, where even Benny and Eve and Lily couldn't guess at his alcohol problem, but this was at least better than drinking in Tarrytown.

Eve and Benny were each drinking a scotch and soda—Benny's choice—Lily was drinking a beer, and Jake had ordered a whiskey on the rocks. Benny had ordered them shots of Jameson when they walked in, but Lily asked if she could make hers a Car Bomb, explaining that she looked it up and all you had to do to make it less offensive was to drop the 'Irish'. So instead, Benny asked for four Car Bombs. The bartender rolled her eyes but made them the requested drinks. They all dropped the shots into the beer and drank quickly and with apparent ease.

Benny had his hand on Eve's lower back as they talked. She just let him have it there, as if it was meant to be there, as if they hadn't just met a day ago. As he often did when he'd had enough drinks, he fantasized about what his life could be like if he'd chosen a different path, or rather if a different path had been granted to him. He imagined himself living in the East Village or maybe in a trendy neighborhood in Brooklyn. He imagined going to coffee shops and bars, meeting girls and being smooth with them like Benny was. He imagined calling home to his mom and dad, both aged and retired now, and telling them about his week. He imagined how proud they would be of him, of Benny, of their two kids they'd gotten to see grow into adults.

"Where are you right now?"

Jake blinked. The bar came into view. He'd been so deep in his fantasy he'd been nearly dreaming. His mouth was slightly open, and a small bit of drool had escaped the side of it. He wiped it quickly as he thought of a response to Lily's question.

"A bar," Jake said. Stupid. Stupid stupid stupid.

"Very funny," Lily said. "But I mean it. Where were you?"

"What do you mean?"

"You were just so zoned out that I thought you might be sleeping with your eyes open. What were you thinking about?"

Jake didn't have the energy to think of a lie, so he started with a partial truth. "My other life."

"And what's it like there?"

"Better than here."

"Oh God, is this one of those existential birthday crises?" Lily said. Jake chuckled, but then Lily must have sensed there was more for him to say, so she said, "What's so wrong with here?" Jake stared at Benny and Eve, and Lily understood, or thought she did. "Do you like her?"

"Huh?" he said, looking back at Lily.

"Eve, do you like her?"

"Oh. I don't know."

"In your other life, is she there?"

"No."

"Am I there?" This conversation was getting far past hot dogs. Jake didn't like it. Then again, it was nice to talk to her like this, even if it wasn't something he would have done sober.

"No," he said. Then, "Maybe. Do you ever wonder what your life would be like if things had gone differently?"

"All the time."

"I sometimes wonder what I would have become if my parents hadn't died. If I hadn't..."

"Hadn't what?"

"Anyway, I wonder how different I would be if I had gone down a different path. What if I was a teacher or a writer or an actor? What if I worked for an ad agency or as a train conductor? Where would I be living? Would I have a girlfriend or a wife? Would it be you? Eve? Someone I've never even met?"

"You know you could have that life. You don't have to keep living this one if you don't like it."

"I can bring my parents back?"

"You know that's not what I meant." Lily put her hand on Jake's leg.

"Jakey!" Benny had risen from his seat. Eve had risen from her own and was grabbing her purse. "I'm going to stay over at Evie's place tonight. I left my card for the drinks, get whatever the hell you want birthday boy. I'll call you tomorrow, yeah?"

Jake didn't respond. He just forced a smile and gave a little nod. Eve hugged him and said goodbye. They walked out of the bar, leaving Jake drunk and alone with Lily.

Jake thought back on the chain of events that allowed this to happen. He went back to the day he stood awkwardly by the door to Philip's hospital room, Eve pushing past him with the ease of someone who'd done it a million times before. He thought of the day she texted him that Philip had been put into a coma. Jake still wasn't sure if he'd caused the worsening of Philip's sickness. He thought back to the day he ran into Eve in the city. She'd fixed his anxiety and inner turmoil with only conversation and her presence. And what if Philip hadn't been awakened yesterday? She never would have met Benny. She never would have known it was Jake's birthday. He wouldn't have had to be in this very situation that he was in. Although isn't all that bullshit? Shouldn't he be blaming himself? If he had told her he was interested in her, maybe things would have gone differently. Or else if he could truly control himself, like he thought he'd been doing all of these years, the snake tattoo on her neck would have been nothing but a splash of black ink and a comical metaphor. Eve. Snake. How could he have missed it? Did he need to see her bite into an apple to figure it out? And now here he was alone again with Lily, whose name was shared with only one other in Jake's mind. How could he have missed the true significance of this, too? O' Lily Scarlett. She'd been here all this time, haunting him, taunting him, tempting him. And it was his fault for being too easily tempted. All of this was his fault and here he sat still unsure of who or what to blame. Is that narcissism or just weakness? What would Job do? All things in Christianity really seem to go back to Job, the poster boy for faith. But maybe the point had been different all along. Maybe Job was an example of what not to do. He gets everything back in the end of the story, but he still has to live with the scars and the trauma that came with the brutality of his God. What if this was a lesson that the devil was, in the end, at the very least not a hypocrite? The devil is what he is, and God is what he says he isn't.

"Are you crying?"

Jake looked to Lily but could only see a blurry shape through the tears in his eyes.

O' God, I'm so tired.

O' God, I'm so sick.

O' God, can't this be the end?

"Is it because of her?" she asked, pointing to the door that Benny and Eve had exited only a minute ago. Had it really only been that long? Jake shook his head and wiped at his eyes, but more tears came. "What is it?" Lily asked. And instead of waiting for his answer, she came toward him and wrapped her arms around him. He nestled his head into her neck and continued to cry.

"Why can't I be more like him?" he sobbed into her neck.

"You don't want to be like him."

He finished crying and pulled away from Lily. "Sorry," he said, "I think I'm just drunk."

"It's brave to cry," Lily said.

"That's just what people say to make criers less embarrassed."

Lily laughed and said, "Yeah. Maybe." Lily turned to the bartender and said something that Jake didn't catch, but then only moments later, she was setting two shots down in front of Lily. "Here. This will help," she said, handing him one of the shots. They took them together and Jake still didn't feel better. Seeing this, Lily said, "Have I told you why I'm really here in Tarrytown?"

Jake shook his head and, more than anything, just wanted to jump off of his seat and head out the door. But something kept him there. Maybe it was because, even in this state, he couldn't leave Lily alone like that again.

"My mom got sick. And she never remarried after my dad left, so I had to come home to help take care of her. Truth is I had stopped calling her years ago. I'd hear from her every once in a while, I'd spend the occasional Christmas with her, but I couldn't be bothered to click on my phone and call her, or jump on a train for a surprise visit. Then, when she got sick, I immediately started researching nursing homes. I even visited one. I didn't tell her; I just went. There was this old woman there who saw me, and her face lit up. 'Bobbie, is that you?' she said. 'Oh my God, Bobbie, I've missed you so much.' Tears started streaming down her face. And then I found myself crying—crying is brave, remember—and I knew I couldn't just leave her in a place like that.

"When I moved back, I struggled a lot at first. She was getting sicker, and I didn't know what the fuck I was doing. So, I came into the church looking for... something. I didn't expect to find faith, but strength or hope maybe. Instead, I found you. A friend. And you might disagree, but friendship, love, companionship—these things are better than faith in something intangible."

Jake leaned in and kissed her. It didn't feel like their first kiss, rather like something he'd been doing all his life with Lily. She tasted sweet like whiskey.

Lily pulled away. "Are you... what about..." Jake put his hand softly around the back of her neck and pulled her back into him. They kissed like this a long time. And at some point, they were in a cab together on their way to Jake's apartment. And then Jake was searching around Benny's bag for a condom. And then they were naked in Jake's bed. Even when they were done and lying together quietly, Jake didn't care what happened the next day. He was no longer willing to let anyone but himself have control over his life. There was no more Lily Scarlett, no more naked shapes bouncing in the rain. He would live his life how he wanted, regardless of the consequences.

CHAPTER SEVENTEEN

The next morning, he and Lily had sex again. Before now, he'd thought the only truly effective hangover cure was whiskey, but ejaculation was coming in at a very close second. He hardly felt the after-effects of last night's imbibement. Nor did he feel any sort of remorse or anxiety about what he and Lily had now done twice. On the floor beside him lay the strings that had held him so long. Once strong and taut, lying there on the floor flaccid, they looked so weak, so flimsy. Had they really controlled him so long? Could that be possible?

Lily was snoring lightly on Jake's chest, his arm around her bare body. It was still early, and Jake, too, considered going back to sleep, but the excitement of the night before and his sudden revelation that none of this mattered kept him wide awake. He wondered what Benny and Eve were doing at that moment. Had they, too, slept together? Would it be naive to think that they hadn't? Now that Jake and Lily had had sex, did that make them a couple? Even with her lying there on him, he couldn't help but picture what Eve would look like naked. What would her breasts look like? What would it feel like inside of her?

"Jesus, ready to go again already?" Lily said half-asleep.

"Sorry," Jake said.

"Oh no, I take it as a compliment." She grabbed hold of it but didn't move her hand. She held it until it eventually went soft. Jake wondered if she fell back to sleep. "Do you have any coffee?" she said into his chest after a while. Jake shook his head, to which Lily looked up to see which way he was shaking it. She huffed. "What kind of adult doesn't have coffee in their house?"

"I never cared for it."

"Don't tell me you're one of those I-don't-need-stimulants-to-wake-up-in-the-morning people." Jake thought of all the mornings he took a swig straight out of a liquor bottle. He thought of the drawer in his office. Instead of answering, he just shrugged. Lily groaned softly. It was an intimate kind of groan. One he didn't think she would have made around him even a day ago.

"There's a 7-Eleven a couple blocks up. I could go get us some coffee." *Us.* Using that word made Jake feel good.

"Would you really?"

"Sure."

"If you do that, I'll let you do anything you want to me when you get back." She said it the way she often said jokes, but Jake got the impression she wasn't fully joking. Could this be his life now? One where someone lets him do anything he wants, within reason, to them?

He walked to the 7-Eleven to grab the coffee. The sky was shining blue, and it looked like it would be a beautiful day. His phone buzzed in his pocket. Instead of feeling a pang of fear, he felt a sense of calm wash over him. It could be spam. It could be the church administration calling, unanswered, for the thousandth time. It could be Beth, calling to say happy birthday. She'd forgotten to call him the day before, though she often mixed the day of his birthday up since Benny's was the day after, only two months later. He let it buzz as he went into the 7-Eleven. He didn't look at it as he left holding two coffees in his hands, one hot, one cold, since he wasn't sure what Lily would prefer. He didn't look at the phone until he got back into his apartment and set them down.

Benny had called. When Jake didn't answer, he'd sent him a text that said: 'How did last night go??' Jake smiled. No one died. No one got hurt. He'd had sex, not once but twice, and everything was just fine.

He brought the coffees into the bedroom to a very delighted Lily, who grabbed the hot coffee and chugged more than Jake could have thought possible given how hot the cup had felt on his hand. She pulled him back into bed with her, where they lay and talked together. Eventually, as morning pillow talk often does, the conversation turned to kissing and then quickly to a third round of lovemaking.

***

It was Saturday. Benny didn't leave until Monday. Jake wasn't sure what to do with Benny for the remainder of their time together, and he so badly wanted to spend more time with Lily, so he was relieved when Benny texted him that morning—coffees resting on the side tables of Jake's bed—'Eve and I want to go into the city. You and Lily down?' Just seeing Eve's name on the phone made Jake's heart start beating more quickly. Why was he so nervous? He'd gotten exactly what he wanted with Lily and, at least for the time being, it didn't feel like it was going away. So why did Eve make him feel this way? Was it that failed kiss? Was it just a lingering obsession? He looked at Lily, who had fallen asleep again beside him, and smiled. Looking at her, he knew whatever the feeling was would go away. He had no real feelings for Eve beyond attraction. Attraction, that tempting little thing, could not compete with love.

"What are you staring at me for?" Lily said quietly.

"Is the whole hot dog bit going to finally be over?" Jake asked. "I mean, now that you've gotten in my pants, it can stop now, right?"

Lily seemed to ponder this for a moment. "We'll see," she said, her pretty eyes revealing themselves under sleepy eyelids. "Mostly, I'm just trying to not make a dick joke. Dicks. Hot dogs. Boring."

"You could never be boring."

Lily wrinkled her nose like she was disgusted at the comment, but she couldn't hide the smile underneath.

"Benny and Eve want to go into the city. Are you up for it?"

She made some incomprehensible sound, something between a groan and a dying goat, and then said, "But what if I wanted to sleep all day?"

"And miss spending time with me?"

"If you're really putting yourself up against sleep, you're going to lose that battle."

"Fair enough," Jake said. He settled back into the bed as if he was going to go back to sleep as well. The room went quiet. And then suddenly, he popped up and lightly dug his fingers into Lily's sides. When was the last time he had tickled someone? When was the last time he'd been tickled? Lily squealed. Lily laughed. Lily hit out at him with deadly fists. And soon enough they were kissing again. Jake didn't have it in him for another round, but kissing, just the kissing, was more than enough.

***

It was early in the afternoon before the four of them made it to Grand Central. Lily had gone home to change into new clothes, jean shorts, and a tucked-in white tee. Benny had the same pants on but had apparently taken a New York Islanders t-shirt from Eve's house. It was big, even on Benny, and it gave him a childish quality that Jake had never, even when they were children, seen. Even when he was messing around like a child, Jake hadn't been able to picture him that way. He was always the older brother. Eve wore long jeans and a black tank top. Was it just him, or did the snake tattoo look faded today? Sun-worn? Maybe even a little smaller?

They took the subway downtown and went to a late lunch at this place that Lily knew. They served mac and cheese egg rolls that Lily said they all had to try. They even split the egg rolls into four pieces, the perfect number. They dipped their treats into the rame-kin of cheese one by one and held them out to the center of the table as if they were knights touching each other's swords. Benny said, "To deep fryers," and the rest of the table repeated before biting into the crunchy, cheesy, greasy egg rolls. All of their eyes lit up with delight as the flavors hit their mouths. They sipped at their mimosas to wash the taste down, and Jake tried not to think about how much he'd been aching for that sip. And he tried not to think about how in the middle of the meal, when the waitress asked if anyone would like another mimosa, he was the only one that said yes. Sensing his unease, Benny changed his mind and ordered another as well with a, "What the hell. Why not?" Jake shrugged this away. After all, what's two mimosas? Nothing wrong with a few lunch drinks.

After lunch, the group wandered around the city. They took Benny to the typical touristy spots: Times Square, the Bethesda Fountain in Central Park, Rockefeller Center. Eventually, they took a train downtown to Washington Square Park and then walked down to the World Trade Center. These were all things Jake had done, but now he wondered how long it had been since he'd really seen the city in this way. For so long, he'd used the city as a place to blend in with the crowd while he refilled his duffel. Had he forgotten how beautiful it could really be?

Benny flirted with both Eve and Lily, though his flirting with

Lily leaned toward friendly banter, while with Eve, he really turned on the charm. They'd stop periodically to kiss, and Jake wondered if he should be doing the same thing with Lily. To Jake, she seemed indifferent, but then he'd never been good at reading romantic situations. Once, looking over the falls of water where the Twin Towers once stood, he put his arm around Lily and pulled her close. She leaned into him. He wondered if this was appropriate, this show of affection at the spot where so much death had happened.

Death.

Had anyone died last night? Where that morning he'd been so sure the curse was broken, unease now crept its way up his body like a hairy spider. Had a God that he didn't believe in attached the strings once more? Had they still been limp on the floor as he and Lily left to go to the train station? He removed his arm from around Lily and checked his phone. Nothing. No calls. No texts. Relief flooded into him, and then so did that unease. They cycled like that as the four of them headed to a cocktail bar. This constant cycling led to a state of nausea, a sort of sea sickness in the concrete jungle.

Cocktails helped. And then the beers after that. And before he knew it, Jake was happy again, no more nausea, only drinks and laughter and—

Kisses. Many kisses. His trepidation at public affection left him completely by the time they had eaten dinner and gone out to another bar. He kissed Lily in-between sips of his whiskey. She kissed him back. She was a good kisser, though Jake didn't have a lot to compare it to. He didn't ever want to stop kissing. He couldn't believe there was a time in his life when he hadn't been kissing anything but liquor bottles to his lips.

***

Jake did not remember making it home. He did not remember pulling out his hidden stash to share with the rest of them. He did not know Eve had only had a few drinks. Benny and Lily only a few drinks more than that. He did not remember the confusion on Benny's face when Jake opened one of his hidden bottles and drank directly from it. Nor the look of disgust when he began to throw it all back up into the toilet.

What he remembered was dreaming that he and Lily were naked and curled up together on the largest bed he had ever seen. His head was on her chest, and she was petting him. There were no sounds. Not even the sound of their breathing. He looked up at Lily and smiled. She smiled back. And then suddenly he felt her pulling away from him. Jake was being sucked into the mattress, grasping for Lily, wordlessly trying to shout out to her. Until suddenly there was only black.

CHAPTER EIGHTEEN

Jake sat in his office, not entirely sure he was there. He could physically see his desk, his computer, his secret cabinet, but he couldn't fully feel himself there. It seemed as if his entire self was only a pair of floating eyes. He saw the time on his computer. He needed to get out to the stage to perform his sermon. What would he say? He tried to sort through some old sermons, but his fingers couldn't perform the task.

Miraculously, his fingers found his cross necklace hanging, apparently, around nothing at all. Invisible arms and hands moved the key to the locked drawer and drew out a half-empty bottle of whiskey. With lips he didn't feel, he sipped the burning liquid. With a throat, *Was it a throat?* he swallowed. A pulse of what felt like a heart illuminated him like neon, but only for a moment. In one flash, he saw his arms and legs and feet, and in another, they were gone again. He took another drink, and then another, until the shining neon of his body became nearly whole. And, when he felt strength enough to do so, he lifted his head to gaze to the doorway he would need to walk through in order to make it to the stage.

Were his eyes lying, or was there a shape there in the doorway? Certainly, there was a shadow of something, but he couldn't fully tell if it was human or if it was the devil or the spirit of God come down to stare into his fading soul. But the whiskey working its way through his body, his eyes eventually focused, and he saw the outline of a tall, suited man. He had a Bible in one hand, his other affixed to the space where his lips would otherwise be.

"You're fonder," the man said. Or, was it, "You're finished here?" Jake couldn't be sure. He took another sip of the whiskey, hoping the figure would disappear.

"Did you hear me?" the man said. Jake shook his head. "I said you're finished here. You'll go up there today and tell them all you have decided to leave and pursue your faith elsewhere. You'll be vague about it. I'll arrange for someone else to step in for you for the remainder of the sermon. As I understand it, Barry has something on hand each week in case someone gets sick."

Jake still couldn't be sure he was hearing all of this right, but feeling revived and alert, now he knew what he needed to do. He'd been a coward. The moment the administration had asked him to fire Kendall, he should have acted. One way or another.

He nodded to the man, who walked off in a blink, and placed the whiskey back in the drawer. Before he could close it, his eyes flashed upon his mother's Bible. He pulled it out and opened it for the first time since her death. In it, he found highlighted passages and, within the margins, numerous questions. *What kind of God would have such ire? Are all sins created equal? Can Benny and Jacob truly be saved?* His own mother, a picture of faith, had doubts in nearly every page of her Bible. At the end of the book of Job, she'd written only a phrase: *God is cruel.* Could it be that she, too, was losing her faith? Were these questions and statements written after the death of his father or even before that? Why had she appeared to believe so voraciously when all of these thoughts had been going through her head? He thought of the time his mother had slapped Benny. Was it really Benny she wanted to slap, or was it herself?

Jake took the Bible with him as he left the room, feeling nearly sober with determination. When he made his way onto the stage, he saw his brother staring at him with a concerned smile. Next to him were Eve and Lily, the latter of whom shrugged when she saw Jake looking at her. He barely remembered pulling himself out of bed that morning, but he thought he'd remembered Lily being asleep in his bed when he left. Benny and Eve asleep in the living room. Only a few days ago, their presence would have filled him with dread, but now he felt almost heightened by it.

"Good morning," Jake said when he made it to the podium. His greeting was returned by the dozens. The words were muted and mangled through mouths full of donuts and coffee. He looked to the back of the room, where the suited shape was staring at him with blazing red eyes. Jake nodded to himself, aware of the long silence he was adding between his greeting and the words that would follow.

"I have some bittersweet news for you all this morning. Effective today, I will no longer be leading this congregation." There were soft gasps and murmurs throughout the room. Benny cocked his head and frowned. Lily beamed. "But before I go, I'd like to deliver one last sermon. One about the Church. Not just this one. The grand Church, all Churches, our religion." The eyes in the back of the room blazed brighter but moved no closer.

"To make my point, let's talk about the big ones, megachurches." He took the microphone off the stand and started pacing back and forth, his mother's Bible still held firmly in his other hand. "Did you know most megachurch leaders never even go to Bible school? No. They study communications, marketing, journalism. They're not worried about God, they're worried about money. Yet, they preach to believers just like you about the unimportance of material wealth. They align themselves with a political party who actively promotes hate against people of color, people in the LGBTQ community. They make millions, tens of millions, some hundreds of millions. And do you want to know what the worst part is? What the point of all of this is? Their success is nothing compared to the larger, all-encompassing *Church*.

"Since pretty much the beginning of time, churches have only wanted one thing. Power. Expansion. That's the only reason they exist. It's the only reason Christianity has more followers than any other religion. It's not because we're *right*. It's because we murdered, we fought, we forced our way into villages and told people they would burn for an eternity in hell if they didn't believe the bullshit we were telling them."

Jake wasn't sure where he would go with this speech. He took in the faces in the crowd in front of him. The horror on them made him want to keep going, to talk forever. He looked down at Benny, who looked like he was watching a boxing match, his face alit with glee and almost glowing with adrenaline. Eve looked confused but interested. Lily continued to beam.

"My point is the Church doesn't exist for you. The Church exists for the same reason Facebook or Apple or Google exists: to make money. Trust me when I say that's all this particular church cares about." The administrator in the back made a move toward the stage, but Jake put his hand out toward him and shook his head. "Weeks ago, I preached about acceptance. That very same day, our beloved Youth Pastor, Kendall, brought her girlfriend to the church. You all probably connected those dots. And the truly beautiful thing is that you all accepted her." He paused a long time. "You did. You all did. I have to say it surprised me.

"I haven't believed a word I've preached you in months. Maybe I never believed. But that day, you all seemed almost nonplussed, as if you'd already known and didn't care one way or the other, and I have to say it strengthened my faith for a moment. Only a moment.

Because shortly thereafter, I received a call from the administrators of the church. The old white fucks that run this place, that own me. They asked me to fire Kendall. They shot off something about the members being uncomfortable about it, but I know what the real problem was: money. *Maybe* some members would be upset. *Maybe* we would lose a few bad eggs. And we can't afford that, can we?"

Jake took a deep breath and felt himself about to say something he wasn't planning to say. He'd meant this to be an attack on the church and a warning for its ignorant congregation that none of them actually mattered to their church. But now something more personal bubbled up within him, and he had to belch it out.

"When I was a kid, week after week, I'd watch my mother scribble away in this very Bible." He held the Bible up high so all could see. "I watched her with fascination as she—" Jake became aware that the audio on his microphone had been cut. Not a problem. He began to yell, "I watched her with fascination as she nodded along to our pastor and wrote along the margins of the Book. What could she be writing? What had moved her so much she felt compelled to write it down?

"I opened this Book for the first time today, well after her death, and I found that all she really had were questions. Just questions. She wasn't moved by what our pastor was saying, she was confused by it. And what's worse? That confusion passed on to me. I was just a kid when my father died. I was still a kid when my mother died. And as a young kid who'd done what he thought were bad things, I thought it was *my* fault." Jake was vaguely aware of tears filling his eyes but didn't care. "This Bible right here. This made me believe that everything had happened because God was punishing *me*. And that trauma followed me all the way to today. Literally, today. I can't spend more than a few hours without having a drink. Maybe you all knew that. Maybe you could all smell it on me and just brushed it off as a silly cliché. Well, I think that's a cliché for a reason. Pastors—priests—can't cope with the fact that all they do for a living is spread lies and false hope and fear. They need a drink. Maybe they need the comforting touch of a *child*. Should I go deeper?"

The administrator was rushing toward the stage now, and Jake knew he wouldn't fight back. So instead, he finished with one last yell. "This church doesn't care about you!"

Jake ran off the stage before the administrator could grab him. He'd caused enough of a scene already; he didn't need people to watch him fight and struggle against this old man. And besides, he'd made his point. He only wished he could have made the same point to his second service. No doubt word of his sermon would reach anyone who'd missed it, but would it make as much of an impact hearing it secondhand? And as he walked back to his office to grab his things, he started to doubt whether he'd made an impact at all.

As he was packing his things—he didn't have one of those boxes with handles like they always use in the movies; all he had was an old Amazon box and some plastic grocery bags—the administrator again came to the doorway of Jake's office. Even now that his hangover had ebbed, the man still appeared to be a shadow in the doorway. Jake couldn't make out his face, nor the color of his suit or tie. He said some things that Jake didn't hear. What Jake could hear was the anger in the man's voice, and this made him very happy. His speech had at had at least angered the person he'd wanted to be angered the most.

Jake stood and pretended to listen until the man stormed off. He received a text from Lily telling him to meet them at Ava's. He thought of the beer that would be waiting for him there. How nice that would feel on his tired, scratchy throat. How his headache, returning now, would slowly disappear with each eager sip. He thought of Lily and her hot dogs. He smiled.

As Jake headed toward Ava's, his car now full of the things from his office, his phone buzzed next to him. It was Lily.

"Hello," he said into the phone. The voice on the other end was crying.

"It's Ava," Lily said through deafening sniffles, "she died last night."

"Lily, what?"

"Thomas is here. He's trying to clear out the restaurant. I think he might be drunk."

"Ok. I'm on my way."

Lily continued to cry without hanging up, so Jake ended the call. He pulled his car over to the side of the road. He stared at the sky. It was cloudless and sunny. Why is the sun allowed to shine so beautifully when people are in mourning? In movies, it was always ugly and raining when people died; why couldn't it be that way in real life?

Jake felt calm. He felt collected. He—Jake smashed his fists into the steering wheel. He punched the window next to him, the console on the other side. He kicked and flailed and screamed. He screamed until his throat felt raw and blistered. When he was done screaming, he cried.

A quarter of an hour ago, he'd felt certain that he'd been wrong about his curse. He'd felt sure that all of it came down to coincidence and toxic faith. Only it happened again. He said to hell with it all and gave in to the temptation he'd been avoiding since childhood, and now someone else close to him died as a result.

No. Not as a result.

Yes. It's your fault.

It can't be my fault. She'd been sick. Thomas said it himself.

And she would have gotten better if you hadn't shed your strings, little puppet.

No!

Jake pulled out his phone and Googled "Lily Scarlet Makes

Breakfast in a Satin Robe." He was surprised to find it still existed. The quality was abysmal but watchable. He unzipped his pants and grabbed his penis.

"It's not my fault," he screamed at his phone and his cock. He pumped and pumped and pumped and pumped and pumped. "It's not my fault," he said again, more weakly this time. And as Lily Scarlet took the man's penis in her mouth, that wonderful feeling came to him and he felt himself release. He reached with his clean hand into the seat beside him where he found his mother's white Bible. With his unclean hand, he smeared his sin onto the front and back covers. He wiped the rest within the pages of the Bible itself, and when he was done, he threw it back into the passenger seat. He turned off his phone and restarted the engine of his car. As he pulled back into the street, he glanced at the Bible, which had fallen open to the book of Job. It was the page where his mother had written, *God is cruel*, the words themselves smeared with his semen. Jake laughed, wiping the last of the tears from his face. Would someone else die because of what he'd just done, or would this be his final act of rebellion? He watched as the cars on the other side of the road sped past him. He imagined one veering quickly into his lane and crashing into him head-on. He noticed he didn't have his seatbelt on; had he done that on purpose? Would he smash through the windshield and end up splayed out and bleeding on the road?

Suddenly, he was at Ava's Diner. He didn't know how he ended up there. He didn't recall turning left on Broadway or turning off of Broadway after that. He didn't remember parking the car or turning off the engine. He didn't recall seeing Lily come out of the diner or hearing her knock on his window. Jake got out of the car and hugged her. Her face was still red and streaked with tears. She cried into his shoulder for a while and then pulled away and looked at him sternly.

"What you said today, did you mean it?" Jake was silent. He didn't know how to answer the question. Was she referencing something specific or his speech as a whole? "Are you an alcoholic?"

There was the word he'd been so afraid of for so long. It didn't sound so scary coming out of Lily's mouth. It was almost a comfort to hear her say it out loud. He reached for her and hugged her again. He put his face in that warm place where her neck and shoulder met. He wondered if he could live there in that space. Could he make himself tiny enough? He felt jealous of the hair follicles that resided there, the skin cells and bacteria that got free room and board. Lily didn't probe him further, instead, she put her hand on his neck and provided what comfort she could.

"How is Thomas doing?" he said, his voice muffled by Lily's shoulder.

"We calmed him down, but..."

Jake nodded into her and then pulled out of the hug. "Come on. Let's go inside."

They walked hand-in-hand into Ava's, where they found Benny, Eve and Thomas sitting at a corner booth with mugs and a half-empty pot of coffee. To Jake's surprise, Thomas was laughing. Benny was regaling him with sone funny tale or another. Benny and Eve didn't even know Thomas before today, and here they were, being a comfort to him after the death of his wife. How strange and beautiful life can be. Jake turned to Lily and gave her what he hoped was a serious and gratifying look. He kissed her. Suddenly, he felt an overwhelming sense of need for Lily. He felt that if she were to leave right now and never come back, he would not be able to go on living. He would either wither and die or spend the rest of his life trying to find her, to bring her back to him. Jake didn't feel as if she belonged to him as much as he belonged to her. He would do anything she asked him to do as long as she would just stick around. Lily ended the kiss and Jake noticed she was trying to hide a smile. She took his hand again and they walked over to the booth where the others were deep in laughter.

"Jakey," Benny said when he noticed his brother, "that was quite a speech. I think I could get into this church thing if it's like that all the time."

"You really pissed off that guy that tried to pull you off the stage," Eve said.

"Surprised no one clocked you," Thomas said with a grin. Presumably, Benny and Eve had been telling him what happened back at the church. "Ava would have given you hell if she'd heard."

"Ava gives me hell for everything," Jake said. He realized too late he'd said 'gives' and wished he hadn't, though it didn't look like Thomas caught on, or else he just didn't mind. Maybe it was even a comfort for him to talk about her in the present tense. He and Lily slid into the booth with the rest of them, and they all continued to talk about what had happened at the church. No one mentioned the comment he'd made about drinking. No one talked about the half-packed boxes littering the diner. They drank coffee until the pot was empty, and then Lily went back to make another. Soon enough, Thomas was telling stories about he and Ava when they were younger. His eyes lit up as he talked, as if there were tiny little lanterns back behind his pupils. They laughed and cried together, and soon enough, all of their stomachs were growling.

Thomas went into the kitchen to cook them all some food. They'd put in their orders as if nothing had changed. He had to unpack some boxes to get the supplies he needed, but he seemed happy to be doing so. Jake wondered if he'd really close the place or if packing it up had been a gut reaction to his grief. He hoped the latter. Though his routine had recently been completely shattered, it would be nice to have one thing still consistent in his new life. As the four of them talked, Thomas brought out a beer for each of them, and no one said anything when Jake gulped more down than the rest of them had. He didn't even sense a look of concern or shame. He knew it would come. If he and Lily continued to see each other, he knew he'd have to change or else she would make him get help. Would he comply? Would he fail? If he didn't get another job, he wouldn't be able to afford alcohol anyway. He wouldn't be able to afford much of anything.

Thomas came back from the kitchen with five plates of steaming hot dogs and an enormous smile on his face. Jake watched as Thomas and Lily shared a look. Still, after everything that had happened, here Lily was taking her hot dog bit a step further. Jake had been looking forward to the burger he ordered, having deviated from his journey across the menu, but when Thomas set the hot dogs down in front of him, he found himself smiling.

"Weirdest-looking Reuben I've ever seen," Benny said, taking a bite out of the hot dog and smiling himself. Eve looked confused but ate the hot dogs anyway. Lily just grinned to herself as if she'd thought of something funny but didn't want to say it out loud.

Before they left, Thomas pulled Lily and Jake aside to tell them when Ava's funeral would be. He said they weren't doing a burial, only a visitation, but that he'd love it if they would come. They'd been great friends to him and Ava, not unlike children they'd never had. "Or maybe more like a niece and nephew," he said with a laugh.

"I hope not," Lily said, "that would make us siblings."

Jake wrinkled his nose at Lily, who smiled at him. He could eat that smile: put it in a bun, throw some condiments on it, and start munching.

"Take care, all of you," Thomas said to all four of them as he receded back into the restaurant.

"Weird afternoon," Benny exclaimed as they walked back to their vehicles. Everyone laughed. "Meet at Jake's?"

"Sorry," Eve said, "I have to go to work in a few hours. I shouldn't have even had that beer."

"Oh," Benny nearly whispered. "Let me say goodbye," he said to Jake and Lily.

Realizing this meant Benny and Lily would be riding with him, Jake was struck with absolute terror. He pictured Lily getting into the passenger seat and finding his mother's Bible. Curious, she would pick it up to leaf through its tainted pages. He pictured the look of horror on her face when she realized what it was that was still wet and sticky within and outside. What would she do then? Would that be it? He could try to throw it in the back seat but then Benny would see it. He'd find it odd at first and then amusing. Which would be worse?

"Give me a second," Jake said, praying to no one in particular that she wouldn't ask what it was he needed to clean. He didn't want to have to lie to her ever again. To his delight, she shrugged and watched Benny and Eve say goodbye to each other. They were talking closely together and kissing with sad passion.

He emptied out the box with his office things in it and put the Bible in the very bottom. His cross necklace tapped the side of the box as he was doing this. He took it off and stared at it a moment. Something he'd once felt was so clever now made him so sad to look at. He wondered if he'd reached a point where he couldn't stop drinking. He obviously had a problem but was it so bad that he physically couldn't stop himself? Would he end up in one of those poorly lit rooms you see in the movies with stale donuts and bad coffee and tokens for milestones? Did those groups meet in churches around here? He didn't think he'd ever be able to step foot back inside a church.

After Jake refilled the box, he moved it to the trunk. Lily smiled at him as he did so. He didn't deserve her smile; he didn't even deserve to be near her. But then, don't good things happen to bad people? What he'd come to learn lately was that good and bad things happen to everyone; how you react to those things is what makes you a good or bad person. Eve waved goodbye to them from afar and Benny walked back to them, a cocky smile on his goateed face. He said, "What a weekend," almost to the air, and then added, "Fucking Tarrytown." Jake and Lily exchanged an amused glance, and then they all got into the car.

They talked little as they drove. Lily asked Jake to drive her home. He didn't like the idea of being apart from her so soon after they'd just gotten together, but he obliged. He'd never been a clingy person—quite the opposite—but with Lily, he felt like wrapping himself physically around her body and never letting her go. He wondered how long it would be until he would see her again. How many drinks would he have? What would happen during that time? He needed to figure out what to do about money now that he was jobless. Was he even qualified for a job outside of the church? So many things to think about while sober and alone. And then he remembered he had Benny, at least for the night.

Lily kissed Jake goodbye and said she'd text him later. He and Benny silently watched her walk to her house. He'd only just learned about why she was in Tarrytown, why she was here at this huge house living with her parents, but looking at her waving back at him from the doorway, seeing that smile, he only found himself excited to learn so much more about her. If only he could hold onto her, and she would let him. He was so used to pushing people away that the thought her letting him seemed outrageous, though somehow also very likely.

When they arrived back at Jake's apartment, Benny threw himself onto the couch and sighed loudly. "What a weekend," he said again, this time directed more at Jake. "What are you going to do for work?"

"That's nice, kick me while I'm down," Jake said. He sat on the floor and leaned his back on the couch, the back of his head nearly touching Benny's stomach. Out of habit, he'd almost gone to pour himself a drink but thought better of it. Could he go a full night without it? Or would he sneak a few swigs when he closed his door at night? The bottles of alcohol he'd hidden under his bed were now strewn about the apartment, but he was pretty sure there were still a few in his room.

Jake moved to grab the remote, but Benny stopped him.

"Let's talk."

Jake felt his throat close up and his breathing become shallow. This was it. This was what he'd been dreading since they had found the alcohol in his room. Since he'd told all of them basically to their faces that he had an alcohol problem.

"What was all that about mom and dad's deaths being your fault?" Benny asked to the back of Jake's head. Jake wasn't sure he could look him in the face if they were really going to have this conversation. "Did you really mean that?"

Jake's first impulse was to lie, but then he remembered he was done with lying. He nodded and hoped Benny could tell it was a nod.

"Remember when dad died? You gave me those binoculars, the kiddy things, and I looked out into the rain. I don't know if you saw it too, but our neighbors were out by the pool. They were naked. Fucking. I made you leave the room so I could... anyway, dad died as I was doing that."

Jake nodded as Benny talked. Was Benny going to say what Jake thought he was going to say? Would he bring up the day their mother died next? What was he doing then?

"I thought I was to blame. I got angry, messed up. I started treating girls like shit for no reason. I was good-looking back then, if you can recall." Jake could feel Benny looking at him for a moment. "That's where you say, 'Oh no Benny, you're still very good-looking.'" Jake chuckled and Benny went on. "Anyway, I'd pretend to be real into a girl and get her to come over and sleep with me. Then afterward, I'd get mean. Sometimes I'd just stop talking to the girl, other times, I'd make them feel like it was their fault I fucked them.

Really nasty shit.

"And then that day mom died, you had left my room and I pulled out this photo of one of the girls. She had an old Polaroid she'd carry around with her at school, and one day I asked—told her to take a naked picture of herself. And the next day she handed it to me and gave me this look like she was, I don't know, it was like she was disappointed in me. Maybe she was disappointed in herself, but really I think it was directed at me. Anyway, when you left the room that night, I took the photo out and started jerking off to it. Not too long after, I heard you screaming."

All this time, Jake felt like he was alone, and all along, his brother had experienced almost the exact same thing he had. They were both messed up, even if it was in different ways.

"I already told you about the time I almost died in college, but the truth was there were a lot of days like that. I barely graduated. And even after I started my career, I was no better." Jake heard Benny sniffle, but didn't want to look behind him to see if he was fully crying. He knew he'd start crying, too, if he saw that. "I lied at the restaurant about always putting the women before the money. In the early days, I did a lot of rough sex scenes. Choking, slapping, gagging. I liked to watch the women struggle. I got some sick Oedipal satisfaction out of it. I still had some drug and alcohol problems, but nothing as bad as the sadistic need to see women in pain, whether it was exaggerated or not."

"It was the opposite for me," Jake finally said. He couldn't believe he was about to tell Benny everything. He told him of the two bodies bouncing in the rain, of Lily Scarlet in her blue satin robe. He told him of Sara and of the panic attack that ensued. He told Benny about getting into the ministry because it was the only job he could think of where people wouldn't question his choice—*Was it his choice?*—to remain celibate. He spoke of his problem with alcohol, the joy and pain it brought him. And, finally, of Lily and of

Eve. And when he was done, Jake asked, "Did you ever get better?"

Jake felt Benny nodding, but he said, "No. I mean yes, but no. I don't like to see other people hurt anymore. I drink but not often to excess, past few nights excluded." They both laughed, and then Jake felt Benny's hand on his forehead. Benny pulled Jake's head backward and kissed the back of it.

"So what's up with you and Eve?"

"What do you mean?"

"I mean you guys seemed really into each other. Where do you go from here?"

"I go home."

"Is Eve okay with that?"

"She knew what this was. Hell, I think she preferred it that way. She's going to be busy soon with work and school, I doubt she'd have time for anyone anyway."

"But won't you miss each other?"

"You've got a lot to learn, bud."

He'd learned so much about himself over the past few months and it pained him to realize that he had so much more to learn. Or maybe it excited him.

Jake found himself drifting off, his head slackening back into the couch and on Benny's stomach. When he woke up, Benny was gone. He wasn't sure how he'd slept so deeply that he didn't hear Benny getting up, packing his bags, and getting out the door, but part of him was glad that he did because he wasn't sure he would have been able to say goodbye without crying. He looked at his phone where a text from Benny was waiting for him: 'Had a great time Jakey. Maybe I'll visit again soon, or you and Lily can come visit me out in L.A. Heard you might be looking for work ;). I'll call you later this week.' Jake closed the text and smiled. He thought about how much had happened in such a short amount of time. How much had changed. Would change. He thought of the lighthouse. Would

Lily be his second lighthouse? Would Benny?

These thoughts made his mind drift toward his aunt Beth. She had texted him to tell him happy birthday the night before, but he had been too drunk to respond. He decided to give her a call.

"Hello?" Beth said tentatively. How had it come to the point where his own aunt, the woman who basically raised him, was confused to be receiving a call from him.

"Hey Beth, it's Jake."

"You know I have caller ID right?"

Jake laughed.

"How are you, Jake?"

"I... I'm... I miss you. Will you come to New York? Or, no, I can come to you."

"Is everything okay?"

"I don't know. I think so. Maybe. I'm sorry I haven't called you much recently. I've been dealing with a lot. Or. I've been dealt a lot."

"It's okay. I love you, and I know you can't always make time for me."

"No. That's not fair. I can make time for you."

"Do you really want me to come visit? You've never asked before."

"Can you?"

"Of course. I'd love to come visit you."

"I need to get some things right in my life, but then I'd love you to come. You'll come?"

Beth laughed. Jake laughed too. "I said I would."

This is about where Jake would typically say goodbye and hang up the phone. What was the longest conversation they'd had since he moved? Ten minutes? Five? So instead of saying goodbye, he asked her about her week. She asked him about his. He told her of Benny's visit, leaving out some of the raunchier details, though Beth had always seemed to be able to intuit those kinds of things.

He gave her an abridged version of what happened at the church the day before, and to his surprise, she laughed. She said she never understood Christians and was glad that her sister hadn't really either, even though she had claimed to be one. Eventually, Jake said goodbye and that he'd call her again soon, or if he didn't, she should call him. He hoped he could keep his promise. He hoped things would be different. All he could do at that moment, before being able to take any real action, was hope.

EPILOGUE

"What's that?"

"What is *this*? *What* is *this*? What *is* this?"

"Shut up and tell me," Philip said through a giggle.

"This, my small, frail friend, is what separates the truly special from the unfortunately ordinary."

"What is it!" Philip cried, unable to keep himself from smiling.

"*Goldeneye*."

"What?"

"James Bond? *Goldeneye*? Only the greatest game ever made?"

"I've never heard of it."

Jake clutched his chest and made a sound of disgust. "I'm physically hurt, Philip."

"Just put it in, old man," Philip said.

"Be careful what you wish for kid."

Jake put the cartridge into the Nintendo, tossed a controller over to Philip, and took one in his own hands. Philip had improved drastically since they'd last seen each other, and he'd be going home any time now. Jake had gone to an old trading card store and found

Goldeneye for sale. It was expensive, probably more than it was when it first came out, but he bought it anyway. He planned to give the Nintendo to Philip. Technically, he'd stolen it from the church, but hadn't the church stolen plenty from him? This made them even. Or, maybe not even, but it at least gave him a small win after a lifetime of losses.

It had been a week since Benny left. In that time, he'd seen Lily twice. They'd had sex once. He drank, but less. He tried not to do it around Lily, but he didn't like the idea of hiding it from her. He hadn't gone to any meetings yet, hoping that the drinking had only been the result of his sexual frustrations and that it would fade with time. Though he also knew that's not how these things typically worked. The problem was he wasn't at a point where he wanted to stop drinking for himself; he wanted to do it for Lily. Maybe it was a start, but at some point, he'd need to want to stop.

Jake taught Philip the controls and how to play. In doing so, he killed Philip eight times and claimed he won the first match. Philip pretended to be mad but still couldn't hide his giggle. Eventually, Philip got the hang of it and the real competition was on.

"Not fair!" Jake shouted when Philip jumped out from behind a wall and shot him directly in the head. "Hey! No screen looking," Jake said when Philip killed him again immediately after a respawn.

"You should be better," Philip said.

"You shouldn't be so cocky," Jake said, and then killed Philip with the Golden Gun. "Only one life left. Use it well, young Padawan."

"I'm not your Padawan!"

Eve snuck into the room as Jake and Philp played on. They didn't notice her come in and she didn't announce herself. She just stood in the doorway and watched them. She liked the way Philip brought out Jake's boyishness. It was like he pretended to be serious all the time, maybe because he thought pastors were supposed to be serious, or maybe because the circumstances of his life had taken his normal childhood away. But when he was out of his head and you really took a look at him, all you saw was the outline of a much smaller Jacob, one who would sit in his brother's room and play video games or watch movies. Eve could see that he and Benny were more alike than either brother knew. Only Benny seemed to have gotten more of a head start on his true adulthood while his younger brother lagged behind. She didn't expect to see much more of Jake. He'd done his time in Tarrytown, and if he could get Lily to leave with him—and as little as Eve knew of Lily, she thought she'd go with him in a heartbeat—then he'd be gone very soon. Maybe he'd go out to Los Angeles to visit with Benny. Maybe he'd go home to Ohio. Eve realized Jake had noticed her and was smiling at her. She gave him a half-wave. He nodded at her and then looked back at the video game. She left the room, head awhirl with thoughts of the future.

When Jake and Philip exhausted their trigger fingers—Jake had won all but one game, which Philip couldn't stop bragging about—they just sat and talked a while. Jake regaled Philip with stories of when he was a kid. Philip talked about how he couldn't wait to be an adult, and Jake didn't have the heart to tell him that things usually get worse when you get older. And then Philip's mom walked in and smiled at them.

"Can I talk to you out in the hall?" she asked Jake, who nodded. When they were outside, Beth looked serious. Jake swallowed. Was everything with Philip not as good as it seemed? "My sister told me what happened." Jake must have looked confused because Beth explained, "My sister. Philip's aunt. The one who asked you to come out here and pray with us?"

"Oh. Sure," Jake said. He'd forgotten all about her. He'd been coming for himself or for Eve so long he couldn't even remember why he'd met Philip in the first place. But then he realized what that meant Beth knew.

"Doesn't matter to me what kind of blow-up you had up on that stage. You've been good to my son. I don't know why you keep returning. Maybe it was that pretty nurse or maybe you got some shit in your own life, but I really don't care. You gave Philip hope. You gave me hope. And I want to thank you."

"Philip gave me hope, too. And courage. More than either of you could know."

"Kid's special that way, isn't he?"

"He really is. I should say goodbye."

"Here's my number." She handed him a slip of paper. "I know adults and kids can't really be friends, but I think he'd like to hear from you every now and then. Call us if you feel like it."

"I will," Jake said. And he meant it. "Oh, I told him he could have that Nintendo. Technically, I stole it from the church, but I don't think they'll miss it. I think he'll have a hell of a time beating his friends at it."

Beth smiled and thanked him. As he turned to walk away, she stopped him. "Jake." Jake looked at her. "It's not any of my business, your drinking. But don't do it around my son."

Jake nodded, sadness filling his gut. That look she gave him. Pity. How had he become this person? Would he ever be able to change?

They went back into the room, and Jake said his goodbyes. Philip looked sad. Happy, but sad. Jake said he would call, maybe someday they could have a real experience outside of a hospital room. He said to make sure to put on some real clothes when they did, though, because he didn't want to see Philip's gross butt hanging out of that hospital gown. This really got Philip going.

***

The rate for the Tarrytown to Grand Central Metro North train had raised a quarter over that summer; hardly enough to cause a stir, but people noticed. A quarter now plus another quarter next summer plus another quarter the next would really add up. Inflation, they say, always inflation, but were the people that had to pay for the train getting paid more money because of inflation? Did people even get real raises without promotions anymore? Had Kendall had a safe move to LA? Where is Tangier located? Remember Cap'n Crunch? These seats are so uncomfortable. Jake allowed his mind to be filled with questions, and he didn't care to know the answers. This was contentment.

He adjusted his duffel bag, which had been falling off his lap, with his left arm. His right hand was busy being held. Lily stared out of the window at the river rushing by. The trees behind it were starting to turn brown and red and orange and yellow, not quite ready to break off and journey down, but soon enough they'd be littering the ground below. She looked either deep in thought or like she was holding in a fart. Maybe it was both. It was another question Jake didn't mind leaving unanswered. He stared at Lily and smiled. She must have felt his gaze on her, because she whipped her head around and gave him her most sarcastic look of suspicion, but broke into a laugh too quickly for it to make an impact. She squeezed his hand, squinted her eyes at him, and then turned back to the window.

The duffel bag was full. He and Lily had gone to the grocery store and made a game out of packing a picnic. Who could pack the bag quickest? He grabbed cheeses. Gouda. Brie. Goat. She got bread, tomatoes, turkey. He got crackers and jam. She got paper plates and plastic utensils. He got wine from the liquor store next door. No one won. No one lost. That was the best part of the game.

The wine rattled in the bag on his lap. He was surprised when she said nothing about it. She looked at it, looked at him, smiled, and started walking to the car. Not a peep or a crooked stare. Jake himself wondered if he should even have any of it. He'd be better off leaving it in the bag. He wasn't sure what would happen after a few sips. Would he convince Lily to leave the park and go with him to a bar? Would he go even if she said no?

They set up their picnic in the Great Lawn in Central Park. It was busy, but then, wasn't it always? In New York, even the tiniest of spaces are good real estate. Lily had a large blanket that fit both of them and their feast. They ate. They took turns taking sips from the bottle of wine. They talked. Lily was in the middle of some bit she'd started about *The Mighty Ducks*. Jake was laughing, but his head was swimming with panicked thoughts of: *Will I be able to hold onto this? O' God, please let me hold on.*

AKNOWLEDGEMENTS

Thank you to all of those in my life that indulged me in writing this admittedly insane novel. To Maggie, Jonny, Conor, Mel, Lauren, and Kassidy, who served as my early readers and had to listen to me go on and on and on and on about how I would one day maybe get this book published. To my cat, Ferguson, who tried numerous times to attack my fingers as I was typing this story. To my parents, of course, who I hope never actually read this book for their own sakes. To my editor, J. Flowers-Olnowich, whose immensely helpful redlines seemed to take up entire pages. And to Kassidy Reynolds, because I am completely without artistic talent and could never have designed such an amazing cover without her.

ABOUT THE AUTHOR

Chris Riffle is originally from the suburbs of Cincinnati, OH. He has been living in New York City since 2016. When he's not writing, he's either out at a bar or working at his job in the advertising industry. *Strings Detached* is his first published work, but he hopes to continue writing novels until his fingers stop working—though by then the voice-to-text technology will probably be so advanced that we'll no longer use fingers to write anyway.

You can find him at:
@chrisriffleauthor on Instagram and TikTok
@criffleauthor on X
www.chrisriffleauthor.com

Due to the nature of this story, many quotes from The Bible are used throughout. Because the featured church is more contemporary, the excerpts were taken from the NIV bible, to which I would like to provide full credit:

THE HOLY BIBLE, NEW INTERNATIONAL VERSION® NIV® Copyright® 1973, 1978, 1984, 2011 by Biblica, Inc.™ Used by permission. All rights reserved worldwide.

www.ingramcontent.com/pod-product-compliance
Lightning Source LLC
Chambersburg PA
CBHW020416110726
47899CB00006B/2010